LET THE GAMES BEGIN

Asia turned back to Erica. "We share fantasies and then what?"

"Then we wait until some guy buys a prop—a movie, a book, a toy, whatever—that relates to our particular fantasy."

"And?" Becky asked, both breathless and bright red.

Erica shrugged. "We approach him. See if he's interested."

Snatching up her foam cup, Asia gulped down a fortifying drink.

Since her first relationship had turned so sour, so . . . *bad*, she'd never gotten to find out what the fireworks were about. She wasn't stupid; she believed awesome sex existed, it just hadn't existed for her.

How would it be to have phenomenal sex with a guy who wanted the same things she did? A man who wanted to please her, not the other way around?

She realized both Becky and Erica were staring at her and she asked warily, "What?"

Becky cleared her throat. "Erica asked if you'd want to go first?"

"Me! Why me?"

Books by Lori Foster

Too Much Temptation
Never Too Much
Unexpected
Say No To Joe?
The Secret Life of Bryan
When Bruce Met Cyn
Just a Hint—Clint
Jamie
Murphy's Law
Jude's Law
The Watson Brothers
Yule Be Mine

Anthologies

All Through the Night
I Brake for Bad Boys
Bad Boys on Board
I Love Bad Boys
Jingle Bell Rock
Bad Boys to Go
I'm Your Santa
A Very Merry Christmas
When Good Things Happen to Bad Boys
The Night Before Christmas
Star Quality
Perfect for the Beach
Bad Boys in Black Tie
Truth or Dare
Bad Boys of Summer
Delicious
Give It Up

LORI FOSTER

TRUTH OR DARE

ZEBRA BOOKS
KENSINGTON PUBLISHING CORP.
www.kensingtonbooks.com

ZEBRA BOOKS are published by

Kensington Publishing Corp.
119 West 40th Street
New York, NY 10018

First Printing: January 2006
ISBN-13: 978-1-4201-4843-5
ISBN-10: 1-4201-4843-5

ISBN-13: 978-1-4201-2265-7 (eBook)
ISBN-10: 1-4201-2265-7 (eBook)

10 9 8 7

Printed in the United States of America

CONTENTS

Satisfy Me

Chapter One

"Do you believe the audacity?" Asia Michaels asked, staring through the dirty window of the company lounge to the newly painted building across the street. Soft pink neon lights flashed Wild Honey with bold provocation, competing with the twinkle of Christmas lights around the door and windows. A porn shop, she thought with awe, right in the middle of their small town. Cuther, Indiana, wasn't known for porn. Nope, it was known for pigs and toiletries, which meant most everyone either farmed or worked in one of the three factories.

Asia worked in a factory as an executive secretary in the marketing department. She liked it, the routine, the security. She'd found independence in Cuther, and peace of mind. Not in a million years had she thought to see a sex shop called Wild Honey erected among the main businesses.

Seated next to Asia at the round table, Becky Harte gaped. She blinked big blue innocent eyes and asked in a scandalized whisper, "You're sure they sell porn?"

Erica Lee, the third in their long-established

group and a faithful friend, laughed out loud as she set her coffee and a candy bar on the table. "Well they're sure not raising bees."

Asia shook her head. Erica was probably the most sophisticated of the three, and the least inhibited. Every guy in the factory had asked Erica out at one time or another. Occasionally, Erica said yes.

Now, Becky, she didn't even look at men, even when the men were staring as hard as they could. Becky's fresh-faced appearance and dark blond curls were beyond cute. Not that Becky seemed to care. If anything, she did her best not to draw male attention. Her best pretty much worked. If Asia had to guess, she'd swear Becky was still a virgin.

Asia took a bite of her doughnut. "We should go check it out," she teased, hoping to get a rise out of her friends.

"Get out of here," Becky rasped, horrified by the mere prospect. "I could *never* go in that place!"

"Why not?" Erica asked. "You refuse to date, so maybe you'd find something that would make your time alone more . . . interesting." She bobbed her eyebrows, making Becky turn three shades of red and sputter.

Laughing, Asia pointed out, "None of us dates, at least not much."

"I date." Erica shook back her shoulder-length black hair. It hung bone-straight, looked like silk, and made every woman who saw it envious. Because her own hair was plain brown and too curly, Asia counted herself among the envious group.

"I just don't meet many guys worth dating twice," Erica explained. "That's all. And it's not like Cuther is a hotbed of eligible males, anyway."

Asia accepted that excuse with silence. Her own reasons for not dating weren't something she cared to discuss. Cuther was a new life, and her old life was well behind her.

Try as they might, none of them could stop looking at the sex shop. "It's rather tastefully decorated, isn't it?"

Becky and Erica stared at her.

"Well, it is." Asia shrugged. "I would have thought the curtains would be red velvet and there'd be lewd signs in the windows. But there aren't." The curtains were actually gauzy, sheer and delicate, in a snowy white, with beige shutters against the red brick. Other than the bright neon sign with the name of the shop, the place looked as subdued as a nail salon or a boardinghouse. And being that it was close to the holidays, there was even a large festive wreath on the door to go with the holiday lights, lending the building a domestic affectation.

Becky leaned forward, motioning for the others to do the same. "When I parked today," she whispered, "I could see inside, and you'll never guess who was in there!"

Erica and Asia looked at each other. "Who?"

"Ian Conrad."

Erica dropped back in her seat. "The new electrician the company hired?"

Becky nodded, making her curls bounce. "He was speaking to the man at the counter."

Erica snorted. "Well, I'll be. And here he acts so quiet."

"Still waters run deep?" Asia speculated aloud.

"I'd like to know what he bought," Erica admitted in a faraway voice.

"Nothing," Becky told her. "That is, he came out

empty-handed. Maybe he was just greeting a new proprietor?"

"More like he went window shopping." Erica made a face, her voice rising. "Men are all alike. One woman isn't enough for them. They need outside stimulation, like a vitamin supplement or something."

"We should be more like them," Asia said, without really thinking. "Can you imagine how a guy would act if a woman started buying up porn?"

Erica looked dumbstruck, then leaned forward in excitement. "Let's do it!"

Becky tried to pull away but Erica caught her arm and held on, keeping her within the conspiratorial circle. "I'm serious! None of us is getting any younger. I'm probably the oldest at twenty-eight, but Becky, aren't you twenty-five now?"

Looking distinctly miserable, Becky nodded.

"I'm twenty-six," Asia volunteered, proud because each year took her one more step away from her past and her insecurities, her lack of confidence in all things.

"You see," Erica said. "We're mature women with mature needs, not silly little girls." She rubbed her hands together and her slanted green eyes lit up with anticipation. "Oh, I'd just love to witness Ian Conrad's expression if he went out on a date with a woman, and afterward, when they were alone, she pulled out the props. Ha! Let him deal with not being enough on his own."

Asia sat back and blinked at Erica. "Whatever are you talking about?" And then with insight, "You've got a thing for Ian, don't you?"

"Absolutely not," Erica sniffed. "I'm just talking about guys in general who think they need all that other"—she waved her hand—"stuff to be satis-fied. As if a woman and her body and her imagina-tion aren't enough."

Becky looked embarrassed, but concerned. "Did a guy, you know, pull out the props on you?"

"Nah, at least not in the middle of things. But I came home once to find him rather occupied."

Becky's eyes widened in titillated fascination. "Ohmigosh."

"You didn't," Asia said, enthralled despite her-self.

"Yep. I'd been gone all of four hours and we'd had sex that morning." She muttered under her breath, "The pig."

Asia frowned. "You know, I don't really think there's anything wrong with a mature, consenting couple making use of toys."

Becky looked ready to faint—or die of curiosity—but Erica just shrugged. "Well, me, either, but he sure wasn't a couple. He was there all by his lone-some, just him and a video and some strange . . . hand contraption thing."

Becky puckered up like she'd swallowed a lemon. "Hand contraption thing?"

Asia tried to hold it in, but Erica looked so in-dignant and Becky looked so dazed, she couldn't. She burst out laughing to the point where half the people in the lounge were staring. When she could finally catch a breath, she managed to say, "I wish I could have seen his face!"

"His face?" Erica raised one brow mockingly. "It wasn't his face that drew my attention. No, ladies. It was the place where that contraption connected."

Becky choked, and they all fell into gales of laughter again.

"So what," Asia finally asked, wiping her eyes, "do you think the three of us should do? Buy our own . . ."

She started giggling again and Becky finished for her, "hand contraptions!"

"Honey, please." Erica affected an exaggerated haughtiness. "That gizmo wouldn't do us any good at all."

Becky had tears rolling down her cheeks, she laughed so hard. "You're so bad, Erica."

"Which is why you love me."

"Yep, I guess that's part of it."

"Okay, so what do we do?" Asia really wanted to know. Not that she intended to go into that porn shop and buy anything. Just the idea made her hot with embarrassment.

Then she realized her own thoughts and frowned. Part of her liberation, her new life, was doing as she pleased, without concern for what others thought. Why should she be embarrassed? The men from the factory had been moseying over there all day! They could appease their curiosity, so why couldn't she?

"First, we'll share our fantasies."

Fantasies! Good grief, maybe *that* was why she couldn't. Asia wasn't sure she had any fantasies.

Not anymore.

Erica had leaned forward to whisper her comment, but still Asia looked around nervously. By necessity, the lounge was large, able to accommodate shifts for the two hundred plus people who worked there. Employees tended to sit in clusters. The managers with the managers, maintenance with maintenance, and so forth.

Asia and her friends always chose the same table

in the corner by the window, separated by a half-wall planter filled with artificial plants. Since Wild Honey had gone in, they often found their favorite table unavailable because everyone wanted to look out that row of windows. Erica had taken to leaving her desk early so she could lay claim to it.

Asia didn't see anyone paying them any mind, although there was someone on the other side of the planter, alone at a table. He wore jeans and a flannel, so she assumed he was one of the workmen, not part of management. But whoever he was, he wasn't listening. He sat alone, a newspaper open in front of his face, his booted foot swinging to music that played only in his head. A half-empty cup of steaming coffee was at his elbow. Even as Asia watched, he rustled the paper, turned the page, and sipped at his drink.

Satisfied, Asia turned back to Erica. "We share fantasies and then what?"

"Then we wait until some guy buys a prop—a movie, a book, a toy, whatever—that relates to our particular fantasy."

"And?" Becky asked, both breathless and bright red.

Erica shrugged. "We approach him. See if he's interested."

Snatching up her foam cup, Asia gulped down a fortifying drink.

Since her first relationship had turned so sour, so . . . bad, she'd never gotten to find out what the fireworks were about. She wasn't stupid; she believed awesome sex existed, it just hadn't existed for her. Not in her marriage.

How would it be to have phenomenal sex with a

guy who wanted the same things she did? A man who wanted to please her, not the other way around?

She realized both Becky and Erica were staring at her and she asked warily, "What?"

Becky cleared her throat. " Erica asked if you'd want to go first?"

"Me! Why me?"

Becky lifted one narrow shoulder. "I'm too chicken, though I promise to try to work up my nerve."

"You will work up the nerve," Erica promised, and squeezed Becky's hand.

Becky looked skeptical, but nodded. "And Erica says if she goes first, she knows neither of us will."

Asia nearly crumbled her cup, she got so tense. But she wanted to do this. It would be one more step toward total freedom. Not that she believed anything would come of it. And thinking that, she said, "We have to set a time limit. I don't intend to visit that stupid place more than . . . say, three times."

"It's Tuesday," Erica pointed out. "You can start tomorrow right after work, and stop on Friday. If no one turns up, it'll be Becky's turn. But we all have to keep rotating turns until we find someone, agreed?"

Asia thought about it, then nodded. "Agreed. But if in those first three times I don't see a guy buying what he'd need to buy to interest me, then it moves on to Becky's turn."

Becky closed her eyes. "Oh, dear."

"Promise me, Becky."

Becky bit her lip, but finally agreed. "Okay," she whispered, and then with more force, as if a streak of determination existed beneath her innocence, "Okay."

Erica laughed. "There you go, hon. So, Asia, what's a fella have to buy to get your motor running?"

This was the embarrassing part. But she'd explain, and they'd understand her reasoning. Asia looked at each woman in turn, then stiffened her backbone. "Something to do with . . ."

Erica and Becky leaned forward, saying in unison, "Yes?"

Asia squeezed her eyes shut, took a deep breath, and blurted, "Spanking."

Cameron O'Reilly choked, then nearly swallowed his tongue. He sputtered, spewing coffee across the front of the flannel he wore today before finally gasping in enough air. A good portion of his steaming coffee went into his lap, but it wasn't nearly as hot as he was.

Spanking! Asia Michaels was into spanking!

As the coffee soaked into his jeans, he leaped from his seat, but at the last second remembered himself and turned his back. He could feel all three of the ladies looking at him, especially *her.* Luckily, he wasn't dressed in his usual suit today. The casual clothes, necessary for the job he did that morning, would help disguise him.

The voice he recognized as Erica Lee muttered, "Klutz."

"Who is he?" he heard Asia whisper and there was a lot of nervousness in her tone.

"Who cares?" Erica said. "Ignore him."

Becky said, "I hope he didn't burn himself." Then they went back to chatting.

Cameron didn't give them a chance to recognize him. He quickly stalked from the lounge. Still poleaxed, he damn near barreled into a wall in his hurry to leave undetected. Asia and spanking! He'd never have guessed it. He groaned, just thinking of Asia with her soft brown curls and big, sexy brown eyes. He'd wanted her for two long months.

But she'd refused to move beyond the platonic acquaintance stage, no matter how many times he tried. She was friendly to him, and ignored any hints for more.

One of the other employees had warned him that Asia was a cold fish, totally uninterested in men. Ha!

He ducked into the men's room and hurried to the sink. In his mind, he pictured Asia stretched out over his lap, her beautiful naked bottom turned up, his large hand on her . . .

And the image ended there.

He just couldn't see himself striking a woman. Not for any reason. But, oh, the other things he'd like to do to that sweet behind.

He grabbed several paper towels and mopped at his soaked jeans. She hadn't known he was listening, of course, or he still wouldn't know her secret. The problem now was how to use it.

He wasn't a kinky man.

He enjoyed sex just like any other guy, but he'd never been a hound dog, never been a womanizer. He'd never done much experimenting beyond what he and his partner found enjoyable, which had stayed pretty much in the bounds of routine stuff, like different positions, different places, different times of the day.

He liked relationships, and he liked Asia.

He wanted her. Soon, and for a long while. He did not want to . . . spank her.

Cameron stared down at his jeans, tautly tented by a raging erection, and knew himself for a liar. He snorted. The idea was exciting as hell, no doubt about that. But mostly because it was sexual in nature. If Asia had said she wanted to roll naked in the snow, that would have turned him on too, and he absolutely detested the damn snow. Give him Florida, with hot sandy beaches and bright sunshine over frigid Indiana weather any day.

Of course, if he'd stayed in Florida instead of taking the new supervisor's job, he'd never have met Asia, and he most definitely wouldn't have overheard such an intriguing confession.

He shook his head. What to do?

First, he had to change into his regular clothes. At least the dousing had helped to bring him back under control, otherwise he might have blown it by rushing things. He'd been sitting there listening to her, daydreaming, imagining all types of lewd things while staring blankly at the newspaper, and he'd nearly worked himself into a lather. Her confession had all but pushed him over the edge. At thirty-two, he was too damn old for unexpected boners.

Yet he'd had one. For Asia.

Which meant the next thing he had to do was be in that shop tomorrow when Asia visited. She wouldn't need three days to find him. Hell, he'd never live that long, not with the way he wanted her.

And no way would he let her go off with some other guy. He'd been fantasizing about her since moving to Indiana two months ago, and here was his chance.

The spanking part . . . well, he'd do what he had to do. And if she enjoyed it, great.

After he warmed her bottom, it'd be his turn.

Chapter Two

Becky looked faint. "Spanking," she said in a strangled, barely there whisper, clutching her throat.

"I have a theory," Asia hurried to explain. "If a
guy gets his kinkier jollies taken care of with props,
then he won't expect to fulfill them with a woman."

Erica dropped back in her seat with a guffaw.
"You big faker! You really had me going there."

Becky asked, still a bit confused, "So you figure if
he buys movies about spanking, he'll have it out of
his system and won't try anything like that with
you?"

"Bingo."

Erica shook her head. "And here I thought you
had a wild side."

"Not even close." Asia thought about it for a moment, then decided it was time for some truths.
She could trust Erica and Becky, she knew that.
They'd understand. "Actually, I had a wild first
husband."

"Get out! You were married?"

"Yes. To a complete and total jerk."

Erica's smile faded. "And he hit you?"

"Not exactly. But he liked to . . . experiment. Everything was geared toward what *he'd* like, whether I liked it or not. And I never did. But he'd claim it was my duty as his wife to try to please him, and I was confused enough then to feel some guilt, because I couldn't please him on my own."

Becky surprised them both by growling, "That bastard."

After giving Becky a long approving look, Erica asked, "How long were you with him?"

"We married right out of college when I was twenty-two. The divorce became final just before my twenty-fifth birthday."

"He did a number on you, didn't he? That's why you don't date."

"Let's just say I like being independent now, thinking my own thoughts and doing my own things. I'm not looking for a relationship, and I don't want—didn't want—any part of a quick affair." She tapped her fingers on the tabletop. "But you're right, Erica. I might be missing out on a lot, and to my mind, I've missed enough already. I deserve some satisfaction."

Erica thrust a small fist into the air and said, "Here's to satisfaction," making Becky chuckle.

"So," Asia said, feeling equal parts triumphant for being decisive, anticipation for what might be, and hesitant about the unknown. "That's settled. I'll head over there tomorrow."

"We'll watch from here," Becky told her, and Erica nodded.

Knowing they'd be close would make it easier, Asia decided. "Your turn, Becky."

Becky blanched. "My turn for what?"

"To share a fantasy."

She winced. "I need time to think about it."

As the unofficial moderator, Erica sighed. "All right. You can have until Friday."

Slumping in relief, Becky said, "Friday." She smiled. "I'll be ready."

Cameron stood in the aisle of tapes, surreptitiously watching the door. Unwilling to take a chance on missing Asia, he'd been there for half an hour. Already he'd studied every cover and description of all the more erotic discipline tapes. Some of them were downright disgusting. Pain and pleasure . . . he wasn't at all sure they really mixed. Not that he intended to judge others.

Not that he'd judge Asia.

He had his eye on one in particular, but he waited, wanting Asia to see him buy the damn thing so there'd be no misunderstandings. The cover sported an older English-looking fellow in a straight-backed chair. He had a schoolgirl, of all dumb things, draped over his knees with her pleated skirt flipped up and her frilly panties showing.

Cameron had chosen it because even though the guy appeared stern, the girl wore a vacuous, anxious smile. She seemed to be enjoying herself and that's what he hoped Asia would do. No way in hell could he make her cry—even if she preferred it— which some of the tapes indicated by their covers.

He was engrossed in fantasies too vivid to bear when the tinkling of the front door sounded like a gun blast in his ears. He looked up—and made eye contact with Asia.

Even from the distance separating them, he felt her shock and consternation at seeing him there.

She immediately averted her face, her cheeks scalded with color.

The blood surged in his veins. Every muscle in his body tensed, including the one most interested in this little escapade. His cock was suddenly hard enough to break granite.

Cameron couldn't look away as she ducked to the back aisle. He'd already discovered they kept a variety of velvet whips and handcuffs there.

She ducked right back out, her face now pale. Damn. He started toward her, not certain what he'd say but knowing he had to say something. He had the wretched tape in his hand.

"Asia?"

She froze, her back to him, her body strangely still. Several seconds ticked by, the silence strained, and then she turned. A false, too-bright smile was pinned to her face. "Yes?" And as if she hadn't seen him the second she walked in, she said, "Cameron! What are you doing here?"

As usual, she reached out for a business handshake, keeping their relationship confined.

With no other option coming to mind, he started to accept her hand, realized he held the damn tape, and switched hands. "I'm just . . . ah, looking around."

In horrified fascination, she stared at the movie now held at his side before finally giving him a brisk, quick shake. "It's an interesting place, isn't it?"

"Yes." They stood in the center aisle with display tables loaded down with paperback books of the lustful variety on either side of them. He propped his hip against a table, trying to relax while his testosterone level shot through the roof. "I'm surprised at the diversity. And how upscale it all is."

He glanced around, feeling too self-conscious. "I'm not sure what I expected."

"I know what you mean." She relaxed the tiniest bit. "I admit, I never expected a shop like this in conservative Cuther."

The tape in his hand felt like a burning brand. He wanted to set the idiotic thing aside, but that would be defeating the whole purpose of being in the shop in the first place. "Cuther is different," he admitted. "More rural than I'm used to."

"And colder?" she teased, because she knew he'd come from Florida.

Idle conversation in a porn shop, Cameron thought. It was a first for him. "I guess my blood has thinned. I'm almost always cold."

"With the wind chill, it's fifteen below. Everyone is cold."

"True enough."

She tilted her head and her long brown hair flowed over her coat sleeve. It looked like dark honey and burnished gold, natural shades for a natural woman.

"What about your family?" she asked, taking him by surprise with the somewhat more personal question.

"What about them?"

She smiled, a real smile this time. "You've never said much about them."

"No." Any time he'd talked to her, he'd been trying to get past her walls. Discussing his family had been the farthest thing from his mind.

"It's almost Christmas. Will you be heading home for the holidays?"

"Uh, no." He wouldn't go anywhere until he'd had her. "My family is . . . scattered. We keep in touch by phone, but we don't do the big family get-togethers. We never have."

Her brown eyes warmed, looked a little sad. Thick lashes lowered, hiding her gaze from him. "I thought everyone wanted to be with family this time of year."

He shrugged, wishing she'd change the damn subject, wishing she'd look at him again.

Wishing he had her naked and in his bed.

"I guess not." Then he thought to ask, "What about you?"

She turned partially away, giving him her profile. Even beneath the thick coat, he could see the swells of her breasts, the plumpness of her bottom.

A bottom she wanted him to swat.

Cameron swallowed hard, willing himself to stay in control. "Asia?"

"I'm not sure what I'm doing yet. Mother is . . . well, she remarried and she gets together with her husband's family. I have one sister, but I think she's making it an intimate occasion. Just her husband and two children."

"So you're an aunt?" He liked learning more about her, but she'd picked a hell of a place to open up.

"Yes. I have two adorable nephews, four and six."

He took a step closer. "If you find out you're not doing anything, maybe we could get together?"

"I . . ." Her smile faded. "I don't know."

He could feel her shutting down, closing herself off from him. He hated it. "I'm free," he said, watching for her reaction, "whatever you decide."

She nodded, but didn't say a thing.

Having all but killed that conversational gambit,

Cameron looked around for inspiration. "This your first time in here?"

"Yes." Her face colored once again.

Drawn to her, Cameron rubbed the back of his neck and tried to keep his wits. "You looking for anything in particular?"

She gave him such an appalled look, he wanted to kick his own ass. Any idiot would know you didn't ask a lady something like that.

But she surprised him. She cleared her throat, lifted her chin, and pointed down at the video in his hand. "I see you made a selection."

It was stupid, but he felt heat crawling up the back of his neck and prayed she wouldn't notice.

Determined on his course, he held the tape in front of him so she'd get a good look at it and see exactly what it was. "That's right. I suppose I should be paying." He took a small step away.

Asia looked after him.

He edged into another step, willing her to say something, anything. He waited.

Nothing.

"It was, ah, nice speaking with you."

Eyes wide and watchful, she nodded. "You, too."

Damn, damn, damn. Had the tape not been risqué enough? "All right, then." He forced a smile, but it felt more like a grimace. "Take care."

He started to turn away, teeth clenched in disappointment, body on fire.

"Cameron?"

He whipped around. "Yes?"

She didn't look at him, but that was okay, because she asked, "Would you like to . . . maybe do something Friday after work? If you're not busy, that is."

His knees went weak with relief. He didn't know if he'd last till Friday, but he said, "Yeah. Sure. That'd be great."

A tremulous smile brightened her expression. "I could cook you dinner."

"No." He shook his head and walked back to her. "I'll take you out to dinner. Someplace nice. All right?" He didn't want their first date to be only about sex.

She teased, "What? You don't trust my cooking?"

"I imagine you're a terrific cook." It was difficult not to touch her, not to grin like a lecherous moron. But, damn, he was hard and there wasn't a thing he could do about it. He wanted her too much. "This week is my treat, though, okay?"

She studied him closely, then nodded. "All right."

"Do you want to go straight from work?" *Do you want to go now, to my place,* he thought, *where I can get you naked and sate myself on your . . .*

"I'd like to go home and change first. If that's okay."

This smile came easier. At least he had a confirmed date, even if he had a two-day wait. "I'll pick you up at six? Will that give you enough time?"

"Perfect." She wrote her address down for him, then accompanied him to the checkout. Time and again, her gaze went to his movie. Was she excited? He wished like hell she didn't have the thick coat on. He wanted to see her breasts, to see if maybe her nipples were peaked with anticipation.

God, many more thoughts like that and he'd be in real trouble. Luckily, he'd worn his long coat today, which concealed his lower body and straining erection. His jacket wouldn't have hidden a thing.

They stepped outside together, his purchase safely concealed in a plain brown paper bag. He felt like a pervert, even though his logical adult mind told him a grown man could purchase whatever he pleased. But he knew what was in that bag, even if no one else did.

The wind kicked up, blowing Asia's hair. It licked against his chin, scented with female warmth and sweet shampoo. He caught a lock and brought it to his nose, wondering if she'd smell so sweet all over, or would her natural fragrance be spicy, like hot musk? He couldn't wait to find out, to nuzzle her throat and her breasts and her belly . . . between her thighs.

His muscles pulled tight with that thought. "You have beautiful hair," he all but growled.

Her lips parted at his husky tone, and her big eyes stared up at him. "I do?"

He wrapped that silky tendril around his finger and rubbed it with his thumb. "Hmmm. It's almost the exact same shade as your eyes."

Her laugh got carried off on the wind. "You mean plain old brown?"

"There's nothing plain about you, Asia, especially your coloring." They had reached her car, and he opened her door for her. He saw her surprise at the gentlemanly gesture, and it pleased him. "I'll see you at work tomorrow?"

"I'll be there."

Pretending to be much struck, Cameron said, "I just realized. You didn't buy anything. I hope my presence didn't inhibit you?"

Her small nose went into the air. "Not at all. I only wanted to see what they had."

He couldn't resist teasing her. "You didn't find anything you liked, huh?"

Those dark mysterious eyes of hers stared at him, and she said, "I found you, now didn't I?"

Cameron stepped back, stunned and so horny his stomach cramped.

She smiled with triumph. "Tomorrow, Cameron."

He watched her drive away. The next two days would be torture, waiting to get her in his bed, open to him, willing. He shook with need, then glanced down at the bag in his hand.

He'd use the time until then to study up on this kinky preference of hers, just to make sure he got it right.

That thought had him grinning. Were there rules to spanking? A time frame to follow? Did you jump right into it, or ease the way? Did the spanking follow the sex, or was it a form of foreplay?

He didn't know, but he'd sure as hell find out.

He shivered from a particularly harsh blast of icy wind, and realized he'd barely noticed the cold while Asia was close to him. Now that she'd left, he felt frozen. He hurried to his own car.

He had some studying to do.

Asia crawled into bed that night and pulled the thick covers to her chin. The sheets were icy cold, making her shiver, and she curled into a tight ball. It had been so very long since she'd felt a large male body in bed beside her, sharing warmth and comfort.

Sharing pleasure.

During her marriage, she'd learned to dread the nights her husband reached for her. Love-making had been tedious at best, uncomfortable and embarrassing at worst. His preferences at trying anything and everything—including discipline—whether she enjoyed it or not, had worn her down. He'd told her it was necessary, that she wasn't exciting enough, her body not sexy enough, to get him aroused without the added elements. After a while she'd begun to believe him, and it had taken a lot for her to finally realize he was the one with the problems, not her.

In the process, she'd gotten completely turned off sex. But she wasn't an idiot. She knew it wasn't always like that.

She didn't think it'd be like that with Cameron.

Thinking his name brought an image of him to mind. She rolled to her back and closed her eyes. Cameron, with his straight black hair. Not as straight or as black as Erica's, but in many ways more appealing, at least to her.

His hair had a chestnut cast to it in the light. And though she knew he was only in his early thirties, a bit of silver showed in his sideburns. His hair was a little too long at the nape, as if regular haircuts weren't high on his list of priorities. And judging by how often it was tousled, he didn't bother much with combs, either. She imagined him showering, shaving, combing his hair—and ending his personal grooming right there. She smiled.

The mental picture of him in the shower lingered, but his suits were so concealing, she could only guess at his physique. He was tall, lean in the middle, and his feet and hands were large. Beyond that, she didn't know.

She liked his eyes best. The many times when they'd spoken, his vivid blue eyes had been very direct. He tended to focus on her with a lot of intensity.

She shivered, but it wasn't from cold.

So many times her mind had wandered while chatting with him. Her heart would race, her skin would flush. She'd thought him dangerous to her, a threat to her independence, and she'd deliberately kept their association as casual, as businesslike, as possible.

But now she'd sought him out.

Would his eyes look that intense, hot from within, when he made love with her? That alone would be nice, she decided, remembering how her husband had always looked . . . distant from her. He'd treated her like nothing more than a convenient body, using her to gain his own pleasure.

Cameron would be aware of her, she was sure.

Was he at home right now, watching that risqué movie? Was he excited? Hard?

Her own soft groan sounded in the silence of her empty bedroom. Rolling to her side, she looked out the window. Snowflakes fell steadily, making patterns on the dark window. She could just make out the faint glow of colored Christmas lights on the house across the street.

Cameron would be alone for Christmas, just like her.

Her heart gave a funny little thump, sort of a poignant pain. The holidays were so lonely, so sad. If she and Cameron were together . . .

No! She wanted this one night of sex, but that was all. She didn't want or need another relationship, and sharing a holiday, especially one as emotional as Christmas, would definitely be a commitment of sorts. Wouldn't it?

She shook her head. Her independence was important to her, and she did just fine on her own. A steady relationship would intrude on that.

Was Cameron watching the movie? Was he thinking of her?

Disturbed by her own conflicting, changing thoughts, she sat up abruptly and turned on the light. Curiosity swamped her, made her body hot and tingly. She reached for the phone and dialed the operator. Cameron was too new to the area to be in the phone book, but the operator had a listing for him.

Asia clutched the phone, daring herself to call him, to ask him . . . what? If he was pleasuring himself? She imagined what that would entail and sensation exploded, like a tide of moist warmth, making her breath catch. She could easily visualize his large strong hand wrapped around his erection. She could see his beautiful blue eyes vague with lust, his hard jaw clenched, thighs and abdomen tensed as he stroked faster and faster . . .

She gasped with the image, feeling her own measure of burning excitement. Shaking, breathing too hard and fast, she bit her lip and dialed the number.

Cameron's sleep-rough voice answered on the third ring. "Hello?"

Asia froze. Oh, God, he'd been sleeping, not indulging in erotic daydreams or self-pleasure! Talk about missing the mark.

Her mouth opened but nothing came out. She'd awakened him when she didn't have a legitimate reason for calling.

"Hello?" he said again, this time with some impatience.

Asia slammed down the phone. Her heart galloped hard enough to hurt her ribs, and her stomach felt funny, kind of tight and sweet. In a rush she turned the light back off and slid under the covers, even pulling them over her head.

Cameron O'Reilly.

He turned her on, no doubt about it. Now if she could just not make a fool of herself, everything might go smoothly.

Cameron stared at the phone. Moving to one elbow he switched on the lamp at his bedside and checked the Caller I.D. Asia Michaels. A small curious smile tipped his mouth. There surely weren't two women in all of Cuther with that particular unique name.

She'd called him—then chickened out.

What had she wanted?

Naked, he eased back against the pillows, plenty warm now, thank you very much.

Very slowly, the smile turned into a toothy grin. Oh, he knew what she wanted, he reminded himself. She wanted sex. She wanted kink.

She wanted him.

Arms crossed behind his head, Cameron glanced at the tape sitting on his dresser across the room. He hadn't watched it yet. Because of what he'd overheard in the lounge, he hadn't gotten much work done the rest of the day. He'd been too distracted with thoughts of Asia and how he'd make love to her.

His preoccupation on the job meant he'd had to bring several files home to finish on his personal computer. By the time he was done, his eyes were gritty and he'd only wanted a few hours' sleep.

Now he only wanted Asia.

He wasn't at all sure he'd be able to wait until Friday. He needed to taste her before that, just to tide him over.

Soon, he promised himself. Very soon.

Chapter Three

"Cameron O'Reilly?" Erica repeated in disbelief, and fanned her face dramatically. "What a hunk!"

"You think?" Asia chewed her bottom lip. *She* thought him sexy as sin, especially now, but did other women think it too? "I mean, I admit I was surprised. He's just such a . . . suit."

Erica snorted. "Honey, all men are the same, white collar and blue collar alike. They're all sex addicts."

"I agree," Becky said. "O'Reilly is hot."

"You been checking him out?" Erica asked in some surprise.

"I'm not blind"—Becky sniffed with mock indignation—"if that's what you mean."

They all chuckled. "I wouldn't mind getting to know him better myself," Erica teased. "But he's never really noticed me. When I talk to him, he's polite, but always businesslike."

Asia fiddled with her coffee stirrer, then admitted, "We've spoken several times." She glanced up, then away. "At length."

"Ah." Erica grinned. "Do tell."

She shrugged. "He sort of . . . sought me out. He comes to my office, hangs around a bit, or catches me in the halls, or right after meetings. I . . . I like him, but I got the feeling he wanted to get more personal, so I . . . brushed him off."

"Are you nuts?"

Asia was sort of wondering that same thing herself, but for different reasons. "I just couldn't see starting something that likely wouldn't go anywhere."

Becky touched her hand. "You were afraid he wouldn't follow up?"

That nettled her new independent streak. "Ha! I wouldn't want him to. It's more likely that I wouldn't follow up."

Erica grinned. "That right?"

"Yes." And then, "Why is it always the woman who's supposed to sit around and wait for a damn phone call?"

Erica said, "Amen, sister. You'll get no argument from me. That's why even on dates, I buy my own meals, and I refuse flowers or gifts. If I want something, I can get it for myself. I don't need a guy. But sometimes I want one. So I go on my schedule, not his."

"Sounds to me," Becky said, "that you both like playing hard to get."

"No playing to it," Erica corrected. "I am hard to get."

Asia chuckled. She wasn't playing, either, though her motivation differed from Erica's. "Most of the guys here understand that I'm not interested, that it's a waste of time to want more from me than casual conversation."

Erica nodded knowingly. "But Cameron was new, so he didn't know, and he's been after you?"

"I figured he'd find out soon enough and leave me alone."

"But he didn't?"

She shook her head. "Whenever we're in the same room together, he watches me, and he smiles if our gazes meet." *And what a smile,* she thought privately, *enough to melt a woman's bones,* so, of course it was hell on her reserve.

"And now you know he has kinky sexual preferences," Erica pointed out with a sinner's grin.

"Now I know," Asia corrected, "that he has a healthy outlet. Honest, all the documentation I read said that what one fantasizes isn't generally what one wants in a real-life situation, which is why it's strictly a fantasy. Fantasies are safe. They are not, however, something we'd ever really try or even want to try."

"I used to think about getting stranded on a desert island with three hunks," Erica mused aloud. "None of us had clothes."

Asia and Becky snickered.

"But granted, I like modern luxuries too much to want to rough it just for male attention. Besides, I imagine one day on an island is all it'd take for me to start looking pretty haggard. No lotion, no scented shampoo, no blow dryer . . ."

"No birth control," Becky pointed out.

"And three men fighting for my body? That could get ugly."

"Maybe they'd just share," Asia suggested.

Erica shivered. "To tell you the truth, it's fine as a fantasy, but the idea of three naked sweaty guys bumping up against one another with me in the middle just sort of ruins the fantasy of them being there for *me*."

They were all still chuckling when suddenly Cameron approached. He had his hands in his pants pockets, a crooked smile on his handsome face.

He looked at each woman in turn. "Afternoon, ladies."

Agog, Becky wiggled her fingertips in a half-hearted wave.

Erica lounged back in her seat and grinned. "Mr. O'Reilly."

"Cameron, please." Then to Asia, "I'm sorry to interrupt your break, but could I speak to you for just a moment?"

Asia felt dumbstruck. She glanced at her friends, who made very differing faces at her, then nodded. "Uh, sure."

"In private." He gently took her arm and headed to the back of the lounge, to the large storage closet. Asia almost stalled. *A closet?* She felt workers looking up in casual interest; she felt Erica and Becky staring hard enough to burn a hole into her back.

She felt excitement roil inside her.

As if inviting her into a formal parlor instead of a closet, Cameron gallantly opened the door and gestured her inside.

She only hesitated a moment. He closed the door, leaving them in near darkness. One narrow window over the door let in the lounge's faded fluorescent light. Shadows were everywhere, from boxes and brooms and supplies. Asia backed up to a wall, a little apprehensive, a lot eager, and waited.

He tipped his head at her, frowning slightly. "I wanted to ask you something."

Oh no. No, no, no! He knew she'd called last night! He'd ask her about it, want to know why, and what the heck could she possibly tell him—

"Would you mind too much if I jumped the gun a little here and . . . kissed you?"

Asia froze, her thoughts suspended, her panic redirected, her heart skipping a beat.

"I know, I know." He rubbed the back of his neck, agitated. "The thing is, I can't stop thinking about it—or you—and I doubt I'll get any work done today if I don't." He looked at her, and his voice lowered. "You see, I'm going nuts wanting to taste you."

Taste her? It was like a dream, Asia thought, far removed from reality. Never had she expected any guy to say such a thing to her.

Asia collected her wayward thoughts and replied stupidly, "You are?"

He gave a slow, considering nod, took a step closer. "Would you mind?"

"Uh . . ." She looked around. They had privacy here in the dim closet, never mind that a crowd of people was right outside the door, oblivious to his request.

Even in the shadows, she could see his beautiful blue eyes watching her, hot and expectant. So very aware of her.

Her pulse tripped. She sucked in an unsteady breath and caught his scent—subtle aftershave and heated male flesh. Delicious scents that made her head swim.

He stepped closer still until he nearly touched her, his gaze now on her mouth, hungry and waiting. She licked her lips and started to whisper, "All right—"

And with a soft groan, his mouth was there, covering hers, gentle and warm and firm. His hands flattened on the wall on either side of her head and his chest almost touched hers. Not quite, but she felt the body heat radiating off him in waves, carrying more of that delicious scent for her to breathe in, letting her fill herself up with it until she shook.

"Open your mouth," he murmured against her lips, and like a zombie—a very aroused zombie— she did.

He didn't thrust his tongue into her mouth. No, he licked her lips with a warm, velvet tongue, gentle, easy. Then just inside her mouth, slowly, over the edges of her teeth, her own tongue.

Asia moaned and opened more in blatant invitation, wanting his tongue. Wanting all of him.

He slid in, deep and slow, then out again.

"Jesus." He dropped his head forward and she felt his uneven breaths pelting her cheek. He gave a short, low laugh, roughened by his arousal. "You make me feel like a schoolboy again."

Her heart in her throat, panting and trembling, Asia managed to say, "Made out in a lot of closets, did you?"

"Hmm?" His head lifted, his eyes burning on her face, still eager, still intent.

She swallowed back a groan. "In school."

"Oh." He smiled, looked at her mouth and kissed her again, a brief, teasing kiss to her bottom lip. "No. No, I didn't. But I did walk around with a perpetual hard-on, and damn if that isn't what you do to me."

Was there a proper reply a lady made to such a comment? If so, Asia had no idea what it might be.

His big rough hands settled on her face, cupping her cheeks, his thumbs smoothing over her temples. He looked concerned. Horny and concerned. "I'm sorry if I'm rushing you."

She almost laughed at that. The way he made her feel, she wanted to be rushed. "Do you hear me complaining?"

"No," he said slowly. "No, you're not." His expression turned thoughtful. "Can I take that to mean you want me too?"

He was so blunt! She hadn't expected it of him. In her experience—admittedly limited—well-dressed corporate types were more reserved. She heard lewd jests from the factory workers all the time. And she heard the maintenance guys make ribald jokes throughout the day. But the suits . . . they generally feared sexual harassment charges and any kidding they did remained very private.

Erica claimed all men were the same when it came to sex, but Asia knew that wasn't true. Some men approached sex as a free-for-all. Her ex-husband had been that way. He wanted it whenever he could get it, whoever he could get it from.

Some saw sex as a commitment, others as a challenge.

And some, she hoped, saw it as a mutual exchange of pleasure, best experienced with respect and consideration.

So far, Cameron struck her as that type of man. Finally, she answered, "Yes."

He let out a breath. "You took so long to answer,

I wasn't sure." He rubbed her bottom lip with the edge of his thumb, smiling. "You've got a masochistic streak in you, don't you?"

"No, I just wasn't . . . sure how to answer."

This time he laughed. "That'll teach my ego to get excited."

She covered her face with her hands. "I'm making a mess of this aren't I?"

"Not at all. You gave me my kiss, and that was more than I had a right to ask for." Stepping back, he said, "I should let you get back to your friends."

But she didn't want him going through the day thinking she *didn't* want him. Because she did. More so with every blasted second.

Forcing herself to be bold, Asia lifted her chin and looked him right in his sexy blue eyes. "Will you give me another kiss first?"

He stared down at her, that charming crooked smile in place. He leaned back against the wall and said, "Why don't you kiss me this time? Just to be fair?"

He kept taking her by surprise! She'd been under the impression all men liked to be in control, at all times. She realized this proved her theory about the sexually explicit movie he'd purchased. Even though he bought a tape that showed a man dominating in the most elemental way, he'd just offered to let her take the lead. She braced herself.

In for a penny . . . Asia put her hands on his shoulders, then stalled. He was so hard.

His suit coat hid some broad shoulders and a lot of solid muscle. She hadn't realized before, but now the proof was in her hands and it was unbearably enticing. Would he be that hard all over?

She shivered. What a thought.

Trailing her fingers downward, she found his biceps and inhaled in triumph. Solid, strong. No underexercised executive here! Cameron O'Reilly was all rugged male.

Eyes closed, Asia flexed her fingers, relishing the feel of hard muscle, strong bones and obvious strength. Her stomach did a little flip of excitement and she stepped into him while going on tiptoe. When he'd kissed her, only their mouths had touched.

But Asia wanted more and she saw no reason to deny herself. She fitted her body to his, soft breasts to broad chest, curving belly to hard abdomen . . . pelvis to pelvis. He groaned low and rough, and then his hands were on the small of her back, pressing her closer, and she felt his solid erection, long and hot, pulsing through the layers of clothes.

"Oh my," she whispered, going well beyond impressed to the realm of awed.

"Give me your mouth, Asia."

No sooner did she comply, kissing him with all the pent-up desire she suffered, than he turned them both so she was the one pressed to the wall. One of his hands slid down her back to her behind, and he gripped her, lifting, bringing her into startling contact with his erection.

He pressed into her rhythmically, rubbing himself against her, setting her on fire, all the while kissing her, soft eating kisses, deep-driving kisses, wet and hot and consuming.

A rap at the door made them both jump.

Erica called in, "Sorry kiddies, but playtime is over. Time to come in from recess."

Asia slumped against the wall and groaned. She'd totally forgotten her surroundings!

Watching her closely, Cameron cleared his throat. "We'll be right there."

With laughter in her voice, Erica said, "If you wait just two little minutes, the room will be clear and you can escape without notice." They both heard the sound of her retreating footsteps.

"I'm sorry."

Asia looked up. "For what?"

Stroking her cheek gently, he said, "I meant only a simple kiss—well okay, not so simple—but I didn't mean to embarrass you."

She sighed even as her heart softened. What an incredible man. "Cameron, you called a halt," she felt compelled to point out, "and I insisted on one more kiss. I'm the one who should be apologizing."

"Are you sorry?" he asked, and he wore that absorbed expression again, which now looked endearing.

"The truth? Nope." He grinned at her and she added, "I've never done anything like this before. It feels good to be a bit naughty."

"Yeah?" He tilted his head, studying her. "Any time you wanna get naughty, lady, you just let me know."

He was full of surprises. "You're not worried about how it might look to others?"

"You're worth the risk."

The things he said played havoc with her restraint. "I'll keep your offer in mind," she whispered as she opened the door, and they were both relieved to see the room was, indeed, empty.

Tomorrow, she decided, couldn't get here soon enough.

* * *

Cameron threw his suit coat over the arm of a chair, kicked his dress shoes into the closet and loosened his tie. All day long, his thoughts had centered on Asia. Damn, but she tasted better, felt better, than he'd imagined. He'd wanted to make love to her there in the closet with the two of them standing, a crowd in the outer room.

He closed his eyes a moment and imagined lifting her long skirt, feeling her grip his shoulders and hook her long slender legs around his waist. He pictured her head back, her eyes closed, her lips parted on a raw cry as he pushed into her.

She would be open, unable to meter the depth of his strokes, and he'd take her so long, so deeply, she'd scream with the pleasure of it. His stomach cramped with lust.

Better not to use the closet, he decided with a rueful grin. He didn't want her stifled in any way, not after the two months he'd spent fantasizing about her. At first, it had been simple lust—she looked exactly as he thought a woman should look. Soft, sexy, capable, and her brown eyes were always bright with intelligence. She was friendly, but not flirtatious. Subtly sensual, with only her natural femininity on display. She didn't flaunt, didn't go out of her way to enhance her looks.

The more he'd gotten to know her, the more he'd wanted her. But she gave him only casual conversation, allowing him to view her generous spirit, her quick smiles and easy nature from an emotional distance. In the two months he'd known her, he'd absorbed all the small glimpses of her character, which had acted as more enticement.

He not only wanted her sexually, he just plain wanted her.

Tomorrow night he'd have her.

He didn't know if he'd survive that long.

He tossed his tie onto the chair with his coat and reached into his pants pocket for the gift he'd bought her. He hadn't meant to go shopping, but on the drive home he'd stopped for a red light, and his eye had caught the festive Christmas display in a jewelry store window. Once he saw the bracelet, he wanted it for her.

For a first date, it was a bit extravagant, he thought, but what the hell. He'd known her two months now, necked with her in a closet, fantasized about her endlessly, and besides, he liked to think positive; he had a gut feeling that this would be the first date of many.

He could call it a Christmas gift. After all, he still had hopes of convincing her to spend the day with him.

The exotic burnished gold and topaz-studded bracelet reminded him of Asia's coloring. As he'd told her, she was far from plain. He put the bracelet back in the velvet-lined box and set it on his dresser, then put the spanking tape into the VCR. He picked up the remote and stretched out in his bed on top of the covers, two fat pillows behind his back, one arm folded behind his head.

He hit play, and settled in to be educated.

As the story—ha! what story?—started, he thought of Asia and knew there wasn't much he wouldn't do to win her over. Including indulging in a little kinky sex.

Chapter Four

Cameron sat behind his desk, a spreadsheet on his computer screen, early the next morning. Steaming coffee filled the cold morning with delicious scents. The windows overlooking the parking lot were decorated with lacy frost, while more snowflakes, fat as cotton balls, drifted down to the sill. The quiet strains of Christmas music from the outer office drifted in.

The knock on the door jarred him and he looked up. "Come in."

Asia peered around the door, smiled at him and asked, "Are you busy?"

Without a single hesitation, he closed out the computer screen. "Not at all."

She inched in, looking furtive and so sexy, his abdomen clenched. Both hands behind her still holding the doorknob, she rested against the closed door. "I hoped you were in."

A glance at the clock showed him she'd come to work almost a half hour early. He'd been there for an hour himself. After watching the tape, he'd found it impossible to relax. He kept seeing Asia in every position depicted by the actors, and when he'd finally drifted off to sleep, he'd dreamed of her. Not since his teens had he awoken in a sweat, but last night he had.

Heart thumping and cock at full attention, Cameron eased out from behind his desk. "Is anything wrong?"

He searched her face, looking for clues to her thoughts. If she planned to break their date for that night, he'd need to find a way to change her mind.

Her cheeks flushed and her beautiful eyes, locked on his, darkened to mahogany. "Do you mind if I lock this?" she asked, indicating the door.

Cameron stepped closer. "Please do."

The lock clicked like a thunderclap, echoing the sounds of his heartbeat. When she turned to face him again, Cameron murmured, "I'm glad to see you, Asia."

She folded her hands together at her waist. Her long brown hair hung loose, like a rich velvet curtain. The ends curled the tiniest bit, barely reaching the tips of her breasts, which were enticingly molded beneath a beige cashmere sweater. Her neutral-toned patterned skirt ended a mere inch below her knees and was trim enough to outline the shape of her thighs. Wearing flats, she just reached his chin, and she looked up at him.

"I thought maybe we could . . ." She stalled, shifted uncertainly.

His testicles drew tight and his cock flexed at the thought of touching and kissing her again. "Yes?"

She lifted one shoulder in a self-conscious shrug. "I liked kissing you yesterday."

"Liked? I'm surprised I didn't catch on fire." He smiled, trying to take some of the heavy desire from his words. He didn't want to scare her off. There were few people in the building yet. Most wouldn't show up for another twenty-five minutes. He had her all to himself. "I dreamed about you last night."

Her lips parted. "You did?"

Cameron couldn't stop himself from touching her. Using the backs of his knuckles, he smoothed a long tendril of hair—right over her breast. Her nipple puckered, and deliberately he rasped it, teasing her, teasing himself more. He heard the catch of her breath. Her eyes were closed, her chest rising and falling.

"Are you wearing a bra, Asia?" he asked, unable to detect one with his easy touch.

She shook her head. "A . . . a demi bra."

"Meaning your nipples," he murmured, lifting both hands to her, "are uncovered?"

Ah, yes, he could tell now as he caught each tip between his fingers and thumbs and pinched lightly. The cashmere sweater was incredibly soft and did nothing to conceal his touch. Her nipples were tight, pushed up by the bra, but not covered. He gently plucked and rolled and she suddenly grasped his wrists.

"I don't believe this," she moaned.

Cameron didn't remove his hands. She wasn't restraining him so much as holding onto him. He leaned close and nuzzled her temple. "This?" he asked, unsure of her meaning.

"I don't . . . I'm not usually . . ."

He had no idea what she wanted to tell him. "You like this?" He tugged at her nipples, making her sway toward him. Her breasts were very sensitive, he discovered, as heat throbbed beneath his skin.

"I do," she rasped, then dropped her head forward to his shoulder, panting. "I'm not usually so . . . so easy."

Cameron pressed his mouth to the delicate skin of her temple, then her cheekbone. "Easy? I've wanted you for two months." He drew the tender skin of her throat against his teeth, careful not to mark her. "I don't call that easy."

"No, but . . ." She sucked in a breath, then cried out. Her fingers clenched on his wrists and her hips pressed inward, trying to find him. "Cameron, I feel like I'm going to—"

Realization dawned, and he stared at her in wonder. "You want to climax, Asia?"

She didn't answer for the longest time while he continued to toy with her breasts, and she continued to writhe against him. "Oh, please," she finally gasped, nearly beside herself.

Cameron released her, ignoring her soft moan of disappointment, and put an arm around her waist. "C'mere," he said, almost blind with lust.

He led her to his desk. She looked at him with darkened eyes, a little unfocused, a lot hungry. "Just a second," he said and reached for her narrow skirt.

She made a slight sound of surprise when he worked the snug material up to her hips, then lifted her to sit on the edge of the desk. She looked up, a question in her eyes, but he stepped between her thighs and took her mouth, devouring her, his tongue licking, his teeth nipping.

She wrapped both arms around his neck and held on.

He hated panty hose, he thought, as he trailed his fingers up her nylon-clad thighs. Stockings that left her vulnerable to him would have been better, but he'd make do.

He teased her, kissing her while stroking the insides of her thighs until she was nearly frantic. Then he pressed his palm against her mound and they both went still.

"Mmmm," he whispered, his fingers pressing gently, exploring. "You're wet."

She ducked her face into his throat.

Blood roared in his ears, but he made himself move slow and easy. "I can even feel you through your panties and your hose."

"Oh, God." She lurched a little when he stroked over her with his middle finger. "This is awful."

He smiled. "You want me to quit?" he teased.

"Please don't!"

With her legs parted, the panties and panty hose couldn't hide her state of desire. He could feel every sweet inch of her, the curly pubic hair, the swollen lips. Her distended clitoris.

He groaned. With one arm around her holding her tight, he used the other hand to pet and finger and tease. Her hips shifted, rolled against him. "Is this good, Asia?" he asked, wanting, needing to know if it was enough.

Her head tipped back, lips parted on her panting breaths, her body arched—and then she broke.

Her eyes squeezed shut, her teeth sank into her bottom lip to hold back the moans coming from deep in her throat.

Cameron felt like a world conqueror, watching her beautiful, carnal expressions, feeling the harsh trembling in her body.

"Yes," he murmured, keeping his touch steady, even, despite her frantic movements and the mad dashing of his heart. "That's it, sweetheart. That's it."

By slow degrees, she stilled, her body going boneless. Cameron gathered her close into his arms and held her. His own desire was keen, but at the same time, he felt a heady satisfaction. She smelled warm, a little sweaty despite the frigid winter storm outside and the nip of the air in his office. And she smelled female, the scent guaranteed to fire his blood.

He rocked her gently and smoothed his big hands up and down her narrow back.

Against his throat, she whispered, "I think I'm embarrassed."

"You think?" He couldn't help but chuckle, he felt so damn good. Sexually frustrated, but emotionally sated. "Please don't be. I'm not."

"This was . . . unfair of me."

"This was very generous of you."

That left her speechless. Cameron tangled one hand in her silky hair and tipped her head up to him so he could see her face. "Thank you."

She laughed, groaned and dropped her forehead to his sternum. "I can't wait until tonight, Cameron. I didn't believe it at first, but I know it's going to be so good."

What did she mean, she hadn't believed it at first? Then the rest of what she said hit him and he stilled. "You intend to make love with me tonight?" He had hoped and planned, but he hadn't expected a confirmation.

She looked up in surprise. "You want to, don't you?"

Bemused, he said, "More than I want my next breath."

Her smile was a beautiful thing. "I'm sorry about doing this now. I'd only meant a few more kisses—more of that naughtiness we'd joked about. But then you . . . you touched me and I lost it."

"I'm not sorry, so don't you be either. I'm glad you're so sensitive, so hot."

She looked down at his tie. "I didn't know I was." Then, "I never was before." She met his gaze with a look of confusion. "I think it's just you."

Cameron didn't bother denying that. He couldn't think of a woman hotter than Asia Michaels. But he'd be damned if he'd explain it wasn't him, taking a chance that she'd find another guy. No way.

"Tonight will be even better," she said, then peeked up at him as if waiting for his reply.

Was this his cue that tonight he was supposed to do something different? Something more . . . forceful? He said, his tone filled with caution, "I want you to be satisfied with me, Asia."

Her eyes brightened, and she threw her arms around his throat again, nearly strangling him. "Thank you." Leaning back, she added with sincerity, "I really am sorry to do this, to leave you . . . unsatisfied. But I never suspected it'd go this far."

He kissed the end of her nose and said, "I'll think of it as extended foreplay."

His phone rang just as she pulled away and began straightening her skirt. Her cheeks were rosy, her eyes slumberous and sated. Watching her, regretting the necessity that kept her beautiful legs hidden from him, Cameron hit a button and said absently, "Yes?"

"You asked that I remind you about the meeting first thing this morning, Mr. Cameron."

"Thank you, Marsha."

He disconnected the line. Marsha was a secretary for the entire floor, which included four supervisors. She kept everyone punctual and was observant as hell.

He looked at Asia. "Do you mind if Marsha knows we're seeing each other?"

She shook her head. "Do you?"

His grin turned wolfish as he stepped past her to unlock and open the door. No one was in the hallway to notice, and for that he was grateful. He wouldn't tolerate gossip about Asia.

"I want everyone to know," he told her, and turned to face her again with a smile. "Maybe it'll keep the rest of the men from pursuing you."

"The guys here?" she asked, and scoffed. "They all know I'm not interested."

"But you are," he reminded her, looking at her breasts, her belly and thighs. "You're interested in *me*."

He waited for her to deny it, but all she did was shrug. "It's strange. You affect me differently."

He sauntered toward her, filled with confidence. "I make you hot."

She looked perplexed as hell when she said, "Yeah."

Cameron shook his head. It had taken her two months to notice the sexual chemistry he'd picked up on within two minutes of meeting her. If it hadn't been for the damned porn shop just opening, she still wouldn't have given him the time of day. He couldn't forget that. Asia with her big bedroom eyes and standoffish ways had a sexual predilection, and last night he'd watched the tape and learned how to appease her.

Her preferences were still foreign to him, but less unappealing. Some of the scenes, in fact, had really turned him on. He'd imagined Asia in place of the overblown actress. He pictured her firm, lush bottom turned up to the warm smacks of a large male hand—his hand. The smacking part didn't interest him much, even though the swats had done little more than redden her bottom, and ultimately prepare her for a hard ride.

But the touching afterward, the utter vulnerability and accessibility of the woman's sex to probing fingers and tongue had made him hot as hell. The actress had remained in the submissive position, bent over a footstool, hands flat on the floor, knees spread wide, and in Cameron's mind it had been Asia, waiting for him, ready for him.

He sucked in a deep breath, drawing Asia's notice.

Her eyes were again apologetic when she asked, "Are you okay?"

"Other than being hard as a spike, yes."

She smiled. "That might make your meeting difficult."

Cameron took her arm and led her toward the door. "Once you're gone I'll get myself in order. That is, if I can stop thinking about tonight."

The hallway was still clear, not a soul in sight. Memory of the movie still played in his mind, and when Asia turned away, he gave her rump a sound smack. She jumped, whirled to face him with both hands holding her behind and her eyes enormous.

Cameron forced himself to a neutral smile,

though the look on her face was priceless, a mixture of surprise and awareness. "I'll see you tonight," he said.

Frowning, rubbing her backside, she gave an absent nod and hurried away.

His palm stung a little, and his cock throbbed. He could do this, he told himself as he went to his desk to gather the necessary files. And if he did it well enough, he'd be able to reel her in.

He wanted Asia Michaels, and one way or another, he'd have her.

Asia thought about that rather stinging smack throughout the day. It meant nothing, she told herself, just teasing gone a little overboard. Cameron had been so gentle, so concerned for her and her pleasure, that she trusted him.

But she'd left his office and gone straight to the restroom. After their little rendezvous, she needed to tidy up. And she couldn't stop herself from peeking once she had her panty hose down in the private stall.

Sure enough, Cameron's large hand print, faintly pink and still warm, showed on her white bottom. The sight of that handprint made her heart race with misgivings . . . and something more.

Long after she'd returned to her desk, she was still aware of the warmth on her cheek, the tingling of that print. It kept Cameron and what they'd done in his office in the forefront of her mind throughout the entire day. She could not stop thinking about him, about the pleasure he'd given her so easily when that type of pleasure had always eluded her. She couldn't put his thought-fulness or tenderness from her mind.

And she couldn't forget that swat.

As she dressed for the date that night, she again surveyed her bottom. But the mark was long gone, with only the memory remaining. It meant nothing, she told herself yet again, but still her heartbeat sped up whenever she thought of it.

Cameron was right on time. The second she opened her door, he leaned in and kissed her. Snowflakes hung in his dark hair and dusted the shoulders of his black coat. He'd dressed in casual slacks, a dress shirt and sweater.

Asia waited for the verdict as he looked her over from head to toe. Her dress was new, a dark burgundy with gold flecks around the low-scooped neckline and shin-length hem. She wore dark brown leather boots with two-inch heels. Her long hair was in a French braid, hanging down the middle of her back, and gold hoop earrings decorated her ears.

"You look incredible," Cameron murmured, then pulled her close and kissed her again, this time with purpose.

Asia quivered with need. When her mouth was again free, she said, "Maybe . . . maybe we should skip dinner?" She didn't want to eat. She wanted to be alone with Cameron, to find out the extent of these amazing sexual feelings he inspired.

She'd told Erica at break that she owed her big time, because if it hadn't been for her, she'd never have discovered the truth. As she'd always suspected, fireworks did exist. You only needed the right man to set them off.

Cameron was evidently the right man.

He took her hand and kissed her palm. She felt the brief touch of his warm, damp tongue and nearly moaned. "Do you need to be up early tomorrow?" he asked.

"No, my weekends are always free."

He took her cloak from her and helped her slip it on. "I hope they won't be free anymore."

Asia had nothing to say to that. She couldn't deny that she wanted to see him again.

"I'll feed you," Cameron continued, "and then we'll go to my place."

She sniffed and turned away, a little put out that he seemed less anxious than she.

Cameron hugged her from behind, chuckling softly. In her ear, he whispered, "The tension will build and build, sweetheart. Just be patient with me, okay?"

She didn't want to be patient, but she figured he had to know more about this than she did. Her experience with sex was that it wasn't much fun most of the time, and other times it was just plain awful.

"All right."

An hour later, Asia was ready to kill him. The restaurant where they had dinner was elegant, expensive and crowded. Festive Christmas music played softly through the speaker system, and fat gold candles, decorated with holly, lit each table.

People talked and smiled and laughed, and Asia felt conspicuous, as if everyone there knew she was aroused but was too polite to point at her.

Cameron kept her on that keen edge, touching her constantly, her cheek, her chin, her shoulders—

touches that seemed innocent but still made her burn because she knew exactly what he could do with those touches, how he could make her body scream in incredible pleasure.

What would it be like when he pushed deep inside her, when he rode her and the friction was within as well as without? She bit her lip hard to keep from gasping aloud with her thoughts.

And still she couldn't stop thinking them.

Feeling his touch through the barrier of clothes had been indescribable, but when he touched naked flesh, would she be able to stand it? When it was his mouth on her nipples, not just his fingers, how much more would she experience? She shuddered at the thought and felt her body turning liquid.

They danced twice, and the way he moved against her should have been illegal. He knew what he did to her, and he enjoyed it.

She was on fire, her breath coming too fast and too deep, and still he lingered at the table, watching her closely, talking idly about inconsequential things. Her heart threatened to burst, and though the wind howled outside, she felt feverish and taut.

"Asia?"

She jumped, nearly panicked by the unfamiliar lust and anticipation. She stared at him blankly.

Cameron just smiled. "I asked you where you got your name."

She squeezed her hands together, trying to concentrate on things other than the way his dark hair fell over his brow, or how his strong jaw moved as he spoke, or the warm male scent of him that made her stomach curl deliciously. His large hands rested on the tabletop, his wrists thick, his fingers long and rough-tipped—fingers that had touched and teased her. Fingers that would be inside her body tonight.

She closed her eyes, remembering.

Cameron smoothed a curl behind her ear, and his voice was rough and low. "Tell me how you got that name, honey."

She swallowed down her growing excitement. "My grandmother's name was Anastasia. My father wanted to name me after her, but my mother thought the name too long."

"So they shortened it to Asia?"

"Yes." Talking required too much concentration.

"It's a beautiful name." His fingertips drifted over her cheek, down her throat, trailed along the neckline of her dress.

She gasped. "Cameron . . ."

"Are you ready to go?" he asked, even as he stood and pulled out her chair.

"More than ready," she muttered. While he tended to the bill, Asia pulled on her wrap and turned to leave. Cameron caught her arm before she'd taken three steps.

They walked in silence to his car. The parking garage was freezing cold and her accelerated breath frosted in the air. Cameron saw her seated, then went around to his side of the car.

They were on the road, only minutes from his apartment, before he asked, "You're not nervous, are you?"

Asia stared at him. She was so beyond nervous, it was all she could do to keep from jumping him. "I'm so excited I can barely stand it."

He kept his profile to her, but that didn't diminish the beauty of his masculine satisfaction. "Good. I want you excited."

Asia thrust her chin into the air. "I want you excited, too."

Without looking her way, he reached across the seat and caught her arm. His hand trailed down to her wrist, then lifted her fingers into his lap. She inhaled sharply at the well-defined, pulsing erection.

"Believe me, I'm excited," he said simply.

Rather than release him when he replaced his hand on the steering wheel, Asia scooted closer. He was a large man, his sex strong and long. She traced him through his trousers, glancing at his face occasionally to see his jaw locking hard, his nostrils flaring. His blue eyes looked very dark, frighteningly intense.

His penis flexed in her grasp, and she tightened her hold. She stroked him with her thumb, forcing the material of his slacks to rub against him. Her thumb moved up and over the head of his penis— and just that quickly, he grabbed her hand and forced it away.

"No," he said harshly, but without anger. "I won't be able to keep us on the road if you do that."

"When we get to your place," she murmured, understanding now why he enjoyed teasing, because she enjoyed it too, "I'll do that to you again. Only you'll be naked."

Cameron gripped the wheel hard, his mouth open as he sucked in air. "I'll hold you to that, sweetheart." And then he turned in toward his apartment complex.

Chapter Five

Cameron kissed her as he opened her car door, kissed her in the parking lot and on the stairs up to his apartment. He couldn't seem to stop kissing her and she didn't try to make him.

Getting his door unlocked was no easy feat with Asia smoothing her soft little hands all over his body, her mouth open on his throat, her fingertips gliding down his abdomen.

He tugged her inside, slammed the door, and fell with her onto the couch. He felt like a caveman, but his control was shot to hell; he'd teased too long.

She shifted around until she laid atop him. "Cameron," she muttered, and then kissed his face, his ear, his jaw.

He caught her, holding her steady so he could devour her sweet mouth. They moved together, hampered by coats and too many clothes and an urgent desire that obliterated reason.

"Damn," he growled, startled as he felt himself sliding off the couch to the floor.

They landed with a thump. He was dumbstruck for a moment, then heard Asia giggle.

"Witch," he groused low, and sat up beside her. He yanked at the fastenings of her cloak and spread it wide. Her breasts heaved, her legs moved restlessly. Cameron lowered himself again, this time with both hands cupping her breasts.

The air filled with their moans and sighs, but again, it became too frustrating. He didn't want to stop kissing her, but he stood up and jerked his coat off, tossing it aside, then pulled his sweater over his head.

Asia stayed on the floor, sprawled wantonly, watching him. When his chest was bare and her eyes were soft and wide, looking at him, he knelt and began removing her boots. "These are sexy," he said low, tugging them off and eyeing her bare legs beneath. His gaze sought hers and he raised one brow. "No panty hose this time?"

She shook her head. Silky fine tendrils of hair had escaped her braid and framed her face. Her lashes hung heavy, her eyes nearly black with lust. "I wanted to make it easier for you to touch me."

Her words were powerfully arousing. In a rush, he plunged his hands up under her skirt and caught the waistband of her minuscule panties. He started to drag them off her, but seeing her face, the anticipation there, he forced himself to slow down.

He had to remember that Asia had special requirements, a refined inclination toward erotic discipline, and if he wanted to keep her for more than a night or two, he had to adjust. Her pleasure meant everything to him, was half of his own pleasure, so he slowed himself. Instead of pulling her panties off, he cupped her through the thin silk.

"Hot, swollen," he said, watching her back arch. "You want me, don't you sweetheart?"

"Yes," she moaned, her eyes now closing.

He petted her, letting one long finger press between her lips, rub gently over her clitoris.

"Oh, God," she whispered brokenly.

Watching her was almost as good as sex, Cameron decided. She was so beautiful to him, so perfect. So open and honest and giving.

He removed his hand and flipped her onto her stomach.

She froze for a heartbeat, her hands flat on the carpet at either side of her breasts. "Cameron?"

"Let me get this dress off you," he explained, and worked the zipper down her back. The bodice opened and he caught the shoulders, pulling them down to her elbows. She freed her right arm, then her left.

Kneeling between her widespread thighs, Cameron eyed her slender back, the graceful line of her spine. In a rush, he pulled the dress the rest of the way off.

Asia half raised herself, but he pressed a hand to the small of her back and took his time looking at her. Her bottom was plump, her cheeks rounded and firm. He stroked her with both hands, feeling the slide of silken panties over her skin.

"Cameron . . ."

"Shhh." He unfastened her bra and let it fall, freeing her breasts. Leaning over her, his cock nestled securely against that delectable ass, he balanced on one arm. With his free hand he reached beneath her and stroked her breasts, paying special attention to her pointed, sensitized nipples. She gave a ragged moan.

Cameron languidly rubbed himself against her, almost blind with need. It would be so easy to enter her this way. She was wet, hot and slippery and he could sink right in.

He groaned and pushed himself away. He had to do this right.

Before he changed his mind, he kicked off his shoes, sat on the edge of the couch, and pulled off his socks.

Asia was near his feet and she turned her head to look at him curiously. Their eyes met and she started to rise.

Cameron caught her under her arms. Her bra fell completely off, and it stunned him, this first glimpse at her bared body. She wore only transparent, insubstantial panties; they offered her no protection at all.

"You are so beautiful," he said with complete inadequacy.

She smiled shyly, reached for him—and he pulled her across his knees.

For a brief moment, she froze. "Cameron?"

When he didn't answer, determined on his course, Asia twisted to look at him. He controlled her easily, his gaze focused solely on that gorgeous behind. He could see the deep cleft, and the dark triangle of feminine curls covering her mound. He traced her with a fingertip, down the line of her buttocks, in between. She stilled, her breathing suspended.

Her panties were damp with her excitement and he pressed into her, feeling her heat, her swollen lips. His eyes closed. He wanted to taste her, wanted to tongue her and hear her soft cries. Her hands, braced on his thigh, tightened, her nails digging into his muscles even through his slacks.

He had to do this right.

Teeth clenched, Cameron opened his eyes, looked at his big dark hand on her very soft feminine bottom, and forced himself to give her a stinging slap.

She yelped.

"How does that feel?" he rasped, lifting his hand for another.

Asia was frozen on his thighs, not moving, not speaking.

He brought his hand down again, doing his best to meter his strength, to let her feel the warmth of the smack without actually hurting her in any way.

His heart thundered and his pulse roared in his ears. He thought he might split his pants he was so turned on, despite the distaste he felt in striking her. After all, they were minutes away from making love and she was a warm, womanly scented weight over his lap, all but naked and so beautiful—

"You bastard!"

Like a wild woman, she launched herself away from him. Stupefied, Cameron looked at her sprawled on the carpet some feet away, her naked breasts heaving, her eyes wet with tears.

Tears!

Her bottom lip trembled and she said with stark accusation, "I thought you were different!"

Very unsure of himself and the situation, Cameron said, "Uh . . ." And then, "I'm . . . trying to be."

"You hit me!"

He had. Cameron looked at his hand, stinging a little from contact with that beautiful behind, and said again, "Uh . . ."

Asia pushed to her feet. Her breasts swayed, full and still flushed from arousal, the nipples tight points. Feet planted apart in a stance guaranteed to make his blood race, she glared at him.

Slowly, very slowly so he didn't spook her or make this bizarre situation worse, Cameron came to his feet. "You wanted me to," he reminded her.

Her eyes widened even more. "What are you talking about?"

He shrugged, gestured toward his bedroom where the damning tape was still in the VCR. He rubbed the back of his neck and felt a sick foreboding close around him. "You, ah, wanted a guy who was into spanking."

She gasped so hard her breasts jiggled, further exacerbating his desire. "You listened!" she accused.

"Not on purpose."

It was as if she hadn't heard him. "You were the guy with the newspaper in the lounge. The guy wearing jeans!"

"Yeah. I, ah, had to work outside that day, to oversee work on the compressors, so my clothes were different." He nearly winced as he admitted that, then thought to add, a bit righteous, "The lounge is a public place and I heard you say plain as day that you were into spanking."

"I said no such thing!"

"Yes, you did." Didn't she? Her face was red, but he barely noticed with her standing there, the body he'd been dreaming about for two full months more bare than not. "You said you would hook up with the guy who bought a spanking tape. Well, I bought the stupid thing."

"Stupid thing?" she growled, and advanced toward him. "You mean you don't watch them?"

"I never had before." He was mightily distracted from the argument by the way she moved, and how her body moved, and how much he wanted her. "But I'd have bought a tape of monkeys mating if that's what it took to get your attention."

She drew up short, a mere foot away from him. "That's sick!"

Cameron leaned forward, his own temper igniting. "No, sweetheart. That's desperation. I wanted you. You barely acknowledged me, except in that too cool, distantly polite voice that kept miles between us. I heard you in the lounge and took advantage. So what?"

She looked slightly confused for a moment, then pugnacious. "You struck me."

"Because I thought you wanted me to. Hell, do you think *I* wanted to?"

"Didn't you?" She gave a pointed stare to his straining erection.

Cameron grunted. "You're almost naked. You're excited and wet and hot, and I've been hard since the day I first saw you."

She blinked uncertainly. "You're saying you didn't want to swat me?"

Hands on his hips, he leaned down, nose to nose with her. "There are a lot of things I'd rather do to your beautiful naked ass than spank it."

She half turned away, then back. Watching him with suspicion, and what appeared to be sensual curiosity, she asked, "Like what?"

Cameron took a small step forward, further

closing the gap between them. In a lower, more controlled but gravelly voice, he said, "Like pet you, and kiss you—"

"My behind?"

"Hell, yes." Moving slowly, he reached out and caught her shoulders. "I can't imagine any man alive not wanting to kiss your behind."

She giggled at the wording, but flushed at the meaning. "My husband would have never considered . . ."

He released her so fast, he almost tripped. "Husband?"

"Ex-husband."

Clutching his heart, Cameron said, "Thank God." It took him a second to recover from that panic. He hadn't heard anything about her being married. "So you're divorced?"

"Yes."

"You still care about him?"

She laughed, which was a better answer than a straight out "no," but she gave him that too.

"I stopped caring about him almost as soon as I said, 'I do.' Unfortunately, it took longer than that for me to admit it to everyone else and to get the divorce."

He didn't want to talk about any idiot ex-husband. Holding her shoulders again, he said, "Know what I want to do?"

Her hand lifted to his crotch, cuddled his cock warmly. Her smile was sweet and enticing. "I can maybe guess."

He drew a deep breath. "You're willing?"

"No more hitting?"

Cameron kissed her. "It took all my concentration to get it done the first time. Believe me, it was for you, for what I thought you wanted. Not for me."

She looked touched by his gesture. "Then, yes, I'm willing."

Disinclined to take the chance that she might change her mind, Cameron lifted her in his arms and started for his bedroom. "I promise to make it up to you," he said. And he meant it. Now that he could think clearly, he'd know to concentrate on her responses, not on the dumb conversation he'd overheard. But that made him think of something else.

"Can I ask you a question?"

"That is a question," Asia replied, but she didn't sound put out. She was too engrossed in his chest, caressing his chest hair, finding his nipples and flicking them with her thumbnail until his knees nearly buckled.

Cameron quickly sat on the edge of the bed, Asia braced in his arms. He kissed her, then against her mouth asked, "Why did you require I buy that stupid tape?"

She tucked her face into his throat while she explained her theories—dumb ones, Cameron thought privately—and when she'd finished, she looked up at him.

"My ex-husband was forever trying to force me to do . . . kinky things that turned him on. He said it was the only way I could satisfy him. I didn't like it, and then he'd be angry about it and call me a prude and a cold fish. I used to wish he'd get his jollies that way with a movie or a book." She shrugged. "I wanted us to just make love, like two people who . . ."

Cameron squeezed her, wishing he had her

damned ex close at hand so he could offer her retribution. But all he could do was say, "Like two people who loved each other?"

She gave a tiny nod. "Yes." Then she shocked the hell out of him by adding, "I haven't been with anyone since him. I needed to prove to myself first that I was independent, that I didn't believe all his garbage about me not being woman enough. He made me feel so low, and in my head, I knew he was a jerk. I knew he was wrong, too. But no man tempted me."

"Not even me," Cameron admitted, more for himself than her. He'd gained a lot of insight tonight, and most of it broke his heart. He'd handled things all wrong. Asia hadn't wanted him. She hadn't wanted any man.

She'd only needed validation, and instead he'd shot down her beliefs by spanking her. Damn, he was a real idiot.

Asia touched his jaw. "That's not true." She bit her lip, then let out a breath. "I think if it had been anyone other than you in that store, I wouldn't have had the guts to go through with it. But it was you, and I liked you already, and respected you a lot."

"You hid it well," he teased, shaken with relief.

"That's because I wanted you, too, though I was afraid to admit it. It scared me to want someone again."

With a trembling hand, Cameron stroked her throat, her shoulder, her breasts. "Let me show you that there's nothing to be afraid of, sweetheart. Let me show you how it should be." *How it'll always be between us.*

"Yes." Asia closed her eyes on a soft moan. "I think I'd like that."

Like a lick of fire, Cameron's kisses burned her everywhere. With incredible gentleness, he tilted her back on the bed and half covered her. She loved the tingling abrasion of his chest hair over her sensitive nipples. She loved the exciting, not-so-gentle stroke of his hand on her body. He seemed to know exactly how and where to touch her. And he found sensitive places she hadn't known about—the delicate skin beneath her ears, her underarms, below her breasts, the insides of her thighs and backs of her knees.

He kissed her, but not where she wanted his mouth most. Her breasts ached for him, her nipples so tight they throbbed with need, but he kissed around them, his tongue flicking out, leaving damp patches on her heated skin. He kissed her belly, tongued her navel until she squirmed, then put tiny pecks all around her sex, not touching her, but she heard him breathing deeply, inhaling her musky scent with appreciation.

She moaned, then caught her breath as he turned her onto her stomach.

"Easy," he whispered, his mouth brushing over her shoulders, down the length of her spine. He caught her panties and stripped them off. Through dazed eyes, Asia looked over her shoulder and saw him lift them to his face and inhale deeply. He gave a rough, growling groan of appreciation, and when his gaze met hers, his blue eyes burned like the hottest fire.

As promised, he kissed her bottom, especially the pink handprint on her left cheek. He murmured words of apology but she barely heard them because his hand slipped between her thighs. His long fingers just barely touched her, teasing and taunting while his mouth continued, so very gentle, so careful.

She couldn't hold still. She pressed her face into the bedclothes and squirmed. "Cameron."

He turned her over again, and this time when his fingers went between her thighs he parted her and pressed his middle finger deep.

Her hips lifted sharply off the mattress and she cried out.

"Asia," he whispered huskily. "Baby, I want to watch you come again."

Oh, God, she thought, almost frantic with need. How was she supposed to answer that demand?

He didn't give her a chance to worry about it. He lowered his head and sucked her nipple into the moist heat of his mouth. His tongue curled around her and he drew on her, even as his finger began sliding in and out.

She moaned and gasped and clutched at the sheets on his bed. Cameron switched to her other breast, licking, plucking with his lips. She braced herself, but he took her by surprise with his teeth, catching her tender nipple and tugging insistently.

"Oh, God."

"Open up for me, Asia," he whispered, and worked another finger into her. "Damn, you're snug."

He had large hands, she thought wildly, feeling herself stretched taut, but with his tongue licking her nipple she didn't have time to worry about it.

He kept moving his hand, deep, harder, and the rough pad of his thumb pressed to her clitoris, giving a friction so sweet she screamed. Her muscles clamped down on the invading, sliding fingers and she shook with an orgasm so powerful she went nearly insensate.

When she was able to breathe again, she realized Cameron had moved and now had his head resting low on her belly, his arm around her upper thighs. With a lot of concentration, she lifted a hand and threaded her fingers through the cool silk of his dark hair. "That was . . ." Words were beyond her. How could she describe such a remarkable thing?

"Very nice," he answered, and she felt his breath on her still-hot vulva. Her legs were obscenely sprawled, she realized, but when she started to close them, he shushed her and petted her back into the position he wanted.

He turned his face inward and kissed her belly, then pressed his cheek to her pubic hair. "I love your scent," he growled, and Asia knew his arousal was razor sharp, that once again he'd skipped his own pleasure for her.

"Cameron," she chided gently, and some insidious emotion too much like love, squeezed at her heart. He kept saying her name, giving to her, pleasing her. He didn't take her for granted. She wasn't just an available woman. He wanted *her*.

"Bend your knees for me, love," he said.

Asia blushed at just the thought, and the pleasure of being called "love." She shifted her legs slightly farther apart.

He pulled them wider, bent her knees for her. He stroked his fingers through her curls, tweaked one, smoothed another. "You're beautiful," he said, looking at her too closely. "All pink and wet and swollen. For me."

She tipped her head back, staring at the ceiling and trying not to groan. But she was fully exposed to him, overly sensitive from her recent release, and it was unbearably erotic even while mortification washed over her.

Cameron repositioned himself directly between her thighs, urging them wider still so that they accommodated his broad shoulders. Using his thumbs, he opened her even more and just when she thought she couldn't bear it another second, he lowered his head and his rough velvet tongue lapped the length of her, up to but not quite touching her clitoris.

Her hips rose sharply off the bed as her back bowed and the breath in her lungs escaped in a rush. "Cameron."

He licked again, and again. His mouth was scalding, his tongue rasping against already aroused tissues. Asia gripped the sheets, trying to anchor herself, trying to keep still, but she strained against him, wanting and needing more.

He teased and tasted her everywhere except where she most wanted to feel the tantalizing flick of his tongue. "Please," she barely whispered.

And with a soft groan, he drew her in, suckling at her clitoris, nipping with his teeth. Asia moaned with the unbelievable pleasure of it, her entire body drawing tight and then melting on wave after wave of sensation.

She didn't know she'd cried until she felt Cameron kissing the tears from her cheeks, mur-

muring softly, reassuringly—and sinking deep into her body with a low, long groan.

"Oh," she said, and got her eyes to open.

"Hi," he whispered, withdrawing inch by inch, and then pressing in again. He filled her up, stretched her already sensitive vulva unbearably, and the friction was incredible.

Dark color slashed his cheekbones and his blue eyes burned with an inner fire, intense and wild and tender.

"You're making love to me," she said, awed and a little overwhelmed because she'd thought her body was spent, as boneless as oatmeal. Yet she couldn't stop herself from countering his every move.

"I'm making love *with* you," he corrected.

"But I'm not doing anything," she said, thinking of all the ways she should have kissed him and touched him in turn.

His beautiful smile made her heart do flip-flops. "You're you— that's all you need to do."

"Cameron." She lifted limp arms to wrap around his neck and squeeze him tight. He kissed her lax mouth, and she felt his smile and kissed him back.

After a minute or two of that, she felt the need to shift and did, only to find the one position that really gratified was wrapping her legs around his waist.

He groaned, then drove a tiny bit harder, farther into her, until it was both an awesome pleasure and a small pain, a joining so complete that she was a part of him, and he of her.

She answered his groan with a gasp, her hips lifting into his, urging him on.

"That's it," he said, and cupped her buttocks in his hands, working her against him, his face a fierce study of concentration.

Incredibly, the feelings began to well again, taking her by surprise with the suddenness of it. "It can't be," she said.

And he said, "Hell, yes," and started driving fast and deep and faster still.

Asia tightened her hold on him, overwhelmed with it all as she experienced yet one more orgasm, this one deeper, slower, longer, not as cataclysmic, but still so sweetly satisfying she wanted to shout aloud with the pleasure of it.

No sooner did she relax than Cameron rubbed his face into her throat and began his own orgasm. She heard his rumbling growl start low in his chest, felt the fierce pounding of his heart, the light sweat on his back and the heat that poured off his naked body.

"Asia," he groaned, and his body shuddered heavily, then collapsed on hers.

Too lethargic to move, Asia managed a pucker to kiss his ear, then dozed off.

Ten minutes later, Cameron levered himself up to look at her. She snored softly, making him grin like the village idiot, and she looked beautiful, melting his heart. *Mine,* he thought with a surge of possessiveness that took him by surprise. Asia Michaels was his, in every sense of the word.

As gently as possible, he disengaged their bodies and removed the condom. He doubted she'd even noticed when he'd rolled it on, she'd been so spent. Smiling, he located the sheet at the foot of the bed. Asia stirred, rolling to her side and curling up tight from the chill of the air.

The lights were still on and he could see the fading imprint of his hand on her soft bottom. He closed his eyes, wanting to groan but not wanting to awaken her. What an ass he'd been.

Tomorrow they'd talk more, he'd tell her how he felt and give her the bracelet, and with any luck at all, she'd understand.

He reached over and flipped off the lights. She turned toward him, snuggled close, and resumed snoring.

Oh, yeah, she was his all right. Now he just had to let her know that.

Chapter Six

Asia stirred, smiling even before her eyes were open, and feeling good—achy but good—all the way down to her toes. Cameron O'Reilly. Wow. The man really knew how to makc love.

She rolled to her side and reached for him, but found only cold sheets. Jerking up in an instant, she looked around, but he was gone. Her discarded clothes from the night before were now neatly folded over a chair, waiting, it seemed, for her to get dressed.

The blankets, which had been irreparably tossed during their lovemaking, were now straightened and smoothed over her, keeping her warm.

She looked out the wide window and saw snow and more snow, and a sun so bright it hurt her eyes.

She groaned. It was two days till Christmas Eve. Of course, the man had things to do, yet she'd slept in. In his bed. Inconveniencing him.

Humiliation rolled over her. Some independent broad she turned out to be. She'd spent the night when she hadn't even been invited. What must he think? Was he wondering how to get rid of her?

She'd just shoved the covers aside and slipped one naked leg off of the bed, shivering at the touch of cool air on her bare skin, when Cameron opened the door. He paused, standing there in nothing more than unsnapped jeans and a healthy beard shadow. His blue eyes were sharp and watchful.

As if shaking himself, he continued into the room and said, "Good morning."

Asia didn't want to meet his gaze, but she refused to be a coward. Attempting a smile, she said, "Give me a minute to get dressed and I'll get out of your way."

Strange after the night of incredible, uninhibited sex, but she suddenly felt naked. Cameron didn't help, staring at her with blatant sexual interest. She could use the sheet from the bed, but again, that seemed cowardly. She had no modesty left, not with this man.

"I'm cooking breakfast," he said. "I was hoping you'd stay and eat with me."

She held her dress in her hands. It was tangled, the sleeves inside out, and wrinkled almost beyond repair. She stared at it stupidly, not even sure where to start.

Cameron pushed away from the dresser and took the dress, tossing it aside. He retrieved a flannel robe from his closet and held it out to her.

Not seeing too many options, especially since her brain refused to function in any normal capacity, Asia slipped her arms into the robe. Cameron wrapped it around her, tied the belt and rolled up the sleeves.

"It makes me hot," he said, "to see you in my things."

Asia stared at him. Her mouth opened, but nothing came out.

"Almost as hot," he continued when she stayed mute, "as it made me to wake up this morning with you in my bed, warm and soft." He touched her cheek. "I could wake up like this a lot, Asia."

Thrown for an emotional loop, she started to turn away, but Cameron caught her arm and led her out of the room. "I'm fixing bacon and I don't want it to burn."

His apartment was slightly smaller than hers, with a kitchen-dinette combination. Asia sat at the thick pine table and watched Cameron complete the meal. Barefoot and bare chested, he moved around the small kitchen with domestic ease. Her ex-husband had never cooked. He didn't even know how to boil water.

Cameron's hair was still disheveled, hanging over his brow with a rakish appeal. Muscles flexed in his shoulders and arms and down his back as he bent this way and that, turning bacon, pouring juice, as he turned to wink at her occasionally, or smile, or just gaze.

He asked her if fried eggs were okay, and how she liked her toast.

Asia answered more by rote than anything else. With the memories of the night, and Cameron in the kitchen looking sexy as the original sin, food was the farthest thing from her mind. But when he set her plate in front of her, she dug in.

And he watched her eat, smiling like a contented fool, his big bare feet on either side of hers.

Finally, she laid her fork aside. Nothing had happened quite as she'd expected and she felt lost. "What," she grouched, "are you staring at?"

His smile widened. "You." He reached out and smoothed her hair, his fingers lingering. "I've never seen a woman with smudged makeup and tangled hair look quite so sexy."

His compliment put her over the edge. She shoved her chair back and stood up.

Cameron came to his feet, too. They stared at each other over the table, facing off.

Asia drew a deep breath. "This is ridiculous."

"I know. There's so much I want to say to you, but I'm not sure where to start."

She blinked, then covered her ears. "Stop it! Just stop . . . taking me by surprise."

Holding her gaze, Cameron rounded the table until he could clasp her wrists and pull her hands down. "I want to see you again, Asia."

"You mean you want to have sex with me again."

"Hell, yes. I want you right now. I wanted you the second I woke up. I'll want you tonight and to-morrow too."

She laughed, a near hysterical sound. "Will you stop?"

"No." Shaking his head, he said, "Not until you tell me how you feel."

"I feel . . ." She wasn't at all sure how she felt, and gestured helplessly. "Frustrated."

Cameron stroked her arms, bending to look her in the eyes. "I didn't satisfy you last night?"

Her laugh this time was genuine. "You did! Ohmigod, did you satisfy me."

"Well, then . . . ?"

"Cameron." She pulled away. She couldn't think,

and she sure as hell couldn't talk, when he touched her. "This was all a . . . lark. You overheard my ridiculous pact with Erica and Becky, and because of that, you reacted and we had . . . better sex than I knew existed."

Cameron's jaw locked, but he kept quiet, letting her talk.

She drew another breath to fortify herself. "But that's all it is, all it was meant to be. You didn't intend for me to spend the night and intrude on your life."

"Are you done?"

He sounded angry, confusing her more. "Yes."

He went to the kitchen windowsill and lifted a small package wrapped in silver foil paper and tied with a bright red ribbon. "Everything you just said is bullshit and you know it. I've wanted you since the day I met you. And yes, it started out purely sexual, and it'll always be partly sexual. You turn me on, Asia, no way to deny that when I get a boner just hearing your name. But I like you a lot, too. Hell," he said, rubbing his neck the way he always did when he was annoyed, "I'm damn near obsessed with you."

Asia bit her lip, doing her best to keep her eyes off that gaily wrapped gift.

"I want you. It makes me nuts to think about any other guy with you." He paced away, then back again. "I want you to spend the weekend with me."

"But . . . it's Christmas."

"That's right. And if you stay with me, it'll be the nicest Christmas I've ever had."

"You don't have any other plans?"

"If I did, I'd change them." He handed her the gift. "I bought you this. Before we slept together, because even if things hadn't gotten intimate so soon, I still wanted you to have it."

She held the gift with fascination. "Why?"

"Because you're special to me. The way you affect me is special, and the way I feel around you is special. I wanted you to know it."

"Oh."

"Well," he said, once again smiling, although now his smile looked a bit strained. "Open it."

Sitting back down in the chair, Asia pulled aside the crisp paper. She felt like a child again, filled with anticipation. When she opened the velvet box and saw the bracelet, tears welled in her eyes. "Oh, Cameron."

"You like it?" he asked anxiously.

"I love it." She looked up at him, seeing him through a sheen of tears. "It's absolutely perfect."

Cameron knelt down in front of her, lifted the bracelet from the box and clasped it around her slender wrist. "You're perfect. The bracelet is just decoration."

"Cameron?"

He lifted his gaze to hers, still holding her hand.

"May I spend Christmas with you?"

He sucked in a breath, then let it out with an enormous grin. "You may. You may even spend the entire week with me."

Giggling with pure happiness, Asia threw her arms around him. "You're so wonderful."

He squeezed her tight. "I know you want to take things slow and easy, honey. So I'm not rushing you." As he spoke, he lifted her in his arms and started back down the hall. "Your ex pulled a number on you, and I'd like to demolish the bastard. But I want you to know I'll be patient. We can do whatever you want, however you want. You just tell me."

Asia felt ready to burst. "I really do care about you, Cameron."

He froze, shuddered, then squeezed her tight and hurried the rest of the way to the bed. "That's a start," he said, lowering them both to the mattress. "Do you think by New Year's you might be telling me you love me? Because Asia, I . . ." He stopped and frowned. "I'm rushing you, aren't I?"

"You think you love me?" she asked in lieu of giving him an answer. "Is that what you were going to say?"

"I know how I feel." He untied the belt of the robe and parted it, looking down at her body. "And yes, I love you." He bent and lazily kissed her breasts. "Hell, I'm crazy nuts about you." He started kissing his way down her belly, and Asia wasn't able to say another thing. All she could do was gasp.

Epilogue

"A Valentine's Day engagement." Becky sighed. "How romantic."

Asia smiled in contentment. "I'm so happy. I didn't know a man like Cameron existed, and now I've not only discovered him, I have him for my own."

Erica gave her a smug grin. "You see how well my plans turn out."

"What I see," Asia said, leaning over the lounge table to wag a finger at her two friends, "is that neither of you have fulfilled your end of the bargain."

Erica laughed. "We were too amused watching things unfold for you. You and Cameron have stolen the show."

"Uh-huh. I think you both just chickened out."

Erica said, "No way," but Becky just looked around, as if seeking escape.

Erica and Asia both caught her hands. "C'mon, Becky," Asia teased, "you know it's well past your turn!"

Looking tortured, Becky said, "I don't know if I can."

"Trust me." Erica patted her shoulder. "You can."

"And you should," Asia added. "I mean, look how it turned out for me."

Becky folded her arms on the table and dropped her head. She gave a small groan.

Asia and Erica shared a look. "'Fess up, Becky," Asia urged. "You've had two months instead of two days to think about it. So let's hear the big fantasy."

"I know I'm going to regret this," came her muffled voice. "But if you both insist . . ."

"We do!"

She lifted her head, looked around the lounge and leaned forward to whisper into two ears.

"Wow," Asia said when she'd finished.

"All right!" Erica exclaimed, and lifted a fist in the air.

Cameron showed up just then, forcing the women to stifle their humor. He bent down and planted a kiss on Asia's mouth. "You want to leave right after work to pick out the ring?"

Erica shook her head. "In a hurry, big boy?"

"Damn right."

To everyone's relief, Cameron got along fabulously with both Becky's timid personality, and Erica's outrageous boldness.

Asia couldn't imagine being any happier. Now, if only her two friends could find the same happiness. She eyed Becky, who still blushed with her confessed fantasy. Maybe, she thought, doing some silent plotting, she could give Becky a helping hand. She tugged Cameron to his feet and said good-bye to her friends.

Once they were in the hallway, she said, "How well do you know George Westin?"

"Well enough to know he's got a reputation with the ladies. Why?"

"I think he may just be perfect."

Cameron narrowed his eyes. "For what?"

"No, for who."

"Erica?"

"Ha! They're both too cocky. They'd kill each other within a minute." She smoothed her hand over his shoulder, then patted him. "No, I was thinking of Becky."

Cameron shook his head. "I don't know, sweetheart. She's so shy, he'd probably have her for lunch."

Asia just grinned. There was no one else in the hall, so she put her arms around him, loving him so much it hurt, and said, "You, Cameron O'Reilly, haven't heard Becky's fantasy. I'm thinking George might get a big surprise."

Cameron kissed her. "If it's half as nice as the surprise I got, then he's one lucky cuss."

"I love you, Cameron."

He patted her bottom in fond memory. "I love you, too, Asia. Now and forever."

Indulge Me

To Jackie Floyd,
Thanks for providing the fun background information.
I know your night out was much more fun than mine!

Chapter One

Becky Harte inched through the doorway of the risqué sex shop, Wild Honey, with a great deal of trepidation. Warmth and the subtle scent of incense greeted her. She knew her eyes were huge, but she couldn't manage a single blink.

It was still something of a shock that the small, conservative town of Cuther, Indiana, had such a shop in its midst.

It was doubly shocking that small town, conservative Becky would be visiting that shop.

Her heart pounded, her face was hot, and her hands shook. Never ever in her life had she expected to do such a thing. Yet here she was, not only inside Wild Honey, but on a sexual mission. A mission designed by her two well-meaning friends, Asia and Erica. Becky knew they were both watching her progress from the company lounge across the street, in the toiletries factory where they all three worked.

Before the door closed behind Becky, she peeked over her shoulder and, sure enough, she could see the twin pale faces of Erica and Asia pressed to the window on the second floor of the factory. She couldn't back out because they'd both know and she liked them too much to want them to consider her a coward.

The three of them had made a pact, and by gosh, she'd keep to her end of the deal.

Drawing a steadying breath, Becky released the door and it swung shut with a tinkling of chimes and a sense of finality that made her jump. Becky held her coat tightly closed at her throat and looked around. What she saw was . . . unexpected.

Wild Honey was actually pretty elegant. It was clean and neatly organized and colorful. There were display tables laden with books and tapes, every wall lined with shelves of more books, magazines, and some boxed items. Biting her lip, Becky forced herself to take a few steps. A woman behind the counter greeted her. "Hi. Can I help you find something?"

Good Lord! Surely the saleslady didn't expect her to discuss such things. Numb, Becky shook her head and turned away, hurrying to the back of the large room. An open door that led into another room offered her a place to hide. She ducked inside.

And immediately stalled.

Mouth falling open, Becky stared about in mingled horror and fascination at the items hung from the walls. Why, there were things that looked like . . . like penises. Enormously large penises. Blue, white, and black penises. Penises in every color of the rainbow. Two-foot long penises, for crying out loud. Double-headed penises.

Without realizing it, Becky drifted closer, mouth still gaping, eyes so wide it was a wonder her eyeballs didn't fall out. This had to be a joke. Sure, she wasn't experienced, but she wasn't an idiot either, and there was no way all those penises could be . . . functional. No way. It was impossible.

She looked away from the display of artificial penises with a disbelieving shake of her head and a barely audible snort. They were probably gag items, used for bachelor parties and such. That made more sense than anything else.

Her attention got snagged on a new contraption and she studied it. She had no idea what it might be, but there were boxes stacked beneath the one on display, with instructions printed on the back. Made of what looked to be hard plastic, the device had several elastic straps and little pointy rubber things sticking out here and there, and a place for batteries. Becky studied it, then picked up the box to read the description.

Gasping, she dropped the box, jerked around—and ran full tilt into a tall, hard male body.

She would have screamed if she had any breath. As it was, she staggered back from the bruising impact and almost fell over the stacked boxes. At the last second, the man caught her and held her upright.

"Hey, easy now."

Becky froze. Dear God, she recognized the voice that had haunted her most carnal dreams for two years now.

Big hands settled on her shoulders, steadying her, and with a wince of dread, Becky slowly looked up—into familiar mocking black eyes.

Oh no. No, no, no. Not someone she knew. Not this particular male someone.

He bent to meet her eye level, one glossy black

brow raised, one side of his sensual mouth tilted up in a smile. "You okay, Ms. Harte?"

Becky squeezed her eyes shut, praying that not seeing him might help. It didn't. She was oh so aware of him standing there.

"Becky?" His voice was gentle, insistent, rough, and masculine. Her skin tingled from his touch and her heart lodged in her throat.

Using the edge of his fist, he tipped up her chin, which effectively closed her mouth, too. After a second, he chuckled. "You know, you're so damn red you're going to catch the place on fire."

Becky swallowed hard and rallied her scattered wits. In a whisper, she admitted, "I'm mortified."

"Yeah? How come?"

She tucked in her chin, refusing to look at him again. George Westin was the man of her dreams, the epitome of everything dark and erotic and forbidden. Whenever she thought of how sex should be, she thought of George.

He had the most compelling eyes—dark, daring, filled with carnal knowledge and challenge. He looked at a woman, and she felt his attention like a physical stroke.

He was looking at her now. Becky gulped.

All the women at the factory adored George, and they all whispered about him. Becky had heard the rumors about his astounding reputation and the validations by a couple of the women he'd dated. By all accounts, George had . . . a lot, and knew how to use it. Becky wasn't entirely certain what a lot meant, except that he could make a woman very, very happy in bed.

For the two years that she'd known him, she'd done her best to hide her own reaction to him.

She hadn't wanted him to see her as just one more woman who lusted after his gorgeous body and his sexual knowledge. She'd pretended an indifference to him, pretended to see him only as a supervisor, not as a man.

In truth, being anywhere near him made her tongue-tied.

Now here she was, not a foot away from him, his hot hands touching her, standing in the middle of a *porn* shop with pleasure probes behind her.

Becky groaned.

Apparently amused, George released her, only to throw a heavy arm around her shoulders. He led her a few feet away, his hold easy but secure. "Take deep breaths, Becky. It'll be all right."

At his casual familiarity, Becky peeked up at him again. His neatly trimmed, silky black hair was disheveled by the blustery wind outside, and his cheeks were ruddy with the cold. He must have just come inside. And of course, she had to literally run into him.

He leaned around to see her face. "I can call you Becky, right? I mean, the situation lends a certain intimacy, don't you think?"

Think? She was supposed to think? He had to be kidding.

"Becky?"

He was incredibly tall. And he smelled incredibly good. She wanted to lean into him and inhale his wonderful scent.

At work she always made sure they stayed on a professional footing. George had often tried joking with her; he'd tried flirting with her a little, too, teasing her. But she'd known there was no future in it, that she couldn't get involved with him.

She'd kept things friendly, because she'd rather have at least that much with him than nothing at all. If she'd encouraged him, he was the type of man who would have wanted sex.

Incredible sex.

Naked, sweaty sex.

And she couldn't do that.

So he'd backed off. Not completely, because he still chatted with her and he sought her out more than most of the men she worked with. But he seemed to have accepted her unspoken decision—to be friendly associates, but nothing more.

The poor man had no idea she lusted after him every single night.

After clearing her throat—twice—Becky managed to say, "We're not at work, Mr. Westin, so sure, you may call me Becky. There's no reason to be formal . . ." She strangled on the word *here*.

"Exactly." George gave her an approving smile, likely because she'd succeeded in stringing more than two words together. "And do call me George."

Like a sleepwalker, Becky allowed herself to be led through the shop. When she'd agreed to this daring scheme with Erica and Asia, she had envisioned running into some unknown, never-to-be-heard-from-again man and getting through the whole ordeal with a modicum of remote familiarity. Not once had she envisioned running into George.

Tomorrow, she'd see him at work, probably several times. He was a supervisor, not over her floor, but they had contact on and off throughout the day. He'd look at her, and he'd know she'd been here, checking out . . . penises and pleasure probes and God only knew what else.

She'd never survive the embarrassment.

George halted them next to a very small curtained booth well away from the wall displays. "Better?"

Becky drew a breath and forced herself to stop behaving like the backward and inexperienced hick she actually was. "I'm sorry. I'm just . . . well, I'm obviously not used to being in places like this."

"Obviously." George released her and shoved his hands deep into his pants pockets. His coat and suit coat parted over his middle, showing a flat abdomen, a wide chest. His hands pulled his slacks taut, and she noticed other, more interesting things.

He cleared his throat, and Becky jerked her gaze away from his belt buckle and the heavy weight of his sex beneath. Being in a porn shop must have muddled her senses to have her staring at him *there* like a lecher.

At his leisure, George lounged back against the wall, next to that dark curtain. *He* wasn't embarrassed. In fact, he still looked amused as he studied her face in that scrutinizing way of his. "Looking for something in particular, are you?"

At first, she thought he was referring to where she'd just been staring—at his crotch—and her mouth fell open in shock. Then she realized he meant his comment in a more general sense, concerning her visit to the porn shop. Her reaction to that wasn't much better. Only sheer force of will kept her from running away. "I was just . . . curious," she lied.

She wasn't about to tell him the truth, that she was here to meet a man.

A specific man.

A man with precise sexual predilections, which

would finally enable her to get rid of her virginity without distress.

"Uh-huh." George grinned, showing white teeth and a dimple in his cheek.

To Becky's mind, George was already too handsome for his own good. The dimple was overkill.

Even Erica had made note of him several times, and Becky trusted her opinion since Erica knew a whole lot more about men than she ever would. But Erica had also called George a rogue, a womanizer, even a sex addict.

Becky remembered that Erica had smiled when she'd made those accusations.

Asia, now madly in love with Cameron, had commented on George, too. In fact, Asia had commented on him several times recently, as if she'd been determined to make sure Becky noticed him. Becky shook her head. It wasn't likely any woman could not notice George, considering he stood so tall and was so dark and emanated such raw sex appeal.

She figured him to be in his late thirties, and judging by his reputation, he'd lived those thirty-odd years to the fullest.

"Cat got your tongue?" George cocked his head to the side. "Or are you considering buying one of those pleasure probes?"

Becky reeled back, scandalized, horrified, embarrassed beyond belief at the mere suggestion. "Of course not!"

George chuckled, but his chuckle dwindled into a warm smile when he looked at her mouth. He kept looking, his expression so fixed Becky began to fidget. "Calm down, Becky. I was just teasing."

The front door chimed and several more men

from her workplace wandered in. Becky blanched at the thought of being recognized yet again. "Oh good Lord."

George glanced at the men. "Don't want to be seen here, huh?"

Panicked, Becky searched around for a place to hide. "I'd rather not, no."

"Then I'll be your white knight." So saying, George took her upper arm and moved the curtain aside. He stepped into the booth, dragging Becky with him. "We can hide in here until they're gone."

The curtain dropped back into place, leaving them in darkness. Becky went utterly still, more aware of George as a man than she'd ever been of any man in her life. Of course, she was sequestered with him in a tiny booth, in the darkness, in a porn shop.

How in the world had she gotten into this predicament?

She and her friends had made the deal—they'd each go to Wild Honey, find a man who shared an interest in her fantasy, and approach him.

The idea had been to get back into the sexual swing of things. Not that Becky had ever been in the swing. She was twenty-five and a blasted virgin, as innocent as a child, without a single speck of experience.

But not for the reasons her friends assumed. Yes, she was shy. Yes, she was moral and believed in love and marriage. But that had nothing to do with why she'd avoided any intimate contact with a man.

The real reason was a shame that ran bone-deep, an . . . affliction she'd dealt with using avoidance.

Until now.

Her proclaimed fantasy, that of bondage, had everything to do with it. If a man was tied up, well then he couldn't control anything. Like the lights. She could keep the room black as pitch. She could even blindfold him and there'd be nothing he could do about it. He'd probably even like it.

She'd be able to find out what all the hoopla was about sex, without worrying that he'd see her, or touch her. She'd be able to look at him, to sate herself on his body, to touch him and taste him and yet she'd keep her own appearance, her body, her flaws, private.

He'd never know.

Asia had gone first, and for her things had worked out perfectly, to the point where she was due to marry Cameron soon. Not that Becky expected to get married, not now, not ever. But she was so lonely, so hungry. She wanted to share love-making. She wanted to experience mind-blowing sex. She craved so, so much.

All she needed was the right man to indulge her.

Becky drew a breath, trying to reassure herself. Instead she breathed in George's scent again. It turned her insides to mush.

George moved beside her in the cramped space, and she heard a clink, like the dropping of change, then a small hum. Two seconds later, the booth lit up and a film played on the wall in front of them.

Becky stared. "This is a movie booth?"

"A place to see previews of the different videos before buying one." George studied her, strangely alert, as he waited for her reaction. "You pop in a quarter, pick the number of the film you're interested in, and you get to see a few minutes of it."

"My, um . . . what a good idea."

Becky turned away from George's scrutiny to watch the movie, and felt the increased acceleration of her heart. Fascination gripped her as the lights flickered and shifted. She saw a well-built man, dressed only in worn jeans, wander into a darkly lit room. The film was poor quality, gritty. But it still held her enthralled.

Beside her, George shifted again, moving behind her, watching the show over her head. He seemed to take up too much space in the small room, with his shoulders that were twice as wide as hers, his body big and solid and hard.

Tension tightened all her muscles, from the movie, from George's nearness, from the rapid way things were progressing. Becky could smell him again, the delicious scent of cologne and hot male flesh.

The man on-screen moved into a room—where a woman was tied to a bed. Becky started in surprise. Why, this movie was about *bondage*. Had George chosen it on purpose?

The woman was atop the covers, completely naked. Her legs were held wide apart, secured to the foot posts on the bed with black cords. Her arms stretched out over her head and were also tied. She was vulnerable, fully exposed. She wore a blindfold, and as she sensed the man's approach, she moaned softly.

Unable to look away, Becky drew a strangled breath—and felt her back touch George's chest.

She started to jerk forward again, but he settled his hands at either side of her throat, keeping her in place.

"Shhh. If you make too much noise," he said close to her ear, "they'll know we're in here."

Shaken by the touch of his warm breath in her ear, Becky whispered, "Who?"

"The guys from the factory."

"Oh." That's right. The reason he'd led her into this booth in the first place was to avoid detection by others. "Thank you."

The man in the movie knelt on the bed beside the naked woman. She squirmed, a little frantic, her bare breasts jiggling with her efforts, rising and falling, but the ropes held her tightly. She couldn't move more than an inch.

She couldn't move away from him.

The man trailed his fingertips over her arm, up and down, over her ribs, making the woman twist and moan some more. Slowly, very slowly, he cupped her breast and gently squeezed. Becky's own breasts tingled, her nipples pulled tight.

George leaned down and this time his warm breath teased her temple. He spoke in a drawing whisper that made her eyelids feel heavy, her insides warm and liquid. "You ever watch a dirty movie, Becky?"

She could barely speak, didn't dare blink. She shook her head, her gaze fixed on the movie so she wouldn't miss a thing.

George's fingers caressed her shoulders, subtly, with encouragement. "I know women," he whispered, "and you, Becky Harte, like this particular film."

Was she really so obvious? Did she even care?

"I . . ." *I want to do that to you.* Becky knew she couldn't say that, so she said nothing.

"Some people are turned on by dominating, some by being dominated."

Becky swallowed hard. "He won't hurt her?"

"Of course not. That has nothing to do with bondage, or with pleasure."

George spoke with confidence, making Becky wonder if he had firsthand knowledge of this. "I . . . I see."

The man began kissing the woman. His mouth touched her nipples, first softly, then sucking until she cried out. He rasped her with his thumbs, and laughed when she tried to escape him. He kissed her again, licking everywhere, her throat, over her breasts, down her stomach . . . between her legs.

The woman jumped.

So did Becky.

"Shhh," George murmured, making Becky shiver in reaction.

The woman arched, but her movements were limited because of her restraints. She cried out, bucked, and bowed but the man stayed with her, his mouth on her, against her sex, his hands holding her hips steady, and seconds later she found her release in a long raw groan that had Becky catching her breath and shaking uncontrollably.

"Becky?"

Feeling almost feverish, Becky wavered, and found herself flush against George's body.

George had an erection.

On-screen, the woman moaned in soft acceptance. Inside the booth, Becky did the same. She could feel George, long and hard, firmly pressed against her behind. It was a first for her.

Everything today was a first.

"Watch," George insisted, and Becky could have sworn she felt his mouth touch the rim of her ear. She all but melted into a puddle.

Since she couldn't seem to draw her attention away from the film, George's instruction was unnecessary.

From one frame to the next, the setting of the film changed, and now the woman sat astride the man, while it was his arms stretched high and tight, tied to the bedposts. His head was tipped back, his chest muscles starkly defined as the woman rode him hard and fast.

Becky breathed too hard in reaction. This was what she wanted. Oh, she wanted it so much. The man in the movie wasn't blindfolded, and he wasn't nearly as appealing as George. But Becky could pretend he was. She could pretend that he'd take his pleasure with her, and not be able to see her, not be able to touch her.

Suddenly the woman's mouth opened on a scream and Becky knew it was a scream of pure excitement. The woman shuddered, climaxed . . . and Becky felt George's hand slip around her to settle beneath her left breast. His fingers were hot, long, curving on her rib cage. His hair brushed her cheek, cool and silky. His heart rapped against her back.

Awareness and need held Becky perfectly still so George wouldn't stop touching her.

"Your heart is racing, Becky."

This time she knew for certain his mouth touched her. He placed a gentle kiss on her temple—and the film died.

Neither of them moved. The sound of her

breathing filled the small booth. Becky had no idea what to do or what to say, so she did nothing. George's big hand was still on her, beneath her coat, right below her breast, not moving, just resting there, warm and sure and confident.

"I think I know what section you were looking for, Becky."

In that moment, more than anything, Becky wanted him to touch her breast. It was insane, but she craved his touch. "You . . . you do?"

"Oh yeah. You want some restraints, don't you, sweetheart?"

He'd called her sweetheart. "Um . . ." Should she just blurt it out? How did a woman go about telling a man she'd like to tie him to her bed? And she did want to do that.

With George.

Becky was now very glad she'd run into him, and not some other man. This small incident felt right in a way she knew it wouldn't have been with anyone else. She'd been wanting George for a long time, so now was her chance.

It was possible that he'd chosen that particular film because he was into bondage, and wanted her to know it. Becky found it hard to imagine that George—sexy, gorgeous, experienced George—would be willing to leave himself at her mercy. But the idea was a very tempting one.

The pros and cons of having sex with a man she worked with winged through her head in rapid order. But before she could find the right thing to say, George moved the curtain aside. "C'mon. I'll help you."

Again, Becky found herself being led by him. He drew her to the back of the store toward another isolated room. Along the way, Becky looked around at all the amazing contraptions. One particular item caught her interest and she turned her head to stare.

Beside her, George paused. With his dark gaze on her face, he said, "It's for female pleasure. Most of the stuff in here is geared for women."

"Really?"

At her surprise, George narrowed his eyes. "It's not always as easy for a woman to climax as it is for a man."

He spoke so casually that Becky blinked, still looking at the small contraption and trying to figure it out. There were so many things in the shop that seemed to require an instruction manual. "I see."

"Do you?" When she didn't answer, he expounded on his explanations. "Just having a man inside a woman doesn't always do it for her. She needs to be touched other ways, other places."

Becky opened her mouth, but nothing came out. She tilted her head, studying the ridiculous device, but still it didn't quite make sense how it would work.

George made an impatient sound. "You can't be that naive."

Becky turned to stare up at him.

He ran a hand over his head, further mussing his hair. Then, to her horror, he snatched up the device and held it in front of her. "See this opening? It fits over a man's cock. When he rides a woman, this part right here strokes her where she's most sensitive. Because it vibrates, if he goes deep inside and just holds still, it'll work too."

Becky was floored by this outpouring of sexual

instruction. George didn't seem the least bit shy about discussing things with her. It was astonishing and embarrassing and very educational.

She wasn't sure if she should thank him or not.

When she remained silent, he frowned. "Becky, do you understand?"

"Yes, I think so."

"You think so?"

Her curiosity overrode her shyness. "Have you ever . . . ? You know."

"What?" He waved the thing under her nose, then tossed it back on the shelf. "Worn one of those? No way. I don't need them." He looked at her mouth and his dark eyes glittered. "Any man worth his salt knows how to make a woman come without all these gizmos."

Ohmigosh, ohmigosh. Becky gulped. Would he illustrate that for her, too? She sort of hoped so.

His gaze moved down her body, to her lap. "Remember the guy in the video? There are better ways to ensure a woman's satisfaction."

There it was, his explanation and that look that felt like a physical touch, given with his blatant suggestion that he enjoyed kissing a woman . . . *there,* and Becky's knees went weak. She caught the shelf for support, refusing to crumble in front of him, even over the idea of oral sex.

Trying to sound as cavalier as George, she changed the subject. "It was designed by a doctor."

He smiled. "Yeah."

"Wouldn't you think most doctors had medical emergencies or something to occupy their time?"

This time George laughed outright. "Amazing."

"What's amazing?"

He didn't explain, he just took her hand and

finished leading her to the other room. Becky looked around in awe. Velvet-lined handcuffs, dark blindfolds, satin ropes and restraints of every style and extreme decorated the walls, some even hanging from the ceiling. "Oh my."

George crossed his arms over his chest. "Did you bring your charge card?"

"No." She didn't want any legal documentation from her trip here. "But I brought plenty of cash."

Looking very pleased, George said, "Then allow me to guide you through a few purchases. And, Becky?"

"Hmm?"

"When we're through, we'll set a date to get together."

Becky whipped around to face him. "A date?"

"Oh yeah." He touched her cheek and tucked her hair behind her ear. "You see, Becky, we're of a similar mind. And I think we'll get along real well, don't you?"

Chapter Two

George watched that intriguing color darken Becky Harte's soft cheeks again. God, but he loved the way the woman blushed. Since he was still touching her, he even felt the heat. Would she flush all over like that when he had her securely bound to his bed, naked and hungry and waiting for him to give her a screaming orgasm?

He had a feeling she would, and he could hardly wait.

What a little fraud she was.

He'd worked at the factory as a supervisor for two years now. In that time, he'd gotten to know Becky well. Or so he'd thought. She was very young—too young he'd sometimes thought. And though at twenty-five she should have had her share of experience, Becky still had "sweet and innocent" stamped all over her in a way that made a man's primal instincts go on red-hot alert.

From her big blue eyes, to her bouncing blond curls, to her sweet small-town accent, she exuded artless naïveté. She was the type of woman who—

he'd thought—would want to get married if she got intimate with a man.

Still, he thought of her nearly every day, and wanted her more often than that. At work, he couldn't help stopping to chat with her whenever possible. She was so sweet, so open, damn near every man at the factory felt drawn to her, himself included. But Becky never seemed to notice.

And she never seemed to want male attention.

She'd certainly turned him down. She hadn't been rude or inconsiderate about it, but rather she'd feigned misunderstanding. He'd tease, and she'd give him a blank look, then call him Mr. Westin in a way that made it clear she considered him a supervisor, a casual work friend, and nothing more.

In many ways, her youth, her fresh-faced candor, and her disinterest had made her more appealing, to the point he nearly felt obsessed with her. Of course, her body had helped in that, too.

He absolutely burned with the need to see beneath her conservative clothes.

Her long skirts and buttoned-up blouses couldn't quite disguise a sweetly rounded figure ripe with curves. The way she tried to conceal herself only made his imagination go wild. More often than was wise, he'd fantasized about getting her into bed.

And now he knew the truth. Sweet, innocent Becky wasn't into marriage. No, she was into bondage. She wanted to be tied down, she wanted to be vulnerable. She wanted to be at a man's mercy.

Yet she still blushed, and she honestly seemed to be clueless about things sexual in nature.

What an intriguing conflict.

Becky Harte wanted to be dominated—and George was just the man to accommodate her. He sure as hell wasn't going to let any other guy do it.

With her bottom lip caught between her teeth, Becky turned away from him to study the wall of blindfolds. George studied her ass.

He could hardly wait to get his hands on her.

Today she wore a beige denim skirt that hung clear to her ankles, but he could see that her feet were small, her ankles trim. Her bulky coat over a loose thick sweater hid her waistline, but couldn't hide the thrust of her full breasts.

George's palm tingled as he remembered slipping his hand beneath her coat to feel her heartbeat. She'd trembled gently, her heart thumping hard and fast, her breast a warm firm weight against the back of his hand.

He'd wanted to slide his fingers higher and cup her breast. He'd wanted to stroke her nipple until he felt it puckering tight.

She'd wanted the same.

But not teasing her now would get him further later, so George had controlled himself, and in the process, he'd controlled her, though she might not have realized it. All in all, sexual preferences aside, he was experienced enough to know that she was innocent, and that delightful mix of timidity and hot sensuality had him hard and more than ready.

And here he'd considered Cuther, Indiana, a dull place. He grinned. With Becky Harte wandering loose, there was nothing dull about it. Since first meeting her, he'd wanted her. Against his better judgment and her apparent disinterest, he'd wanted her.

Now he'd finally have her.

George watched her pick up and examine a black velvet blindfold with shaking fingers. She peeked at him out of the corner of her eye, then lifted her chin, tucked the box under her arm, and moved on to the handcuffs.

His thoughts mired in carnal speculation, George followed.

If she wanted to wear a blindfold, that was fine and dandy with him. He liked her big blue eyes, but it was her body he was dying to see.

Maybe it would help her to hide, to not see what he was seeing. He realized now that much of her past reticence was due to inexperience. Her shock at the items sold in Wild Honey had proven that.

Or maybe she liked the idea of being blindfolded because she thought it would heighten the sense of touch and anticipation. Maybe it would feed her need to be controlled. George shrugged. He would happily oblige her.

He'd leave her wanting more.

When Cameron, another supervisor at the factory, had first approached him with this bizarre plan, George had been skeptical. He assumed Cameron had seen his lust for Becky, and was pulling a joke on him.

Cameron was due to marry Becky's friend, Asia, and he'd claimed the women had some goofy dare going that was centered around the porn shop. Cameron had refused to reveal the details behind his and Asia's circumstances, but he had explained that it was Becky's turn, and Asia wanted to make sure Becky wasn't hurt.

George wanted to make sure, too.

Both Cameron and Asia thought that by ensuring Becky's partner—him—they could protect her from other, more unscrupulous men. Smart. The thought of Becky going off with anyone else set George on edge.

She'd been unattainable, a fantasy, for too long. Now that he was part of this plan, he'd already begun to think of her in his bed, already begun to imagine all the carnal fun he'd give her. Until she indulged his craving for her, he damn sure didn't want any other man touching her.

After they were through . . . well, he just didn't know, didn't want to think about that right now. The idea of Becky getting down and dirty with anyone else felt repugnant.

Cameron had told George that if he was willing—*ha*—he was to meet Becky at the shop and show an interest in bondage wares. That had nearly floored him, but Cameron, damn him, had been so blasé about the whole thing, George had refused to show his shock.

Becky Harte and bondage—a combination guaranteed to give any guy a steel boner.

Now he was beyond glad he'd taken up the challenge. Bondage wasn't something he'd explored much in the past, but hey, if that's what it took to finally get Becky into bed, he was willing, able, and ready. Actually, now that he'd thought about it— and he hadn't been able to think about much else—having Becky tied to his bed appealed to him in a dozen different ways.

"There's so much to choose from."

George watched the expressions flicker across her face when he asked, "Do you want it rough or gentle?"

Her eyes widened comically before she gathered herself. She cleared her throat and made a point of not looking at him. "I don't think the idea is for anyone to be roughed up, do you?"

That was a relief. He wasn't into manhandling women at all. Just the opposite. Once he had Becky bound, he'd worship her body until she cried with the pleasure of it. He could hardly wait.

"How about the velvet cuffs? They close with Velcro, so they'll be quick and easy to use." And he'd have her snared before she even knew what he was doing.

His cock throbbed with that thought and the accompanying image of Becky spread-eagle, naked atop his mattress, taut, trembling, waiting for what he'd do to her.

Her chin lifted. "Good idea." She snagged up the box and held it.

"Why don't you let me carry those for you?"

Face averted, Becky thrust her packages at him. "Thank you."

With every second that passed, George got more turned on, more eager. He rubbed his chin and thought about everything he wanted to do to her. He eyed her legs, then made another suggestion. "There are ankle cuffs too."

She wore a considering frown. "Do you think they're necessary?"

Oh yeah. "That's up to you."

"Yes, of course." She bit her lip, snagged up the package, and tossed it at him.

"Anything else?"

"Like what?"

Her determination was adorable. "I don't know. It's your show, Becky. You tell me."

That startled her, then she beamed. "Yes, it is,

isn't it?" She looked around, her brow puckered in a frown, then shook her head. "No, I think that's it for now."

"Becky?"

She peeked up at him.

"Do you want me to pay for these?"

Her shoulders slumped in relief. "Would you?" She dug in her purse and pulled out several bills. "I have to admit, the idea of getting caught at the register doesn't exactly thrill me."

George didn't take the money. She'd be fulfilling a two-year long fantasy for him, so letting her pay didn't seem right. "This'll be my treat."

His offer stiffened her spine. "Oh no, it's my expense."

Seeing that she wouldn't change her mind, George shrugged. "All right then."

"But aren't you going to buy anything?"

He'd already given due thought to his own purchase. "Yeah, I think I'll get the video we watched. We only saw a small portion of it. Wouldn't you like to see the rest?"

Becky flushed. "If you'll watch it with me."

"Absolutely." He'd watch her watching it. Seeing the fascination on her face was better than anything on-screen.

Her breath came fast. "When?"

George could see she was anxious, which fed his own urgency. "Friday night?"

It took her a moment before she screwed up her courage. "All right, yes. You can come to my place. I'll order a pizza if that's okay."

He'd rather have her in his house, on his ground. But it wasn't worth debating the issue. "Do you have a VCR?"

She bobbed her head. "Yes."

They'd watch the movie, then get those restraints out of the box and break them in proper. God, he could hardly wait. Though today was Thursday, it felt like Friday was more than a month away.

George forced a smile. "Six o'clock?" They both got off work at five, so that'd give her an hour to get home and get ready for him.

"All right."

By silent agreement, they started making their way to the register. Becky kept watch for other customers, and when they neared the front of the store, George took pity on her and told her to wait out front for him. She smiled and quickly ducked through the door.

When he joined her minutes later, he caught her waving to the factory. He looked up, but saw no one. "Your friends?"

She yelped and whirled to face him. "What? Oh, yes. I think I saw . . . uh . . . Erica."

"Erica Lee?"

"Yes." Becky frowned in suspicion. "Do you know her?"

He knew both Erica and Asia, mostly because Becky hung out with them every day during breaks and lunch. "Just in passing."

"Erica's dated nearly every guy at the factory." She glanced up at him, then away. "You've never been out with her though."

"Nope." Erica Lee was a pushy broad, demanding and too damn independent. She epitomized what many men termed a ball buster. She was sexy, no doubt about that, but he liked gentler women.

He liked Becky.

They walked across the street to the parking lot for the factory. When they reached Becky's car, George handed her the bag. She took it, smiled up at him, and said, "Thank you."

His gaze settled on her mouth. Damn it, he couldn't wait another second. For two years he'd wondered what it would be like to kiss her, how she'd taste, how she'd fit against his body. "Friday is too damn many hours away."

Becky gave him a look of confusion.

"I'm going to kiss you, Becky."

Her eyes widened and she stumbled back a step. "You are?"

"It'll be all right," he murmured, leaning down slowly so he wouldn't startle her. "Consider it a small prelude to tomorrow night, all right?"

Her lips parted. "But . . ."

He cupped her nape, turned her face up to his. Her blond hair was as soft as he'd always imagined. It felt warm against the back of his hand. "Just one kiss, Becky."

Her eyes drifted shut. "Yes."

She had one of the prettiest mouths George had ever seen, soft and full, always ready to smile. She never wore lipstick, but that was fine by him. He loved the way her naked mouth looked.

The moment his mouth settled on hers, he realized she tasted wonderful as well. She was breathing too hard and fast, as if she'd never been kissed before, but George decided it was anticipation that had her nearly panting. He understood that, because he wanted her so badly right now, he felt near to exploding.

Her bag dropped to the ground with a thump.

One of her hands touched his chest, fisted in his coat. The other curled over his biceps.

George slipped an arm around her waist, pulled her up close against his body, and sank his tongue deep with a groan. Her mouth wasn't only pretty, it was delicious, too. Sweet.

And damn, she was hot.

She went on tiptoe and kissed him back, awkwardly at first, but with enthusiasm. She stroked his tongue with her own, even sucked at his tongue a bit.

It was a caress guaranteed to make him nuts.

He wasn't just kissing a woman, he was kissing Becky. And she was wild for him.

Finding himself overwhelmed with rioting sensation for the first time in ages, George hugged Becky closer until their bodies pressed from knees to chest, until he could feel the wild beat of her heart and the gentle cushion of her belly. He wanted to absorb her. He wanted to take her right here, right now.

Lost in the sensuality of the moment, he drifted his hand down to that curving bottom of hers. She was a sexy handful and Friday night she'd be his.

Her ragged moan brought him to his senses. George lifted his head and looked around. Thankfully the lot was empty, but it was still a public lot, still out in the open and visible to anyone driving by or coming in or out of the building. Cold wind blasted his face and tossed Becky's hair, but it had little effect on his lust. He teetered on the ragged edge and knew it. "Jesus."

Becky, still clinging to him, still burning hot,

stared up at him with vague eyes and a damp mouth and rosy cheeks. "George?"

He wanted to drag her behind a parked car, lift her long skirt, open his pants, and sink into her. He just knew she'd be wet. And tight. And she'd groan. . . .

He had to stop. Now.

Damn it, he wasn't a man who went crazy with lust. He wasn't a man who took women in parking lots in the middle of cold winter weather. He was a man used to control, and Becky, more than most women, wanted his control. She wanted him to restrain her with velvet bonds.

He shook with that thought and the resultant carnal images.

"I'm sorry." He drew a ragged breath and tried for a smile. "We're out in the open, baby."

Her eyes were large and dark and hungry.

George muttered another curse. "Look, Becky, maybe you should just come home with me now. We're both free tonight, right?"

"Oh." Becky stiffened, looked around in appalled awareness of their surroundings. The warm flush of excitement was replaced by the hot wash of embarrassment. "Oh no, I can't. Not yet."

"Why?" George was so tense he'd never live till Friday. He wasn't sure he'd survive another two minutes.

"I'm not . . . ready."

Not ready? The hell she wasn't. She'd been clinging to him, all over him, with him every step of the way.

George drew himself up on an ugly suspicion. Did she have another date for tonight? Had he just warmed her up for another man? No way in hell was she going to crawl into bed with another guy who'd get to tie her up and watch her burn.

The mere thought had George outraged, and that bothered him, too. What she did away from him shouldn't concern him—but damn it, it did. He frowned. Maybe they should get a few things straight right now.

But Becky was back to blushing and she turned to fumble with her car door. The second she had it open, she slid into her seat and stuck the key in the ignition.

George picked up the bag she'd dropped and handed it to her. Leaning down into the car, eyes narrowed, he said, "Listen, Becky . . ."

She locked her hands on the steering wheel. "I have to hurry. Asia and Erica are, um, coming over tonight."

Asia and Erica? Well, that was different. She could visit with all the women she wanted to. Then it occurred to George how close the three women were. They spent every break, every lunch hour together at work. Would Becky tell them everything? Would she share every intimate detail? Would they know he intended to restrain her with hand- and footcuffs?

Women could be so damn gossipy. George wasn't sure he wanted his private affairs discussed—especially before he'd even had the private affair. He frowned and rubbed his jaw. "Erica and Asia, huh?"

Becky nodded so hard, her curls bounced wildly. "Yes. But I'll be ready Friday. I promise."

She looked eager to escape him. George gave up. "All right." But he added, his tone tinged with warning, "I'll see you at work tomorrow."

That idea seemed to horrify her. She gave him a sickly smile, slammed her door, and started the car. George stepped back and Becky, with an airy wave and unnecessary haste, drove away.

Friday. About twenty-four hours. He could wait, just barely.

But no way would he allow her to avoid him at work. Regardless of her kinky preference for bonds, Becky was naive, so she probably didn't understand what they'd started. He'd have to let her know that they were now on a new footing. They had something going, and he expected to reap the benefits of their new association for as long as it lasted.

In fact, the sooner they got that straightened out, the better.

Becky barely got to the top of the stairs leading to her second-floor apartment when she felt the stairs shaking. She knew even before she turned back to look that it was Asia and Erica thundering up the steps after her. She unlocked her apartment door and waited.

Asia and Erica burst onto the landing. Asia looked ripe with curiosity, and Erica was grinning like a loon. They both saw her, grabbed her, and screamed together, "You did it!"

Becky couldn't help but laugh. They knew how shy she was, knew that she never dated. For her to have actually gone through with her end of the pact was nothing short of a miracle. "Shhh. Come inside before my neighbors call the police. They'll think you're both accosting me."

The women moved inside, still huddled together, and shut the door. The second they all had their coats off, Asia enfolded Becky in a tight hug. "Becky, that kiss. Oh man. We watched from the window, and shew. Talk about a scorcher. Even Erica was impressed. That man's ears were steaming."

Erica snatched her up for a hug, too. "And you were in the shop for so long." She held Becky back and teased, "Had to check it all out, huh?"

"No! Of course not. It's just that . . . well, George and I got to talking . . ."

"And?" Erica squeezed her. "Did you buy any bondage stuff?"

Blushing, Becky gestured toward the bag. "Actually, George went through the checkout for me. Wasn't that sweet of him?"

Both women went mute. Asia rolled her lips in and stared at Erica with a worried frown.

Erica finally laughed. "George Westin, sweet? Now, Becky, honey, don't get disillusioned. He's a wolf, a hunk, the baddest of the bad boys and sexy as they come, but no way in hell would any sane woman call him sweet."

Becky thought he was very sweet. And very sexy.

"Becky," Asia cautioned, "he'll eat you for dessert if you're not careful."

Becky's face flamed at that unintentional double entendre. If they only knew how partial George had seemed to that idea. She remembered the way he'd stared at her lap while claiming he knew exactly how to make a woman happy in the sack.

She lifted her chin, not about to let them talk her out of her decision. She wanted George, and he was willing. That was good enough for her. "He's the one."

Asia surprised her by nodding in satisfaction. "I just knew it."

Erica frowned at her. "What do you mean, you just knew it?"

"I, ah, well, I could tell he was a bit kinky and because he obviously knows women, he'll be the perfect man for Becky. That's all I meant."

Becky wasn't quite convinced, but then Erica dumped out her bag. "Oh my. Look at this stuff."

Being fair-skinned was a curse, Becky thought, as she felt her face turn hot yet again. At this rate, she was going to give herself a sunburn.

Planning to handcuff a big muscular man to her bed for sexual purposes, and actually discussing it with her friends, were two different things. Normally she told them everything, but now, because it was George—her secret fantasy man—the idea of discussing him made her feel disloyal.

Erica, correctly reading her hesitation, looked at her with a wide smile. She pulled the velvet-lined handcuffs out of the box and let them dangle from her finger. "I can just see Geoge now, all stretched out and naked, straining, sweaty, sexy . . ."

Becky snatched the cuffs from her and stuffed them back into the bag. "Are you two staying around awhile?"

Erica folded her arms and looked at Asia. "Is she trying to get rid of us?"

Asia lifted one brow. "Probably wanting to moon over George."

"She can moon with us, right?"

"We'll give her pointers."

Erica laughed. "Have you ever tied up a man, Asia?"

"Well . . . no."

"That's what I thought."

Asia flipped her long brown hair over her shoulders. "I have a good imagination though."

"You'd have to, because I can't see Cameron letting you tie him down any time in the near future." She heaved a sigh. "Looks like it's up to me to instruct her."

"And I suppose you have experience in bondage?"

"Why certainly." Erica winked. "Men are most enjoyable when controlled, you know."

Becky ignored her friends and headed for the kitchen. She tied on a starched white apron over her denim skirt. "I'll put on some coffee," she called to Erica and Asia, "to go with the cookies I made this morning."

While her two friends continued to debate sexual experiences, Becky pondered the wonders of experiences to come. Though she was nervous, she could hardly wait. *Stretched out naked, straining, sweaty, and sexy* . . . Oh yeah, she could hardly wait to see George that way.

In between conjuring up images of George naked, George touching her, George kissing her again, Becky remained aware of Asia and Erica sitting at her small kitchen table. They blustered back and forth, teasing and joking. Erica claimed to have a lot of sexual experience, and neither Becky nor Asia disbelieved her. She was a strong, confident woman, and she knew what she wanted where men were concerned. But they still liked to tease her about her hard-nosed ways with the guys.

Asia on the other hand had gotten involved with Cameron during her foray into the porn shop. In whirlwind fashion, they'd both fallen hard, and subsequently gotten engaged on Valentine's Day, a mere month ago. The wedding would follow just as soon as they could get everything arranged.

As Becky measured coffee, she considered Asia and Cameron. Unlike Erica, Becky didn't doubt for a minute that Cameron would let Asia do whatever made her happy, even if it meant tying him up.

"When's the big date, hon?" Erica asked.

Drawn from her thoughts, feeling the tiniest bit melancholy because Asia had found something so special, Becky shrugged. "Tomorrow. After work."

Asia flopped back in her seat. "So soon?"

Erica snickered. "I don't remember you and Cameron waiting. And why should Becky wait anyway? If George is willing, and it looks like he is, why then, I say go for it."

The coffee machine began spitting and Becky got out three cups. She set them on the table near the matching sugar bowl, then filled the small creamer. "If I wait, I'm liable to chicken out."

Erica looked at the cloth napkins and silver spoons Becky arranged on the table. "You're such a Suzy Homemaker. It's a wonder some guy hasn't talked you into marrying him yet. Men adore the domestic types. Makes them secure."

Without meaning to, Becky heard herself say, "George is already secure."

"Oh Lord." Erica tangled her hands in her blue-black hair and groaned. "She's singing his praises and the man hasn't even made it to her mattress yet."

Becky frowned. "Well he is."

"And she's defensive of him too!"

Asia shook her head. "Erica, not all men are weak asses."

"No, only most of them."

Asia threw her spoon at her. "You, lady, are a sad cynic."

Erica merely laughed. Trying to ignore them both, Becky got up to pour the coffee. She'd just finished filling all three cups when her doorbell rang.

She froze. Somehow, with absolute conviction, she knew who was at her door.

Asia and Erica stared at her, then Asia took the coffeepot from her and set it on the hot pad. "Expecting company?"

"No."

Erica rolled her eyes. "Well, do you suppose you ought to see who it is?"

"Uh . . ." Becky wrung her hands together. She knew who it was, she just didn't know what he wanted.

Asia pushed back from the table. "I'll get it."

"Wait." Becky hustled after Asia, and Erica fell into a hurried trot behind her. En masse, in parade fashion, they quick-stepped it to the door. Asia turned the doorknob just as Becky reached her.

Provocative as the original sin, George lounged in the door frame with a devil's smile. His long-lashed, black eyes were glittering with intent.

At the sight of him, Becky drew up short. Erica plowed into her. They both knocked into Asia.

"Hey, easy now." George, somewhat startled by the unexpected greeting, reached out and kept them all three from toppling. He ended up with his arms full of females—and to Becky's eye, he didn't seem to mind in the least.

Chapter Three

George chuckled as the women began righting themselves. He didn't exactly hurry to get them out of his arms, but then, hey, he liked holding women. "Helluva greeting, ladies. Thanks."

Erica, the black-haired witch, managed to send her elbow into his middle before pulling away. George grunted, but refused to give her the satisfaction of rubbing at it.

Asia gave him a chiding look and muttered in all seriousness, "Behave."

Becky just stared up at him with that adorable look of innocent shock that seemed to melt his heart, his common sense, and his touted self-control. She didn't move away, and he damn sure wasn't going to insist. They stared at each other, and finally she blinked her way into speech. "George. What are you doing here?"

Her blond curls were mussed—a typical state for Becky, he was beginning to realize—and he went about smoothing them back into place. As badly as he wanted her naked and under him, he enjoyed simply touching her, too.

He ignored Erica, and only winked at Asia to re-assure her, then said to Becky, "You forgot your change."

"My change?"

"From your . . . purchases?" George wasn't sure if she'd told her two coconspirators about the bondage stuff yet, so he didn't want to let the cat out of the bag. All in all, it was a weak-ass excuse to be calling on her now, but it was all he could come up with.

Erica rolled her green eyes and drawled, "He means the cuffs and the blindfold, Becky."

Predictably enough, Becky gasped, embarrassed by the mere mention of the items.

George wanted to smack Erica, but Asia saved him the trouble. She shouldered the other woman and frowned fiercely. Erica gave her a "what?" look that wasn't the least convincing.

George decided to continue ignoring that one. "Remember, I paid with your money. You had change coming." He pulled out the bills and coins and put them into Becky's hand.

She stared at the money. "Thanks."

Asia shoved her way between them. She caught George's arm and pulled him through the door-way, then pushed the door shut. "We were just hav-ing coffee, George. Why don't you join us?"

"Yeah." Erica grinned. "Join us. Becky even made cookies."

George eyed Becky in the frilly little apron, and all sorts of fetish images flooded through his already taxed brain. Hell, it was only an apron, and if he remembered right, his grandmother used to wear one.

But damn, it sure looked different on Becky than it had on Gram.

Sandwiched between Asia and Erica, he allowed them to drag him to the kitchen. They seemed awfully eager to keep him around, but then, it had been Asia's idea, according to Cameron, that he should be the man to hook up with Becky.

He owed her big-time, he decided, then he noticed how the apron tied snug at Becky's waist emphasized the flare of her hips. Usually her clothes were concealing. He cleared his throat and sought casual conversation.

"You bake, Becky?" Somehow, that fit. He wouldn't be at all surprised to find out she knit and canned, too.

"They're just chocolate chip cookies," she mumbled. "No big deal."

"My favorite." Along the way to the kitchen, George took in the sight of her apartment. It was small, a little crowded with knickknacks and photos. Her sofa was floral, her curtains frilly, everything spotlessly clean. It was so like Becky that he liked it instantly. Her home felt warm and cozy and comfortable.

It felt like a . . . home.

They stepped into the small kitchen and George held out a chair for Asia, who was charmed, then Erica, who was sardonic.

Becky bustled about, looking like a very sexy Martha Stewart clone, getting out another cup and saucer, arranging the cookies on an ornate plate—studiously avoiding eye contact with him. George decided to let her get away with that for now. Once he had her alone, he'd show her there was no reason to be shy with him.

"Asia," he asked, again seeking mundane conversation to ease the tension, "how's Cameron doing?"

"He's great."

"He's exhausted," Erica corrected. "Wedding plans and all that, you know."

George set his teeth and smiled at Asia. "Things moving right along?"

"A few glitches. Nothing major." She snatched up a cookie as soon as Becky put the plate on the table. "That's typical of every wedding, I suppose."

Erica snorted. "Every marriage, too."

"Someday," Asia told her, "some guy is going to make you eat those words."

"Right. Don't hold your breath."

George picked up a cookie, handed it to Erica, and said, "Here. Something useful for your mouth."

She grinned shamelessly. "Honey, my mouth can be used for a lot of things more interesting than eating . . . cookies."

She'd used just the right amount of hesitation so George couldn't miss her meaning. He raised a brow. "At the kitchen table?"

"Why not?" She popped the cookie in her mouth and eyed him up and down. "You a prude?"

Despite himself, George laughed. "Okay, let me rephrase that—at the kitchen table with two women present?"

Erica held up her hands. "I concede. A woman has to draw the line somewhere."

"Indeed." George glanced up and saw that Becky was disgruntled by the sexual banter. Damn, he hoped she didn't think he was flirting with Erica.

He had been, he supposed, but not out of interest. He'd merely felt compelled to hold his own against her, sort of a male against female thing. Dumb.

He wondered how Becky could stay such close

friends with Erica. Their personalities were so different. He took a bite of cookie, and groaned in appreciation. "Damn, Becky, that's good. You even put walnuts in them."

Becky stopped dumping sugar in her coffee and gave him a stony stare. "Thank you. I'm so glad you like them."

Her words sounded anything but pleased. Was she jealous? Normally that would annoy the hell out of him, because grasping women drove him nuts. But this time George found himself fighting a grin. He kind of liked the idea of Becky being jealous. After putting him off for two years, she deserved it.

Becky sat opposite him at the small table, with Asia and Erica at his sides. He wanted to touch her, to reassure her, but the other women were watching him like they expected him to sprout horns at any moment.

Moving slowly so they wouldn't notice, George stretched out his legs. His feet bumped Becky's. Before she could withdraw, he caged her legs with his own. Beneath the table their knees touched, his outside hers. He watched her over his coffee cup and saw her go still, then draw in a deep breath. Her gaze lifted and locked with his.

For long moments, they stared at each other.

Erica chuckled. "You two are embarrassing me. I think it's time Asia and I hit the road."

Asia agreed, but Becky jumped to her feet. "No. I mean, you haven't finished your coffee."

"Caffeine keeps me awake." Erica drew her close and hugged her, then said in a stage whisper that the birds in the trees outside could hear, "If we don't go now, George is liable to self-combust.

The man is all but salivating and it isn't over the cookies, no matter what he tells you."

George continued to watch Becky when he replied to Erica. "How astute of you."

Erica flapped her hand at him in dismissal. "Nah. Men are just so easy to read."

"More infamous words," Asia complained. She grabbed Erica and towed her away. "Bye, Becky. Behave. And call me later."

"Call us both! But do not behave."

Seconds later, George heard the front door close with a quiet click. He set his coffee aside and came to his feet. Becky backed up.

He rounded the table.

She bumped into the counter.

"Are you afraid of me?" He wasn't worried about it, because he'd come to the conclusion that Becky's decision to incorporate a little bondage into her lovemaking was based on sheer curiosity and daring. No way did she have enough sexual experience to be bored and looking for a new kick. Under the circumstances, he expected her to be a bit nervous. Beyond being a real turn-on, it was sort of endearing.

She flattened her hands on the counter at either side of her hips, bracing herself. Standing there in the frilly apron, eyes wide, lips parted, she made a very tempting picture. "No, I'm not afraid of you."

"Good." George advanced on her until his legs were on either side of hers, his cock pushed up snug against her soft belly, and his hands over her hands on the counter, effectively holding her captive.

Damn, he liked this game. He liked it a lot.

He stared at Becky's mouth. "No matter what we do," he told her, thinking of how she might feel when he had her tightly bound on the bed, legs open, unable to move, "no matter what I say, you don't ever have to fear me. All right?"

Becky frowned.

"Believe me, Becky."

She nodded slowly. "Yes, all right."

He let out his breath in relief. "I need another kiss."

"All right." She closed her eyes, turned her face up, and pursed her lips.

Grinning, George smoothed a finger over that delectable mouth. Patience, he told himself. She might be ready to try new things, kinky things, but she lacked any real experience. It was up to him, regardless of his urgency, to guide her gently.

The idea of tutoring her gave him another rush. "I want to taste you, babe. I want you to suck on my tongue again."

Her eyes popped open and she blinked. "You do?"

"Mmmm. Becky, open your mouth for me."

Her lips parted the tiniest bit, more out of surprise than because of his instruction, but it was enough. George groaned and took her mouth.

The second he tasted her, his intentions regarding gentle guidance went straight out the window. He licked his way inside, tasting her deeply, eating at her mouth, pushing her lips farther apart with a hunger that quickly shot out of control.

After a small, shocked sound, Becky struggled to free her hands. Frustrated, George released her and lifted his head, ready to apologize.

She launched herself at him.

Her hands were frantic on his chest and shoulders, his neck, his face. She seemed to enjoy touching him, and she definitely enjoyed kissing him. Her mouth landed on his with inept exuberance until George helped by turning his head and adjusting the fit. Becky made a hungry sound and gave him her tongue.

Now, without their coats between them, he could feel her nipples stiffened against his chest. He wedged a hand between their bodies and cuddled her lush breast in his palm.

They both groaned in raw appreciation. Becky was full and firm and so soft, her heartbeat galloping madly. He was pretty much in the zone of no return when he stroked his other hand down her narrow back and gripped her rounded behind. He lifted her into his groin and pressed against her in a tantalizing rhythm that mimicked sex but wasn't nearly as satisfying. She felt good, smelled good, tasted good.

Against her mouth, he whispered, "God, Becky, you are so beautiful."

And like a wet cat, Becky screeched and thrust him away.

Dumbfounded, all his wits now gathered below his belt, George stared at her and tried to figure out what the hell had just happened. One minute she'd been attacking him, and the next she acted like she'd been attacked.

Even now, she appeared panicked, while George simply struggled to catch his breath. They were still pressed tightly together, his cock still throbbed, and his body still thought sex was the best solution.

Becky disabused him of that notion when she

flattened her hands on his chest and tried to push him away. He regretted her change of heart, but no way in hell was he going to let her put any major distance between them. Not yet. Not until he figured out what was wrong.

He caught her shoulders and held her still. "Becky?"

She turned her face away, her voice trembling, her eyes closed. "Let me go."

He hesitated, unsure about what to do. "All right. But can you tell me why?"

She wouldn't look at him. "I . . . I'm not ready yet."

What was the big deal about getting ready? He tried to sound reasonable. "Ready for what?"

"For . . . whatever you were trying to do."

"What exactly do you think I was trying to do?"

"I don't know!" She glared up at him, defiant and shaken. "You were grabbing my . . . my . . ."

"Your ass?" His voice dropped and he said with great and inadequate sincerity, "Becky, honey, you have a fantastic ass. A premier ass. A world-class ass."

She appeared startled, then laughed and covered her face with her hands. George relaxed a bit; that was more like it.

Gently, he eased her against him and began rubbing her back, not in a sexual way, but in a soothing way. She was trembling—and still snickering. His chest felt tight with an emotion that definitely wasn't sexual in nature.

He kissed her temple. "Becky? If I promise not to do any more ass grabbing, can I kiss you again?"

Her words were muffled against his chest. "That . . . that wasn't the problem."

Hmmm. Not exactly the answer he'd expected, but at least now she wasn't pushing him away. In fact, she leaned on him in a way he chose to call trusting. What a mix she was, buying handcuffs, going wild when he kissed her, then freaking out for reasons he couldn't begin to fathom.

Despite his current frustrated state, figuring her out would be a treat.

"How about we sit down and finish our coffee and cookies?"

Her forehead dropped to his sternum. "You don't mind?"

Teasing her had worked, so he tried it again. In a low sexy rumble, George said, "You've got great cookies, too, Becky."

She actually giggled, then groaned. "I'm embarrassed again."

"Why?"

"Because I acted like an idiot."

"Oh, I dunno." He nuzzled against her hair, breathing in her soft, baby-fine scent, loving the feel of her silky curls. "If some guy grabbed my ass like that, I'd probably act the same way."

She slugged him, and now she shook with laughter. George smiled, too. It amazed him, but despite a raging hard-on that by all accounts wouldn't be appeased any time soon, he was actually enjoying himself.

He kissed her hair again and moments later felt her shoulders stiffening, felt her bracing herself. Becky was shy, but she wasn't a coward. When she raised her face, he saw the determination in her gaze. "I didn't know you were so funny, George."

Cautiously, because he didn't want her to go

hiding against his chest again, he said, "I didn't know you were into bondage. I suppose there's a lot we can learn about each other."

She didn't look away, but she did bite her lip.

"C'mere, Becky." George led her to her chair and seated her. Startled amazement crossed her face when he knelt down in front of her, but he wanted to see her eye to eye, to read her reactions and make sure she understood. "I'm dying to make love to you. Don't ever doubt that. But I'm not a pig. If you want to wait a bit, it doesn't have to be tomorrow. We can just . . . I don't know, go out if you want."

Amazement turned to disbelief.

George frowned at her. "I don't want you to feel rushed."

She covered her mouth with her hand.

"And as for all this bondage stuff, hey, it's fine by me, but only if you're into it, okay?" Her hair had gotten tangled by his hands when they'd kissed and now he smoothed it, tucking it behind her ears. He adored her hair and couldn't wait to feel those soft curls drifting over his chest, maybe down his abdomen when they made love. . . .

"I . . . I'm new to this."

Her admission brought him out of his sensual revelry. "I figured that out." How new was what he really wanted to know. But then he assumed he'd find out soon enough.

"I want it to be tomorrow, I really do."

Thank God. "Okay, if you're sure that's what you want."

"It is. It's just that I want everything to be . . . right." She looked down at her hands, then back up. "And I want . . . I want the bondage stuff. I want to use the handcuffs and . . . the blindfold. Okay?"

It was a wonder he didn't come in his pants. As it was, George had to take two deep breaths, close his eyes, and count to ten. And still he hurt.

"All right." It sounded like he was strangling.

Becky smiled and touched his jaw. "You're pretty terrific, George, you know that?"

At the moment, he felt pretty damn terrific, like friggin' Superman, with superhuman patience. Only a real hero could take this kind of temptation and still survive. The inquisition could have made use of little Becky Harte.

"Cookies." He straightened, grimaced at the discomfort from a straining boner, and moved to his seat. "I'm going to eat my cookies, drink my coffee, then go home before I insist on kissing you again." He raised his cup to her in a salute. "You, babe, are pure fire."

Becky looked down at her hands folded on the tabletop. "But I'm not." And then, in a whisper so low he could barely hear her, "I'm not beautiful either."

George stared at her in surprise. So that's what had bothered her—a compliment. Judging by the seriousness of her expression, she really believed what she said. She also looked more vulnerable than any woman should ever look.

Trying to lighten her mood, he raised his hands and studied them.

That got her attention. "What are you doing?"

George lifted one shoulder. "I'm looking to see if I've got any visible burns so I can prove to you how wrong you are."

"Burns?"

"You are hot, lady. Believe me, I know. So hot, in fact, I would've sworn my fingertips were singed from touching you."

It was so ridiculous, but so sweet, Becky couldn't help but smile. George blew on his fingers and she laughed out loud. He was an incredible man.

"That's better," he told her, and he snagged another cookie.

Becky looked at him sitting across the table from her—a place she'd never, ever expected to see George sitting. Because it was getting to be late in the day, he had a dark beard shadow. She'd felt it when he kissed her, knew she had a few slight burns on her throat, her cheeks. Amazing. She'd never had whisker burn before. In many ways, it felt as though she'd been initiated.

George caught her staring and grinned. "What?"

Her smile lingered. "I was just . . . wondering about you."

He leaned back in his seat, a cookie in his hand. "Yeah? Like what?"

Becky shrugged. "I don't want to pry."

"No, it's okay. We might as well use this time to get to know each other better, right?"

She loved that idea, but having a personal relationship with a man was new to her. Having a relationship with George defied all her expectations. "You're sure?"

"Well hell, you're making me curious with all this hesitation. What are you going to ask me anyway? My social security number? How much money I make?"

"Of course not." She was insulted that he'd suggest such a thing. "I don't care about that."

His eyes narrowed a bit, making his dark gaze sharper. "Some women do, you know. What a man makes ranks right up there with the size of his cock."

Becky sputtered on the drink of coffee she'd just swallowed. He kept taking her by surprise with the things he said, his unregulated speech.

"You okay, honey?" He made to stand and Becky waved him back into his seat. If he touched her now, she was liable to attack him and then everything would be ruined. Twice now, she'd lost her head with him, in the parking lot, in her own kitchen. He was under the ridiculous assumption she was beautiful, and she didn't particularly want to dissuade him of that notion. If any of this was to go right, it had to be as she'd planned, with the bondage.

And with the blindfold.

George stared at her, must have decided she wouldn't choke to death, and shrugged. "Sorry. I didn't mean to shock you."

Becky didn't believe that for a second. It seemed to her that he took maniacal delight in shocking her. Besides, she'd already heard plenty about his dimensions. Women would whisper about him, pretend to swoon, and get all flushed.

Becky had always found it all rather silly.

And intriguing.

She cleared her throat. "Let me reassure you, I don't care . . . about what you make."

His grin was slow and suggestive, wicked. "But you do care about the size of my cock, huh?"

Deciding to face him down, to give him a little of his own, she lifted her chin and nodded. "The thought has occurred to me a few times. Especially since you're supposed to be . . . impressive."

"Yeah?" He took a bite of the last remaining cookie, for all appearances unconcerned with the idea that his private male parts had been discussed around the break room. "When have you thought about it?"

Good grief, he wanted details? Becky sought words that would explain, but wouldn't be too graphic. "Like when you were . . . you know, against me."

"Mmm." He gave her a sage nod. "Go on."

"And with all the . . . well, the talk." She shrugged. "I suppose it was natural for me to be curious about it, don't you think?"

He stared at her for a moment, then burst out laughing. He grabbed his coffee to wash down the cookie, and nodded. His eyes were still twinkling and his words were broken with chuckles. "I hate to break it to you, Becky, but truth is, I'm really quite average."

That stunned her. "No way. I felt you." Her brows puckered. "Surely that's not . . . not average."

His laughter dwindled, then died. Suspicion made him frown. "Becky, exactly how much experience do you have?"

She wasn't about to admit her experience was zilch. Nada. That other than the video he'd shown her earlier, she'd never seen a naked man.

"That's a personal question," she replied, trying to sound prim rather than evasive.

George barked a disbelieving laugh. "And the size of my dick isn't?"

That stumped her. "Well you're the one who told me to ask my questions."

"But it doesn't go both ways, huh? I'm to bare my soul and my manly measurements, but you get to keep private?"

She felt guilty, darn it. "On some things." As if to appease him, she said, "I'll tell you my bra size."

He looked at her breasts. "I'd say a thirty-six C. Right?"

Darn. That was right on the money—the man knew women much too well. She frowned, but didn't reply.

"We'll never get to know each other better unless we share, now will we?"

He had a point. "I suppose not." Then, "Do you want to . . . you know, get that familiar? I mean, you don't just want to do . . . what we planned to do . . . tomorrow night?"

That idea seemed to ignite his temper. "One night? Oh no, Becky, you can forget that right now. It'll take a damn month at least for me to even get close to getting enough of you."

"Oh." A whole month of having sex with George? The idea made her giddy. But would he continue to let her restrain him that long?

George's scowl grew darker. "Okay, this is how it's going to be. An even exchange. You can ask me a question, but for every one you ask, you have to answer one. Deal?"

She blanched at that suggestion. "I refuse to discuss past lovers." She couldn't discuss something that didn't exist. If he found out he was a guinea pig of sorts, he might lose interest or back out.

His eyes narrowed in annoyance. "Fair enough. That question is taboo—for both of us."

Well, darn. Becky sat back in a huff. There were at least three women at work who claimed to have been intimate with him. She wanted to know if there were others, if half the women there had carnal knowledge of him, and what exactly he'd done with them. The curiosity was killing her. But now she'd seem really petty if she pushed the issue. "All right," she muttered. "It's a deal."

He sat back with a satisfied nod. "Good."

Becky waited. And waited some more. "Well?"

"Well what?"

"How big is your . . . you know."

Being a complete cad, George asked with false confusion, "My what?"

Exasperated, Becky pointed.

"My waist? Thirty-four."

"No, not your waist."

His gaze was intent, taunting. Sexy. "Say it, Becky."

"Why?"

His voice changed, went husky. "Because I love it when a woman talks dirty."

Huh. She'd gotten that bit of information for free. Would she have the courage to talk dirty to him tomorrow? What kind of language qualified as dirty? With what he considered appropriate table conversation, it'd have to be pretty explicit to be dirty to him. She'd have to think about it. Or maybe ask Erica.

No, she couldn't do that. He and Erica seemed to get along a little too well to suit her.

She drew a steadying breath. "How big is your . . . penis?"

That slow grin reappeared. "Penis?" He laughed. "What a spoilsport you are. My cock is about seven and a half inches. Erect. And that's length by the way, not circumference."

"I know that!"

He laughed and finished off the last cookie.

Becky tried to picture a seven-and-a-half-inch penis—which was much smaller than the rubber penises she'd seen on the wall at the porn shop. But since she'd never seen a real one up close and personal, she decided she'd have to get a ruler out later to get a good visual. "Thank you. And you say that's average?"

"Close enough."

"Then why do they make the fake ones so big?"

George rubbed his face, and Becky suspected he was laughing. "I'll explain that to you after."

"After?"

He dropped his hands. Nope, there was no sign of amusement in his expression. "After we've had sex."

"Oh." That shut her up. She couldn't think of another single thing to say.

George leaned forward and propped his elbows on the table. "My turn."

Becky braced herself.

"Have you ever thought about having sex with me? I mean, before now. Anytime over the last two years?"

Oh, unfair! How did he come up with such a question? The last thing she wanted to do was admit that she'd fantasized over him a lot.

She frowned, and he just waited. She had agreed, so she met his gaze and nodded.

"Yeah?" His eyes turned hot with her confession, and he leaned closer still. "How often."

"That's another question."

"So I'm one ahead. Answer it."

Deciding a good offense was her best defense, Becky stood to pace. "You're an incredibly attractive man, George."

"Thanks. How often, Becky?"

She glanced at him, but saw no irony in his watchful gaze. She continued her pacing. "You're also very nicely built."

"Is that right?"

Becky bobbed her head. "Sure. You're tall and lean and muscular." She peeked at him. "Women like that."

"Like men like great asses and big breasts?"

Every feminine bone in her body was offended by such a cavalier, sexist comment. But once again, he'd gotten her. She'd started this stupid conversation, after all. Eyeing him, she muttered, "I suppose."

"Go on."

"You also have an astounding reputation."

To her surprise, George shook his head. "Women and their damn gossip. Believe me, I've heard some of it, and only half of it is true."

"Really? Which half?"

George settled back with an aggrieved sigh. "Is that your question? Because I have to tell you, it seems like a roundabout way of questioning me on that taboo topic we agreed to avoid."

Flustered because he was right, Becky busied herself with refilling his coffee cup. When she started to move away, he caught her wrist. "Besides, Becky, you still haven't answered my question."

"Oh?"

"Yeah." He took the coffeepot from her, set it on the table, and tugged her into his lap. With his arm locked around her, she knew she couldn't escape, so she just held herself erect. "Now, let's talk about these fantasies of yours. Particularly how often I played a part in them."

With the back of his finger, he teased her cheek, the side of her neck. Becky gulped. "All right." She glanced at him, then away. "If I have to be truthful, then I've thought about you often."

That teasing finger went still. "How often?"

Every day. "Often enough. I'm glad you were there today, and that we seem to have a similar interest."

His hand dropped to her waist. He squeezed, caressed. "In bondage?"

"Yes." Becky felt him shift and came to a startling realization—he still had an erection. And he felt bigger than seven and a half inches to her.

Eyes agog, she said, "You're still hard."

He looked pained. "Yeah. Believe me, I know. And as long as you're talking about bondage, or sitting in my lap, or . . . hell, just breathing, I'm probably going to stay hard."

Fascinating. "Will you stay like that for long?"

His mouth curled with suggestion. "As long as I need to."

"Oh." She shivered at that dark promise. "Oh no, I meant tonight, after you leave here." And then a horrible, awful thought occurred to her and she frowned at him, outraged. "You're not going to be with another woman tonight, are you?"

George pulled her down for a ravenous kiss. When he lifted his head, his voice was raspy and deep. "I want you, Becky, not anyone else. Until we're through with each other, we'll both keep it exclusive, agreed?"

Relief washed over her. "Yes."

He dropped his head to her chest. "Thank God. Now, I have to go because if I don't I'm going to lose control." He lifted his face to smile at her.

Becky, taking the hint, scrambled off his lap and stood in front of him. He came to his feet as well.

He cupped her head between his big hands and kissed her nose, her chin. Against her lips, he asked, "Will you think about me again tonight, babe? About what we'll do?"

"Yes." She'd think and dream and fantasize and plan.

George stepped away. "Until tomorrow, then."

It was raining when he left, a cold miserable rain, but inside her lonely apartment, Becky burned. She went to the couch, picked up the handcuffs, and began figuring out how she'd get them on him.

At least she had a four-poster bed, just like in the video. She was certain that was going to be a big help.

Chapter Four

George waited outside the women's rest room for Becky to emerge. He'd been so damn busy all day in meetings he'd scarcely seen her at all. But this was her last break of the day, and they'd both be getting off work in two hours.

He was so keyed up, so tense and impatient, he'd had to fight to concentrate on his work instead of on sexual thoughts. But always there in the back of his mind was the tempting picture of Becky submitting to his will, bound for his pleasure—and hers.

George locked his knees and concentrated on not getting hard. Damn, he couldn't wait to explore her body, to sate himself on her. He felt like a kid again, ready to get laid for the first time.

But it was more than that, too. He'd really enjoyed himself yesterday; chatting with her was always a pleasure because Becky was so unique, so different from most of the women he knew. But getting to know her more intimately, getting a few clues to her secrets, had been exciting in a way he hadn't expected.

The door swung open and Becky, Asia, and Erica walked out. Becky was carrying a wooden ruler, of all things, and Erica was laughing, Asia shaking her head. Becky fell silent when she saw him, and she nearly tripped over her own feet. Not so with Erica.

She moseyed right up to him, patted his chest, and said, "You stud, you! I'm so impressed."

George had no idea what had brought that on, but obviously whatever professionalism had existed between them on the job was now gone. He pushed away from the wall and grinned. "That's Supervisor Stud to you, Ms. Lee."

In the next instant, Becky swept past them, nearly knocking him down in her haste. Erica leaned forward and said, "Now you did it."

"What did I do?" He watched Becky's fast retreat.

Asia scowled at both of them. "You know she's shy. You should quit baiting her by flirting."

Erica shrugged. "If I wasn't flirting, what would I do?"

George saluted them both and took off after Becky. He caught her at the soda machine. She'd just popped the top on a Coke when he rounded the corner. She didn't know he was watching and she tipped up the can and guzzled it all in nearly one long gulp. Afterward she fell back against the machine, put the back of her hand to her mouth, and burped.

George laughed. He had a feeling the way she'd guzzled that Coke was her rendition of tying one on. "Have I driven you to drink already?"

Becky slanted him a narrow-eyed look. "What do you want?"

"You."

Her mouth opened, then closed. Her eyes glittered in her pique. "Oh. And here I thought you might want Erica instead."

He'd never heard that particular nasty tone from Becky before. It was all he could do to hold back his grin. "No way. Erica scares me." He inched closer.

"Yeah, I can see you shaking."

"I'm a man. Men don't shake no matter how terrified we are."

Becky rolled her eyes. "Yeah, well, Erica might be scary, but she's also plenty knowledgeable about men." She smacked him in the chest with the wooden ruler. "She said seven and a half inches is *not* average. You lied to me."

George rocked back on his heels, and to his chagrin, he felt himself going hot. Jesus, he hadn't blushed since he'd been a green teenager. "You told her what I said?"

"Well yeah. I mean, look at that!" She held up the ruler, marked by her thumb at exactly seven and a half inches. "I was . . . worried."

George looked around, and thankfully, the hall was empty. "Worried about what, damn it?"

"Fit."

"Fit?"

Looking equally embarrassed and mulish, Becky said, "I don't think you'll fit."

George no longer cared if anyone was around. He caught her shoulders and backed her into the machine. Against her mouth, he said, "I'll fit, Becky, believe me. I'll make sure you're nice and wet first, so no matter how snug it is, it'll feel great for both of us." He kissed her open mouth before she could say anything. "Two more hours, Becky. Two hours that'll feel like a week. Don't back out on me now."

Her eyes glazed over. He loved how quickly she reacted to him. Taking advantage of that, George cupped her breast, teased her nipple. It stiffened against his thumb. "Tell me you want me there, Becky. Tell me you haven't changed your mind."

"I want you there." The words were whispered and then she was kissing him, holding him tight, accidentally prodding him in the back with the stupid ruler still held in her fist.

Luckily George wasn't so far gone that he'd totally lost track of their surroundings. He stepped away from her just as two other employees started around the corner. He caught Becky's hand and dragged her along in his wake. "Six o'clock, Becky. Be ready for me."

"George."

"What?" He kept walking, refusing to let her back down on him now because of some ridiculous anxiety over his size. Hell, he'd thought she'd be turned on, as most women were, or he never would have told her a damn thing. At thirty-seven, he felt no need to brag about his endowments.

He shook his head. When Becky found out he was actually bigger than that, that he'd shortened the dimension out of modesty, well, he could only imagine her reaction.

He wondered again at her lack of experience, but it was far too late for him to change his mind.

"You're dragging me in the wrong direction."

George stopped and struggled for breath. It was unheard of, the way she affected him. "Right." He looked up and down the deserted hall. "Give me another kiss to tide me over then, and I'll let you get back to your work."

Becky grinned. She went on tiptoe, kissed his chin, his jaw, and finally his mouth. "Six o'clock." And teasing him as Erica had, she added, "Stud," and tapped his chest with the damned ruler.

George watched the sexy sway of her backside as she walked away from him. Before his very eyes, Becky's inhibitions were wearing away. He'd done that to her, he realized, and she was sexier for it. Very sexy.

He had to stake a claim before every cursed male in the factory noticed. When the night was over, Becky wouldn't have a shy bone left in her sumptuous little body.

And *she'd* be telling *him* that they were a perfect fit.

In more ways than one.

He showed up twenty minutes early. Becky was in the process of attaching the hand- and footcuffs to the bedposts, thinking that it would be less awkward that way than trying to set things up once they were . . . in business. She hid the handcuffs with the bed pillows, the footcuffs with the turned-down sheet. Her hands shook, her heart pounded, and her stomach felt very funny, sort of fluttery and tight and tingly.

She was going to have sex. And not with just any guy, but with George.

She closed her eyes and held her hands to her belly, trying to calm the stirring there.

The bed was all prepared, she decided. She'd drawn the drapes to leave the room dark. And on the nightstand—on her nightstand—was a condom and the blindfold. She felt faint with expectation.

When the knock sounded on her front door, she actually jumped and let out a small screech. Heavens, she was nervous. And eager. And excited.

She rushed from the room, but forced herself to slow, to take two deep breaths so George wouldn't know how anxious she was. She'd dressed in a button-down sweater and a long casual corduroy skirt. The sweater would be easy to remove, the skirt easy to lift. She'd left off pantyhose and instead wore lacy ankle socks—again, because they'd be easy to take off.

Her door rattled with another heavy knock and Becky peered through the peephole. George stood there, tall and dark and so handsome her toes curled inside her slip-on shoes.

She turned the locks, braced herself, and opened the door.

Trying to sound calm and cavalier when she was anything but, she said, "Hello, George—umpf!"

In one movement, he stepped in and scooped her up, then kicked the door shut. Held high against his chest, Becky had no choice but to grab hold of his shoulders and hang on. "George!"

His arms were trembling, his dark eyes piercing and hot. He leaned forward, nuzzled her hair, kissed her ear, gently bit her neck.

Becky jumped again, unprepared for such an onslaught of sensual attention. She had thought they'd . . . talk. That they'd . . .

"Where's your bedroom?" His voice was an aching rasp that curled through her on a wave of heat. Urgency beat inside her, matching the tempo of her suddenly racing pulse.

"My bedroom?"

"God almighty, Becky, I can't wait another single second." He strode forward though he obviously had no idea which room was hers. "Forget the movie. Forget the damn pizza." He peered into her bathroom and kept going, peered into the small guest room she used as a den. "Where is your bedroom?"

Becky lifted one limp arm and pointed to the last door in her small hall. Two seconds later George stepped into the room. This door he left open, which allowed the hall light to spill in. Becky wanted to protest but when he reached the bed, he dropped her. Her shoes fell off and tumbled to the floor.

Trying to ground herself, to get her bearings, Becky started to rise up on one elbow. She never made it. George threw off his coat, came down on top of her and started kissing her again, touching her, moving against her.

It was something of a shock, feeling a man lying on top of her, all heavy and hot, hard and lean. It took her a single heartbeat to realize it was also wonderful and Becky squirmed, better aligning their bodies. He caught her hips and held her still. His mouth traveled from hers to her throat to her chest.

She yelped when he nuzzled her breast through her sweater.

"George." She didn't mean to, but her body arched in reaction.

He grappled with her buttons, finally just shoving the sweater down so it caught beneath her breasts. With an expert hand, he released the front catch on her bra and the cups parted.

Breathing hard, George reared back to look at her. His cheekbones were dark with color, his eyes glittering and intent. "Damn." He cupped her breasts in both hands, stroked her nipples with his thumbs, caught and held them, tugged. Her nipples felt achingly sensitive, and his touch jolted through her.

Never in her life had Becky expected so much sensation from such a simple caress. A raw moan escaped her, and then another when he bent and sucked her right nipple deep into his mouth. She clasped his head and held him to her.

Wonderful. Beyond wonderful. She was lost in feelings too exquisite to describe when his hand went beneath her skirt, up the outside of her left thigh.

Becky panicked. "No."

George stilled. He lifted his head to look at her. Confusion warred with the lust and other emotions that Becky couldn't decipher.

She tried a smile, tried to remember everything she'd planned. Voice shaking, she touched his chest and said, "This is my show, George, remember? You were going to . . . indulge me."

His gaze went from her face to her naked breasts. He breathed hard, closed his eyes for a long moment. When he opened them again, some of that devastating emotion was banked. "Right."

Gently, Becky pressed against his chest until he fell to his back. Still struggling for breath, he put one arm over his eyes.

Becky slid on top of him, liking that position almost as much as being beneath him. A distraction was in order, so before he could cool down and start questioning her, she kissed him.

His hands went to her back, keeping her close as she tasted his throat, the side of his neck. "I love how you taste, George."

His fingers contracted on her in reaction. Encouraged, Becky kissed his ear and breathed, "I want to see you, George. All of you. I've been fantasizing over your body for a long time."

He groaned.

Slipping to the side, Becky touched his chest, light and curious and teasing, through the open collar of his shirt. "Will you get naked for me?" Her face heated as she made that request, both with a tinge of shyness and with anticipation.

His mesmerizing gaze locked on hers. "Oh yeah. Whatever you want, Becky." Without further instruction, he started on his buttons.

It was a slow striptease and she loved it. Having George remove his clothes for her delectation was a dream come true. Becky didn't want to miss a single thing.

As he worked the buttons free, she saw the dark hair on his broad chest, the way it narrowed down his trim abdomen and curled around his navel. The sight of the downy hair below his navel, leading to his sex, made her heart race. He was full and hard, and she could hardly wait to see that part of him.

He pulled his shirttails free of his slacks, and with a taunting smile, opened the button on his pants and cautiously slid the zipper down.

He smiled at her wide-eyed fascination. "You, too, honey."

"Oh." She glanced down at her still-exposed

breasts. Her nipples were puckered, darkly flushed, still sensitive. Yes, she could do that. If he enjoyed seeing her upper body, that was fine. If he wanted to touch her there again, or suck on her again, even better. "Okay."

Becky watched him watching her. Her fingers seemed far clumsier than his had been, but he didn't rush her. Instead, still glued to the sight of her breasts, he curled forward, raising his back from the bed. Using his fist, he reached back and grabbed a handful of his open shirt, then yanked it off over his head and down his long arms. He balled it up and tossed it over the side of the bed to the floor. Becky paused in the middle of her stripping.

Wow, he looked good. His shoulders were hard and sleek and muscled, his chest hairy but not too much so. He looked so . . . manly, so edible, beyond mere sexy.

Becky accidentally popped the last button on her sweater, then just stared at him.

"Take it off." George leaned back on his elbows. "The bra too." As he waited for her to comply, he toed off his shoes and let them fall over the end of the bed. They hit her carpeted floor with a soft thunk.

There was no embarrassment, not yet, not with the hungry way George watched her. Using the excuse of putting her sweater and bra on a chair, she crossed the room to the door and shut it. Shadows enveloped them.

George asked, "Where's the light?"

"We don't need the light." Becky peeled off her sweater and bra and strode back to him.

There were two heartbeats of silence. "Now, sweetheart, how can I see you without a light?"

He spoke so gently, his tone cajoling, that Becky wished she could relent. But she couldn't, so she teased as she slipped back into the bed with him. "And here I was under the impression you already knew where everything was." She reached out, felt his chest, and pushed him flat. "Isn't that right?"

"Becky . . ."

She trailed her hands down his body to the top of his slacks, effectively cutting off his protest. He drew in a sharp breath and his hands caught hers.

"Let me," she said.

His hands dropped to his sides. "You're pushing me, babe. And I'm already on the edge."

"Good." She loved the idea that she, Becky Harte, could drive a man to the edge.

"Not good. I want you with me."

"I'm right here." She shoved the material over his hips. "Lift up."

He lifted, but said, "No way, Becky. You're eons behind me."

She got his slacks all the way to his ankles and pulled them off with his socks. Taking a deep breath for courage, she explained, "I've thought about how I want to do this at least a hundred times, George. And that's just since yesterday. Please, just lay back and let me have my fun, okay?"

His hesitation was thick and unnerving. Then with a growl, he dropped back. "Somehow, I just know I'm going to regret this."

His legs were so long, she wondered briefly if he'd overreach the length of the footcuffs. As she touched his legs, she felt how his muscles had tensed, his thighs hard as steel. She glanced up at his face, but all she could really see was the glitter of his eyes. "Relax, George."

"Ain't gonna happen, babe."

She stroked the inside of his thigh. "Try." Becky cleared her throat, then touched his erection through the soft cotton of his boxers.

They both flinched, then both groaned.

"Damn."

Becky said, "Yeah." She touched him again, explored his length. "You feel even bigger than I remembered."

"A figment of your imagination." He sounded suspiciously anxious to convince her of that.

Before she could chicken out, Becky caught the elastic waistband of his underwear and dragged them off him. George shifted his legs to help, and again reached for her.

Becky decided it was past time she got him contained before she forgot herself and everything got ruined.

She fell on top of him, kissed him wildly to divert his attention. He went still for a moment in surprise before his big hands closed over her naked back and hugged the breath right out of her. The feel of his chest hair against her nipples was incredible. Becky closed her eyes and absorbed the tantalizing stimulation.

"Becky." He started to stroke his way down her back. "You're still wearing your skirt."

"Mmmm." Becky shifted to kiss his chest, to lick her way up to his shoulder, to his biceps. She loved his various textures—crisp hair, sleek warm skin, bulging muscles. His arms went slack and she trailed her fingertips to his wrists, then stretched his arms up over his head. The position had her hovering over him, her breast near his mouth.

"Lean down a tiny bit, babe."

She did, at the same time he lifted his head. His mouth closed over her nipple hungrily. It was enough to leave Becky witless with pleasure.

It wasn't easy, but she forced herself to remember the plan. She pushed his right arm higher, fumbled for the cuff, and closed it around his wrist.

George went still. He released her breast.

Quickly, before he could get cold feet, Becky did the same with his right arm. She pulled the Velcro tight but his wrists were so thick, there was barely enough length to the cuff to wrap around and hook.

"Uh, Becky . . ." He sounded bewildered, and Becky felt him tug experimentally against the restraints.

Thank God they held. Her hands had been shaking so badly, she wasn't sure she'd fastened them right.

She sat back, which meant she literally sat on his abdomen. "Can . . . can you see me, George?"

Again his arms strained. "Damn right I can see you! What the hell are you doing?"

Uh-oh. Becky leaned over him and felt on the nightstand for the blindfold. "Here, let's get this on you."

"No! Damn it, wait a minute . . ." He twisted, but Becky easily got the elasticized band hooked across his eyes. "Becky." There was a wealth of warning in his tone.

Becky bit her lip. She wasn't quite sure what to make of his new attitude. "You promised, George."

"Like hell I did!" He jerked hard, making the

bed shake and almost tumbling Becky from her perch on top of him. "You're the one who wants to be restrained, not me."

Becky gasped. "That's not true! You said you understood, that you'd indulge me. You said we were in agreement."

"We agreed I'd tie your sexy little ass down. I didn't say jack-shit about this being done to me." He yanked hard again and Becky thought it was a wonder the bedposts didn't crack. "Now unfasten the damn things."

Her heart beat too fast and her face burned. Becky moved off him so she was no longer astride him. "Oh no. This is just awful."

"It's going to get a lot more awful if you don't undo these damn things right—now."

He sounded so outraged, Becky wasn't sure it would be wise to let him loose. "George, please calm down." She sounded near tears and hated herself. "It's a misunderstanding, that's all. And I'm sorry. I'll unfasten you if you promise to just go."

"Go?"

"I don't want to argue about this and I don't want a huge confrontation. I'm embarrassed enough as it is . . ."

He'd stopped struggling halfway through her diatribe. "What the hell are you talking about? I'm not going anywhere." His voice dropped to a growl. "We're going to make love."

Becky stared through the darkness at him. "Oh no. We can't now."

He practically vibrated with tension, with anger, then burst out, "Fuck. Fuck, fuck, fuck . . ."

"George!"

He groaned, he cursed again. Finally, he took a deep breath. "You're saying you won't have sex with me unless I let you keep me this way?"

Becky bit her lip. He was definitely outraged. She nodded her head, realized he couldn't see her, and said, "I'm sorry."

"Why?"

"Because I didn't mean to mislead you."

"No, I mean why do I have to be restrained. Did some asshole hurt you? Are you afraid *I'd* hurt you?"

"What? No!" His misconceptions further flustered her. "It's nothing like that." She leaned over him and cupped his face. "I trust you, George. And I want you. I want you so much, it's killing me. But it'd have to be this way or . . . or not at all."

She felt him breathing, felt the rise and fall of his chest beneath her. Then he spoke, his voice husky, his words enticing. "Are you wet, Becky?"

Oh, she knew this new tone. He was interested again, rethinking things. Becky touched his mouth with her fingertips and answered in a barely there whisper. "I don't know."

"Take the rest of your clothes off, okay, sweetheart?"

She was almost afraid to hope. "You've changed your mind? You're going to make love to me after all?"

"Yeah, I'm going to make love to you." He laughed, a sound of irony and frustration. "Or rather, you're going to have to make love to me, all things considered."

Becky kissed him very gently. "I'd like that."

His voice deepened even more. "Then finish taking your clothes off."

"Is it okay if I fasten your ankles first?"

He groaned. "Yeah, what the hell. If that's what it takes."

To Becky, he sounded in pain. She twisted around and quickly caught each ankle to a bed-post so that his long strong legs were held open. Curiosity got her, and she trailed her fingertips up his thighs until she located his erection. "Is it okay if I do this too?"

"God yes."

His hips lifted with her first tentative touch. She lightly wrapped her fingers around him, amazed at how big he was, how he filled her hand.

"Harder."

Thrilled with the instruction, Becky used both hands to hold him, and stroked. Now he definitely sounded in pain, but she wasn't so innocent that she misunderstood. He was painfully aroused, and he was enormous.

"I'm going to take my panties off, George."

She could hear his labored breathing in the otherwise quiet room. His head turned toward her, but Becky knew he couldn't see her. The room was dark enough without lights; under the blindfold, he wouldn't be able to distinguish a single thing, much less her scarred leg.

Still, she left her skirt on. It wouldn't hinder their lovemaking in any way.

"Becky?"

"Yes?"

"If you're going to touch my cock, then I want you to sit on my stomach, with your back to me."

Naked beneath her skirt, shivering at his sexy suggestion, Becky climbed back into the bed. "How come?"

"I want to feel you, wet and hot, on my belly."

Her muscles all clenched at the provocative way he said that. He was pretty good at this business of talking dirty. She liked it.

Breathless, she said, "Okay," and again straddled him, this time as per his instructions. Slowly, her breath held, she lowered herself until she was flush against him, her thighs around his waist. His skin was hot, slightly hairy. She braced her shaky hands on his hipbones. "Like this?"

"Mmmm. Oh yeah. You are wet, Becky, and so hot. You want me, don't you?"

Somehow, this wasn't how Becky had imagined it, with him still controlling things. "I want you a lot. I always have."

"That's a good thing since I'm not at all sure how much control I have left."

Becky began touching him, and he muttered in a rush, "None. I don't have any control left."

"Just give me a few minutes." His penis was hard, throbbing with life. The velvety texture amazed her. She didn't know what she had expected, but this was much more exciting than any fake rubber penis could ever be.

"Becky . . ."

She cupped his testicles, now drawn tight, and cradled them gently in her palm. They felt so different from his penis, she couldn't help but explore them.

George's legs shifted against the bonds. He groaned.

His scent was strong, that of musk and male and sex. Adding that to the combined influences of his size, his heat, his body, and his understanding, and Becky felt swollen with need. She'd had no idea that it would be like this, so personal, so hot and still so tender. She wanted to experience everything and wallow in this opportunity to be with him.

"I love how you smell, George." She bent low to inhale deeply. His abdomen contracted against her mound, he lifted just a bit, pressing closer. She rubbed her nose against him, brushed him with her cheek.

"Becky," he warned again.

She stroked the head of his erection with her thumb, and felt him flex in her hand. "I still don't know how this is going to fit inside me."

"Oh God." He trembled, then growled. "That's it. Turn around, Becky."

She looked over her shoulder. "Why?"

"Because I'm going to come." His voice was low with desperation, urgent. "You have to take me now, babe, or I'm going to embarrass myself."

Becky hesitated only a second before scurrying around on him. He wanted her, needed her, and she was more than ready herself. "Let me grab the condom."

He gave another pained laugh. "Lord help me."

"It'll be okay," she promised.

"Have you ever put a rubber on a guy before?"

"No. But I read the instructions, and I practiced on a banana."

The bed shook with his startled laugh, and his raging lust. "I think I've just been insulted."

"Not at all. It was a big banana." Because she'd already gone through about half a dozen condoms from the box during her practice, she ripped the package open like a professional. She was rather proud of herself. "I also bought the large-sized ones, so at least I know the condom ought to fit."

"You'll fit me too, sweetheart. I promise."

"I need a light so I can see you. Just a sec." She'd thought that out, too, and flipped on a very dim night light. "Can you see?"

He sighed. "Not a damn thing, but I imagine you're getting an eyeful."

Becky stared at his naked body, spread-eagle and bound. There were thick shadows, but they only enhanced the clench of muscles, the length of bones, the texture of hair.

The throbbing of his cock.

"Oh yes." She laid the condom on his thigh and began running her hands all over him, absorbing him, relishing him. "George, you are so incredible."

"Becky." Her name emerged as a raw groan. "You're killing me, sweetheart."

"Could I . . . kiss you?"

He held his breath. "Where?"

"Here." Becky gently pressed her mouth to his erection. He strained against her and for a startling moment, she thought he might break free. Better not to try that again.

She moved over his thighs, held him steady, and rolled on the condom. "Does that feel right?"

"Fine. Great. Now ride me. Right now."

Ride him? The things he said were guaranteed to make her melt. Shoving her skirt out of the way, Becky poised over him. "Tell me if I do this wrong."

She clasped his penis in one hand, braced herself with the other, and lowered onto him. The broad head nudged against her and she gasped.

George trembled, every muscle in his body stark and delineated. "More."

Becky bit her lip and forced herself to settle down onto him. He was barely inside her, and already he felt much too big.

"I don't know about this, George."

His arms were pulled tight against the bonds, his body slightly arched. "You need to . . ." He swallowed hard. "You need to get yourself wetter. Move the head of my dick around, yeah, like that. Oh God . . ."

Becky closed her eyes, liking how that felt.

His teeth clenched. "Now try again, babe."

She did, and this time the head pushed inside her. Becky froze at the discomfort of it. Her muscles clamped down on him, squeezing.

George moaned, "Ah, damn . . . Becky."

She stared at his face, felt him jerk, shiver, and then she knew he was coming. His body bowed hard, lifting her, inadvertently driving him deeper. Becky flattened her hands on his chest and braced herself. He went deeper still, not all the way, but it was too much. It hurt.

One of the cuffs gave way and he grabbed the back of her neck, brought her head down to him and ground his mouth against hers. Becky was too astonished by it all to consider the ramifications of his freed arm.

He kissed her and held her and groaned, and then he was finally motionless, still inside her, his hand still tangled in her hair, his chest rising and falling like a bellows. A little in awe of his fierce reaction, Becky rested her face on his shoulder. He tasted a bit salty against her lips, and he smelled divine. She could have spent the night like that, and probably would have if she hadn't felt him stiffen.

"George?" She started to move.

His arm tightened across her, keeping her close, and then he jerked his other hand free.

With a yelp, Becky realized exactly what was happening and tried to escape, but it was too late. Using only one arm, his strength far greater than she'd suspected, he kept her gently locked to him while he jerked the blindfold away. He looked . . . well, she wasn't sure. There was determination in spades, but also a lingering of lust.

And what looked like tenderness. Maybe even regret.

Refusing to become fanciful, she shook her head to clear it. "George?"

He kissed her lightly on the mouth. "I'm sorry, sweetheart."

"For what?" Did he mean to apologize for losing control? She kind of liked it that he had.

Incredibly, his gaze darkened even more. "For this." In the next instant, Becky found herself on her back. George twisted awkwardly over her, considering his feet were still fastened, but it took him mere seconds to strap the handcuffs around her own wrists, and because she was small boned, they overlapped, holding her tight and secure.

"George, no!" A very real panic set in and Becky struggled wildly.

"Shhh. Easy, sweetheart." He bent and removed his ankle cuffs, only to catch each of her flailing legs in turn. With a smile in his tone, he said, "Ankle socks. I think I'll leave them on. They look sexy." She kicked and fought but again, he was too strong for her. With seemingly no real effort, he wrapped the restraint around each ankle and Becky found herself spread out, wide open. Vulnerable.

Her skirt covered her, but for how long?

Her heart thundered in her ears and her vision blurred. "No."

"Turnabout is fair play, babe." He tickled his fingers over the arch of her foot. "I think I have an affinity for this. 'Course, thinking about doing this to you for so long already had me in a lather."

A sob rose in her throat.

George lowered himself over her and held her face. "Becky, shhh, don't cry, honey. Becky, listen to me."

She didn't want to listen. She wanted to escape, to run away. "Please, George, please don't do this."

He looked very solemn, very resolved, as he kissed her mouth. "Do what? What you did to me?"

"George . . ."

"Right now, all we're going to do is talk."

Becky tried to calm herself, tried to think of how to reason with him. "And then?"

"And then I'm going to do everything to you I've been thinking about for two long years."

"No."

"Oh yeah. Everything. And, Becky, I can promise you're going to love it."

Chapter Five

He could almost see the thoughts scrambling through her mind. She was afraid, mad, embarrassed . . . It was the fear that ate at him.

As if she'd read his thoughts, she said, "You told me I didn't have to be afraid of you."

George stared at the tears glistening in her beautiful blue eyes and felt his heart breaking. Damn, somehow his good old-fashioned, straightforward lust had morphed into something much more complicated. "That's right."

Her lips quivered, her chin quivered. "But you're scaring me now."

"Why?" He rubbed the soft skin beneath her chin, hoping to soothe her. A riot of feelings bombarded him. She was all but naked and tied open beneath him, so lust was there, demanding attention. He hadn't realized quite how much he'd like the bondage stuff, but he had to admit it was an enormous turn-on.

Those deeper emotions were there, too, making him soft in the head, turning his muscles to soup. And the damn tenderness, choking him, making his own eyes damp—he wanted to cradle her close and tell her everything would be okay. But he didn't even know what the problem was yet.

"I won't hurt you, Becky."

She turned her head away until her nose was pressed deep into the lace-edged pillow. George smoothed her hair. He loved her hair.

Shit, he loved her.

No woman had ever plagued him the way she did. No woman had ever turned him on, turned him inside out, and made him generally nuts the way she did.

And right now, she was afraid of him.

To ease the way, he stalled for time. "I'm sorry to subject you to this, but now comes the ickier part."

Her brows drew together and she glanced his way. "Ickier part?"

"Disposing of the condom." He sat up beside her on the bed. He made such an indent in the mattress, her hips rolled toward him. George grinned, grabbed several tissues from the nightstand and peeled the condom off.

Becky watched in fascination. "I hadn't thought about that."

"Really?" At least she wasn't crying now. She was such an inquisitive little ex-virgin. "And you had this all planned so well."

She snorted. "Obviously not well enough." A hard tug on the restraints proved her point.

George dropped the condom into the bedside waste can. "You have more rubbers on hand?"

She sniffed, sounding very put out but also curious as to what he intended to do. She bobbed her head. "I bought a whole box. They're in the drawer."

"I like a woman who thinks positive." George retrieved a few more of the little silver packets—and noticed the wooden ruler in the drawer. "Ah, what's this?"

"What?"

George lifted it out, pleased that she had started to relax enough to converse. He waved it under her nose. "Planned to do your own calculations, did you?"

"Yes." She glared at him and her face was hot. "Before you ruined everything."

George dropped the ruler and rubbers on the top of the nightstand. He turned and rested his hand on her belly. "Ruined things how, babe?"

For long moments, she simply stared at him, utter defeat clouding her gaze.

"Come on, Becky," he encouraged, knowing he couldn't pull back now. "Explain it to me. Maybe things'll turn out way different than you expect."

"I don't want you—any man—to see me."

That totally took George off guard. He wasn't at all sure what he'd been expecting, but modesty over her body? It didn't make sense. He glanced at her sprawled form, which looked beyond delectable even in the dark shadows. Thank God for the night light or he wouldn't have been able to see her at all.

Her long skirt was twisted around her legs, her ankle socks were bunched, but the rest of her . . . well, she was naked.

She was his.

"Why the hell not?" Her pale breasts and belly showed up just fine. "You're beautiful."

"No." She shook her head, mussing her hair once more. For a woman who starched her pillowcases, she sure had a problem keeping her hair in order. "I don't . . . don't look how you probably think I look."

"Is that right?" George cupped her breasts. Even now, when she was frantic to get away from him, her nipples stiffened under his touch and her heartbeat lurched.

"Let's see," he murmured, while playing with her pretty breasts. "These are real, not enhanced. A gift from Mother Nature, and they look even better than I'd imagined."

"George! I didn't mean that."

He slid his hand to her waist—and felt her stiffen. "No girdle," he said, watching her closely. "You're not bone skinny, but your curves are all perfect."

She squeezed her eyes shut.

George moved his palm lower, over her hip and then under her to cup one round cheek through the corduroy of her skirt. "There sure as hell isn't anything fake about this great ass. So that leaves, what? Your belly button? Do you have two? An outie, maybe? Hell, Becky, I like outies. No? That's not it?"

"No."

He'd never heard so much misery in one word. George stroked her right thigh through the skirt—and heard her catch her breath against a cry. He knew he hadn't hurt her, so that had to mean her embarrassment was over her legs. But why? She did always wear long skirts, and even now, when they were in bed together, she had her legs covered. He frowned in suspicion.

Whatever bothered her, it wasn't going to be easy to convince her that he didn't give a damn.

He decided it was best to bypass that topic for

now, and instead reached beneath her skirt and between her legs.

She went rigid, but for different reasons.

"You're awfully tight," George admitted, and pushed his middle finger into her.

She squirmed, gasped. Moaned softly.

"I like that, Becky. I really do. You squeezed me and I lost it." With gentle care, he pressed in and out, rasping against already sensitized, swollen tissues. She was so wet, still excited. He kissed her open mouth. "You were a virgin, weren't you?"

She groaned.

"I like that too, babe, though how the hell you kept your virginity for so long amazes me. A woman as sexy and sweet and beautiful as you is just made to be fucked."

She made a small sound of dazed excitement. George smiled. Becky liked it when he talked dirty to her. He'd noticed that early on, and right now, he wanted her insensate with lust. He wanted her to forget whatever inhibitions remained, whatever troubled her, scared her. He wanted her to trust him.

He wanted her love.

Looking at her with new insight, he asked, "Does this feel good, Becky?"

"Yes." That single word shivered almost as much as Becky did.

She was so precious, so hungry for physical contact and yet such a sweet innocent. The contradictions drove him wild, and made it impossible not to love her. "If I'm going to squeeze back into you again—and you can be damn sure that I am—we need to prepare you a little more. Let's try two fingers, okay?"

Her head tipped back, exposing her pale throat where her pulse raced. "Yes. Okay."

He smiled at her immediate, husky reply. She held her breath as he began working the second finger into her, not roughly, but with insistence. "Take deep breaths, that's it. A little more." Her feminine muscles squeezed his fingers as he pushed forward until he had them completely inside her. "I told you I'd fit."

Her eyes closed. "But you didn't."

"Only because you didn't let me get you ready. Remember me telling you that women need to be touched?"

She swallowed hard. "Yes."

"Especially here." He found her clitoris with his thumb and pressed.

"Ohmigod."

"Yeah, that feels good, doesn't it?" He watched her, loving the way her face, her chest and breasts pinkened. Satisfaction flowed through him as she began to tense. "Next time I slide deep into you, you'll be so wet and ready, you'll be begging me to hurry."

She opened one eye to stare at him in doubt. George grinned and kissed her again. "Now, I'm going to scoot down just a little bit—no, don't get all antsy on me. I only want to get to your breasts. You have very soft, heavy breasts. They turn me on, and I especially love how your nipples taste."

"Oh." She arched, offering herself to him.

George tested her self-control by kissing just below a nipple, around it, touching with his tongue.

"George?"

"Hmmm?"

"Will you . . . um . . ."

"What?"

"Suck on me again?"

He'd already come not more than five minutes ago, and with just a small request, she had him painfully hard once more. "Yeah. You can bet I will." He went back to teasing her.

"George?"

Hiding his grin, he said, "Hmmm?"

"When?"

He curled his tongue around her and drew her into the wet heat of his mouth. Her moan was nice and deep and real. He liked it. He liked helping her forget her silly qualms about her body. What, did she have freckles on her legs? A birthmark? He'd show her that it didn't matter—after he had her mindless with lust and limp from a screaming orgasm.

Within minutes, Becky was squirming and gasping and George knew she was close. He wanted to be inside her when she came, but decided he could be generous. She deserved a lot of pleasure, and he'd enjoy giving it to her.

He kissed her ribs, down her belly.

Becky groaned. She jerked and pulled against the handcuffs, then flopped back in defeat.

"Sorry, babe, but you're not nearly strong enough to free yourself." He dipped his tongue into her navel.

"What . . . what are you going to do?" She sounded both anxious and worried.

He wanted her to enjoy her first orgasm with him, so he didn't push the issue of her skirt. Instead, he spread the skirt out across her wide-opened legs. Becky tried to bring her knees together but the footcuffs stopped her.

"None of that. You're open to me, and I can touch you, taste you, and look at you, as much as I want. Just relax and enjoy."

He ignored her continued struggles, her rasping breaths, and raised just the middle of the skirt, keeping her thighs hidden but revealing her mound. She went perfectly still.

Being the master of understatement, George said quietly, "Now isn't this pretty."

Becky groaned, but otherwise didn't reply.

He fingered the dark blond curls decorating her sex; they were damp with her excitement. "Very, very pretty."

Her heels pressed into the mattress, but she still didn't say anything. Unable to wait a second more, George carefully parted her. "All sweet and pink. You're beautiful, Becky."

"You're looking at me!" She sounded scandalized—and aroused.

"Hell yes." He stroked his fingers over her, opening her more, teasing her. "I love looking at you." He leaned down and kissed her deeply.

Her hips shot off the bed. "George."

He held her steady, keeping her poised high, and continued to taste and tongue and nip at her.

"Ohmigod, ohmigod, ohmigod."

The taste of her, her spicy female scent, filled him. He held her tight so she couldn't lurch away from him, found her clitoris—and suckled.

In that moment, George knew she forgot all about her worries. She thrashed and cried and pressed herself against his mouth, as much as she could, considering she was tightly bound to the bed.

She begged him with words and actions to continue. He stayed with her, carefully attentive to her reactions so he'd know exactly what she liked the most.

"Back inside you again," he whispered against her hot flesh when he felt her begin to tighten, felt her legs tensing. He pushed two fingers deep, out, in again—and she came.

It was pretty damn special, George thought, watching Becky come, tasting her release, hearing her low cries.

When she finally quieted, her body going boneless against the mattress, he reared up, grabbed another condom, and in record time, he was over her. She didn't have time to accustom herself or gather her objections.

George shoved her skirt aside, but kept his gaze locked on her face. Her eyes opened in startled alarm, met his, and went soft and vague as he thrust into her.

"You can take me, Becky," he ground out from between his clenched teeth. "All of me."

Her hands curled into fists, her head tipped back. George kissed her throat, bit her shoulder, and rocked into her. "More," he said as he felt her hips lift, shift in an effort to accommodate him. "More, more, more . . . ah, yeah."

Becky panted, her whole body dewy, drawn taut. He knew he filled her, that she felt strained. She was young and virginal and stretched tight around him, squeezing him, gripping him.

George slowly pulled out, moaned with her, and just as slowly drove back in. "Perfect," he said. "Fucking perfect."

Becky whispered, "Yes," and amazingly enough began to shiver in another release.

He wanted her to come again, with him this time. He slipped his hands under her satiny bottom and helped her to meet the rhythm that would drive them both over the edge.

"Faster," she begged, then, brokenly, on a whimper, "Harder."

George shuddered. The bed rocked with his thrusts. He felt Becky tense, felt her body go rigid, and it was enough. He held her closer, drove deep into her one last time, and they both shook with an explosive release.

George collapsed on top of her. Her body was small and soft and damp beneath his. Her hair tickled his nose. Her gentle breath brushed his sweaty shoulder. Her plump breasts cushioned his chest. He wanted to stay this way forever, the two of them still connected, their hearts beating together.

For the moment, Becky wasn't shy or apprehensive. She was sated. She was his.

He dreaded moving because he didn't want her to start shying away from him again, but he knew he was too heavy for her, and he knew her arms had to be tired.

Forcing his muscles to work, George braced above her. "Mmm," he teased, and kissed her slack mouth. "You're something else, lady."

As if by a great effort, her eyelids lifted. "George?"

Her love-soft voice made him smile. "Did you enjoy yourself, sweetheart?"

Her gaze roamed over his face, finally settling on his eyes. "You're incredible." Her sigh brushed his throat. "And very big."

"But not too big to fit."

"No."

George regretted what was to come. He drew a breath to prepare himself, then cupped her cheek. "Now, let's see what has you so shy, okay?"

All the sleepy satisfaction left her face. Instinctively, her arms jerked, trying to be free. She glanced up at the handcuffs still around her wrists, then back at him. She cried out. Her legs twisted and tugged, shaking the bed.

Disregarding her futile efforts, though they tore at his heart, George sat up. Knowing she watched him, he disposed of the second condom much as he had the first. The sound of her strenuous breathing filled the air between them.

When he finished, he turned on the bedside lamp and faced her. She squinted against the light, tried to twist away from it, from him. Her voluminous skirt was now bunched and tangled around her thighs.

"George, please . . ." she said, without much evident hope.

Her pleading tone ate at him—and strengthened his resolve. He shoved her skirt aside—and froze.

Becky gave a soft sob.

Her entire right thigh was marred with zigzagging scars, some deep, some shallow. The skin was puckered, pinkish in places, roughened in others. They feathered out around the front of her hip, then got worse, uglier, down her leg, her knee, and partially onto her calf.

Acting solely on emotion, George cupped his hand around her knee and bent closer. "Jesus, what happened?"

"Don't touch me."

Her flat voice brought out his frown. "Don't

touch you? You're naked in bed, Becky. I've just finished making love to you, twice. You're the sexiest woman I've ever known, and regardless of what you think of me, I care about you. Of course I'll touch you."

"Go away."

"Not on your life." He was angry at her for not trusting him, for evidently considering him a shallow ass. He was angry that she'd hidden herself for so long, that she'd let it matter too much. Angry that she didn't know what a beautiful, amazing, unbelievable woman she was.

She didn't even realize he loved her.

"Tell me what happened."

Devoid of feeling, she said, "A car wreck."

He caressed her, from the inside of her knee to her groin then back again. Bound as she was, she couldn't do a damn thing to stop him. "How old were you?"

"Twelve."

"Surgery?" His heart threatened to break, thinking of his Becky at the tender age of twelve, so hurt, so emotionally wounded, too.

She managed a shrug despite the handcuffs. "Some. It helped me to walk again, but there was nothing they could do to make it look better."

Very gently, George said, "They're just scars, Becky."

"They're hideous. Kids . . . they used to make fun of me at school. The ones who weren't mean, who didn't tease, just stared instead. They'd look at me with pity." She spoke with no emotion at all. "My mom started buying me long skirts to hide my leg, but by then, everyone already knew."

"So you never dated? Never gave a guy a chance?"

She looked at him, her face almost blank. "I dated a guy once. When he saw my leg, he got sick." Her laugh scared him because it didn't sound like his Becky, didn't sound sweet and shy and innocent. "Needless to say, he never asked me out again."

George floundered for a proper reply, but all he could think to say was the truth. "I'm not him, you know."

"No?"

"Nope. It doesn't matter to me, Becky."

She laughed again.

George decided he'd just have to show her. He gave her a friendly slap on the hip. "You know what I want to do?"

Her gaze turned wary. "What?"

"I want to turn you loose, first. Much as I enjoy seeing you like this"—he leered at her, to make his point—"I know your arms must be getting tired."

"They are." She still looked doubtful.

"Okay then. We'll shower, probably fool around a little more, then I'd like to spend the night." He put his hand back on her belly, this time under her skirt. "Will you let me stay with you?"

"Why?" She appeared genuinely perplexed by his request.

"You mean other than the fact that I haven't gotten nearly enough of you?" He grinned at her expression. "All right, I'll bare my soul again. I'm a man in need of reassurance. I've got that damned reputation to live up to, but you only came twice and then only after I'd already acted like a pig and lost control. I need to know that you still respect me."

"George," she said, almost laughing but not quite.

He tickled his fingertips down her leg to her ankle, back up again to her hipbone. "I need to know that you haven't lost hope, that you'll give me a few more chances to show you that I can be a considerate lover. A great lover. A lover worthy of an awesome reputation." He bobbed his eyebrows. "I can't have you running back to work with tales of my shortcomings."

"Shortcomings?" She smiled past her tears. "You're a nut. You already know you're awesome."

"Awesome enough that you'll let me spend the night?"

The laughter was replaced with hope. "You really want to?"

"Damn straight." He unhooked her legs and massaged them in case they were stiff. He ignored her rigidity when he rubbed over the scars, pretending he hadn't noticed. "Feel better?"

A hot blush colored her face. "Yes."

George unhooked both her arms and went through the same process, rubbing and stroking. Then he looked down at her breasts. "I feel like Pavlov's dog."

She folded her arms around herself. "What do you mean?"

"I see your breasts, and already I'm conditioned to drool." He shook his head, a little stunned, a lot chagrined. "Damn, I want you again. Already. I'm insatiable."

Two heartbeats passed, and then Becky tackled him to his back. She trembled, and she had a death grip on his neck. George, feeling his own throat close with emotion, held her tight. "Don't cry, Becky. I can't bear it."

She sniffed and snuggled closer. "George?"

"Yeah?"

"If I let you stay, you have to let me measure you."

He laughed and rolled her beneath him. "Deal."

George woke to an empty bed. He sat bolt upright in alarm, but Becky was nowhere to be seen. Frowning, he realized sunshine filtered through the drapes. When he looked at the clock, he was stunned to realize he'd slept so late. It was nearly ten, when he almost never stayed in bed after eight. Especially when there wasn't a woman in bed with him.

He frowned—then heard the feminine whispering in the other room. Becky had company, and he could just guess who it was. Asia and that damned Erica. Were they gossiping about him even now?

George grabbed up a sheet, halfheartedly wrapped it around his waist, and slunk to the door to listen. Yep, that strident voice belonged to Erica. Was she trying to talk Becky out of getting involved? She was so damned cynical about men, even when she was being amusing.

Because he couldn't hear anything clearly, George opened the door and slipped halfway down the hall. He heard Asia say, "You let him spend the whole night? Why, Becky, you little tart."

The women laughed, so he knew Asia was only teasing.

"Is it love at first lay, then?" Erica wanted to

know, and George thought about storming out and muzzling her.

But Becky's next words stopped him cold.

"Of course not, Erica. I'm actually amazed that he even wanted to stay the night."

Both Erica and Asia asked, "Why?"

There was a long expectant moment, and Becky sighed. "There's something neither of you know."

George peeked around the corner in time to see Erica bound to her feet. "What did he do to you?"

"No, it's not like that."

Asia touched Erica's arm. "There's something she wants to tell us. Is that right, Becky?"

"Yes." But rather than explain, Becky stood. She straightened stiff and proud, and lifted her nightgown, showing her friends her leg.

George wanted to groan. He knew she expected them to be horrified, to be disgusted. If either of them hurt her feelings, he'd . . .

Asia whispered, "Dear God, Becky, what happened?"

And Erica asked with concern, "Does it still hurt?"

Becky dropped her nightgown back into place. "I was in a wreck when I was young. No, it doesn't hurt, but you see how ugly it is."

Erica turned militant. "Did George think it was ugly?"

"He said not. He said it didn't matter."

"Of course he's right." Asia stood to hug her. "You should trust what he tells you, honey."

Erica laughed. "True enough. George doesn't

care about a few scars on your leg, Becky. He probably only cares about what's between your legs."

The comment sent George right over the edge. Dressed only in a sheet, he stormed into the room. "You don't know what you're talking about, Erica."

Erica stood, too, so that the three women grouped together to stare at him in shock.

Three sets of feminine eyes roved over him, from his naked chest and legs to his tenuous hold on the sheet at his hip.

Asia gulped.

Becky blushed. "George, you're naked!"

Erica recovered first. She gave a wolf whistle, then said to Becky, "Honey, there are some things a woman never complains about. I think this might be just such an occasion."

George was too disgruntled to be embarrassed. "I don't like having you speak for me, Erica."

Asia raised her brows. "You're saying she's wrong? That you do care about Becky's leg?"

Becky looked horrified. "Asia!"

"Of course I care about her leg."

In a united front, Asia and Erica flanked Becky. They looked ready to castrate him. Becky looked devastated.

At the ragged end of his emotions, George stomped forward. When he touched Becky's cheek, his hand shook. "I love your leg, and what's between your legs, and your heart and your hair and your—"

Becky gulped out a laugh. Her face turned bright pink.

Beside her, Asia beamed. "Well now, this is wonderful."

Erica snorted. Before she could say anything,

George reeled on her. "Isn't it your turn to go hang out in the porn shop?"

A heavy silence fell. All three women scrutinized him, Asia with a touch of guilt.

Becky breathed in accusation, "You knew."

George wanted things settled. "Damn right I knew." He cocked a brow. "Or at least I thought I did. You put a definite spin on things that I hadn't anticipated."

Asia and Erica leaned around Becky to look at each other. "A spin? Now that sounds interesting. Do tell."

George rolled his eyes and ignored them. "I didn't really give a damn what your so-called fantasy was, because all my fantasies are about you. No matter what, I couldn't lose."

Erica rubbed her hands together. "Better and better."

George growled, "Will you two go? I'd like to propose in private."

Becky blinked. "Propose? You mean . . . you mean . . ."

Knowing he'd just blown any chance for privacy, George groaned. Then, filled with determination, he cupped Becky's chin and demanded, "Marry me, Becky."

Asia squealed. Erica laughed. Next thing George knew, he was caught in their circle and they were all dancing and jumping and singing their way around the room like a gaggle of loons.

He damn near lost his sheet, and when he made a grab for it, he stumbled. "Damn it, she hasn't said yes, yet!"

They stopped bouncing around. Becky covered

her mouth with a shaking hand. She looked at Erica, looked at Asia. Glowed at George. "Yes."

Satisfaction rolled through George, followed closely by a tidal wave of lust. "Good." He grabbed her wrist with his free hand. "Let's go back to bed."

Erica burst out laughing. "Men. They are so predictable."

George stumbled to an outraged halt.

Asia said, "Uh-oh. Bad timing, my girl."

He turned and stalked back to Erica. "You are next, right, Erica?"

She lifted her brows with mock confusion. "Next?"

"To visit the blasted shop." He had her cornered and they both knew it. He took swift advantage. "So tell us, Erica, what's your fantasy?"

"Wouldn't you like to know," she quipped, but Asia and Becky just crossed their arms, not offering her an iota of help. Asia even tapped her foot.

"You wouldn't understand."

"Why?" George put his arm around Becky, hauling her close. "Because I'm a lowly male?"

Becky said, "He's very understanding, Erica," and George couldn't help but kiss her.

"George will be family, soon," Asia pointed out. "So tell."

Rolling her eyes, Erica blurted, "All right, all right." She put her hands on her hips, thrust her chin in the air, and said, "Prepare yourself, kiddies." Then she named her fantasy with a taunting smile.

Asia and Becky went wide-eyed. George straightened in surprise. Thinking of what she intended, and what she'd likely get, George started to laugh—

until Erica gave him a sloe-eyed, seductive look. He could tell that she expected him to poke fun, to ridicule her. Her opinions on men weren't overly complimentary.

Well, he wouldn't give her the satisfaction of reacting as she expected.

But he couldn't resist saying, "I pity the poor bastard who runs into you. He doesn't stand a chance."

"No, he doesn't," Erica assured him.

Giving up, George turned and dragged Becky back toward the bedroom.

Asia was still laughing when Becky yelled over her shoulder, "I think it sounds wonderful, Erica! You can start on Monday."

George pulled her into the room and slammed the door. He dropped the sheet, picked her up, and crawled into bed with her held close to his heart. "Wonderful, huh?"

Becky touched his chest. "Not as wonderful as you."

George stared into her eyes, watching her reactions as he slid his hands up her thighs, then spread them wide so he could nestle in between. Becky flinched when he touched her scarred leg, but George knew now that she'd get over that in time. In a thousand ways, he'd show her that she was the perfect woman for him. "I love you, Becky." He stroked her thigh. "All of you."

Big tears welled in her eyes. "I love you too."

"Is that right?" He was already hard, but hearing her say that made him burn.

"I've been hung up on you for a long time. What you said about me being your fantasy? You're mine. You've always been mine."

George smiled. "That's all I ever want to be."
He kissed her. "Yours."

"George?"

She sounded so serious, George gave up his
contemplation of her breasts to give her all his attention. "What, babe?"

"Do you think Erica is going to end up hurt?"

He rolled over and pulled Becky on top of him.
"I think Erica is going to learn a very well-deserved
lesson. But if you're worried about her, I can lend
a helping hand."

"How?" Becky groaned as he began fondling
her breasts.

"I'll make sure the right guy knows what she's
up to." Cameron had helped him along, so George
figured it was the least he could do.

Becky smiled. "Ah. And I know just the right
guy."

He scowled, then caught her nipples in a tantalizing taunt. "You wanna rephrase that, Becky?"

She laughed, squirmed, and when he didn't release her, she groaned. "The right guy for Erica."

"That's better. Now enough about Erica. Come
here and love me."

"All right." She peeked at him. "Can I handcuff
you again?"

George's heart pounded and his cock flexed.
Damn, seeing Becky in a frisky, kinky mood was
enough to make any man lose the battle. "You
know, I believe you can."

Drive Me Wild

Chapter One

She'd gotten herself into a pickle this time.

Too distracted to work, Erica Lee slouched back in her office chair and blew her bangs out of her face. Who would have thought that uptight Asia and ultra-shy Becky would have followed through on the dares? Erica sure hadn't. But with only a little prodding both of them had traipsed right over there and done the unexpected.

It boggled the mind, it surely did.

Now her turn had rolled around and hey, it wasn't that she had anything against porn shops or fantasies or the like. But where the hell did they expect her to find a man who wouldn't be a pain in the patoot?

Of course, for them it had turned out great. That is, if one considered marriage great. Erica was still undecided on that particular point. Then again, footloose and fancy-free wasn't really working for her either.

She winced over that sad truth.

In the next second her office door slammed open with startling force. She jumped a foot and almost fell out of her rolling chair. She was alone in the office, and in fact, the entire floor was deserted while employees attended some meeting that she'd managed to opt out of. She'd been so lost in thought she hadn't even heard anyone approaching.

Holding a hand to her heart and ready to blast the noisy offender, Erica looked up—and up some more until she fell headlong into the mesmerizing midnight gaze of none other than Ian Conrad.

Oh, boy. Her heartbeat didn't calm with recognition. Nope. If anything, it tripped even faster. Ian was just so . . . so male.

Hot around the collar and sweaty, clad in blue jeans, a dirty cambric work shirt, and scuffed lace-up black boots, Ian epitomized all that was man. He wasn't particularly handsome, at least not in the classical sense, but that didn't lessen his impact one bit.

His features were bold with a strong, straight, high-bridged nose, a powerful chin, and high, harshly carved cheekbones. His eyes were the darkest blue and piercing in intensity—the type of eyes that froze a woman to the spot whenever he directed his attention on her. His dark brown hair was more straight than not, a little shaggy and unkempt.

Bracing his long thick legs apart, he filled the doorway—and then some.

Well, well. Quiet, masterful, impossible-to-ignore Ian. Erica raised a brow, wondering what had put him in such a temper when in the past she'd never seen him so much as frown—even when she'd deliberately provoked him.

Unlike most of the men she knew, Ian was al-

ways calm and always firmly in control—of himself
and everyone around him.

Not that she'd ever let him control *her*. "I've wit-
nessed more polite entries."

She'd meant to be a smart-ass, of course, but
her attitude got snagged in her throat when Ian
took two long, heavy strides to her desk, braced
strong, lean hands flat on the surface, and bent
down—way down—until his nose nearly touched
hers.

Good Lord, she could see every eyelash surrounding those mesmerizing eyes, feel his warm
breath against her lips, and smell his raw, potent
scent.

"I know exactly what you're up to, Erica."

Her eyes widened over that gravel-deep voice
that seemed to sink right into her bones. Combined
with the heat of his gaze, his rough tone was impossible to misunderstand. It was that man to
woman tone, and sexual awareness rolled over her.
Feeling helpless, she asked, "You do?"

"Damn right." His mouth appeared tight with
annoyance, but still sexy. "Your buddy George was
more than willing to spell it out."

Her gaze snapped back to his. "George spoke to
you?" With Becky as a best friend, and George as
Becky's fiancé, she supposed he could be considered a buddy. That is, unless he'd done something
to irk her—and given Ian's unusual mood, it
sounded like he might have.

In that case, Erica would have George's hide.

"No, he didn't speak to *me*. And that's most of
the problem right there."

Ian's disgruntled scowl was dark enough to
make grown men tremble. No wonder he kept it

under wraps in polite company. Not that Erica intended to tremble in front of him. Later, when she was away from him and remembering how close he'd gotten and how delicious he smelled, she might shake a little. But no way would she let him know he affected her that much.

"Well, if George didn't speak to you, then . . . ?" She let the sentence hang, waiting for him to explain.

"He didn't. But he did tell a couple of other guys what you have planned at that damn porn shop."

Erica's mouth fell open. It took a lot to shock her, and this definitely qualified. She sputtered a moment before finding her voice. "Why, that miserable rat!"

Ian straightened, studied her a second more, and then waved away her indignation. "Forget that. Hell, the whole factory knows what you and Asia and Becky have been up to so it's hardly a secret."

She'd just gotten her mouth shut when it dropped open again. "They don't!"

"You're not naive, Erica. You know something like that can't be kept quiet. Hell, I'd be surprised if all of Cuther doesn't know about it."

Erica shot out of her chair to pace. She, Asia, and Becky had made a deal when the new porn shop, Wild Honey, had opened up in their miserably quiet hometown of Cuther, Indiana. They were each to visit the somewhat titillating establishment with a specific fantasy in mind. As soon as they spotted a man shopping for wares that indicated a similar interest, they had to ask him out.

Asia had gotten off easy when Cameron overheard the initial discussion as well as the fantasy she'd claimed. Without letting on, he'd visited the shop on the right day at the right time and he'd specifically purchased items that would draw Asia to him, as per the dare. Since Cameron had already been half in love with Asia, one thing had led to another and they'd quickly advanced from making love to making wedding plans.

Then Cameron had played big brother and helped set Becky up so she got exactly what she was looking for too—in both her fantasy and her choice of man. George had been something of a surprise, but Erica liked him. Or at least she had before he let the cat out of the bag. Now she wasn't so sure.

Becky and George were currently shopping for engagement rings, while Asia and Cameron had just tied the knot. As the only unattached female still in their circle, that left Erica out in the cold. Not that she wanted to be married, because she didn't. No, sir. Uh-uh.

It didn't matter that George and Cameron made it look so damn appealing with the way they catered to Becky and Asia and kept them both smiling like lovesick saps. Hell, these days it was downright nauseating to be around any of them, they all walked around in such a vacuous fog of romantic bliss.

Fuming, Erica whirled around to face Ian. "Who did George tell it to?"

"I don't know and I don't care."

"What do you mean, you don't know?" She didn't exactly mean to screech, but there were only around two hundred workers at the factory and everyone pretty much recognized everyone else. "What department do they work in?"

He narrowed his eyes. "I didn't see them, Erica. I was in the ceiling wiring the lights when they walked in. They didn't even know I was there and I didn't care to announce myself."

"Never mind, then." She started to go around him. "I'll find out." And when she did, she'd . . .

Blocking the door, Ian crossed his massive arms over his wide chest and glared at her. "It doesn't matter who they are because you're not meeting up with either one of them."

Erica drew to an indignant halt. She hadn't planned to go anywhere with either of the men but, oh, boy, Ian's tone was guaranteed to get her back up. She knew him well enough since they worked in the same company and their paths often crossed. They chatted regularly, too, especially when he'd rewired her office, but then, she chatted with all the men.

Unfortunately, she was more aware of Ian than the others. She couldn't put her finger on it, but something about him just really got to her—and she didn't like that. She didn't want to be drawn to him, but how could she not? When Ian was around, his personality was so quietly dominant that every other guy faded into the woodwork.

Regardless of all that, there was no way in hell she'd let Ian or any other man dictate to her.

Holding his steady gaze, she stalked closer toward him, her stride as long as her leather miniskirt would allow. "I'll see them, and a dozen other men, if that's what I want to do."

"No." He stared down at her from his lofty height. "You'll see *me*."

That drew her up short in mingled shock and affront. He'd sounded so . . . certain, so in charge and imperious. Luckily, she managed to laugh over her reaction. "You?" Her sneering tone sounded just right. "Gee, Ian, I didn't know you were interested."

His expression turned cynical; he even went so far as to shake his head in an indulgent way. "Erica, you assume every guy is interested."

Insults? Now just what did he think that would accomplish?

"This time," he conceded in that deep voice that felt like a tactile rub and sent shivers down her spine, "you're right."

He admitted it? And why did *that* give her such a thrill? She started to deny him, but he didn't give her the chance.

"I think you're interested as well, which is why we need to bypass this foolishness with the porn shop."

Foolishness? Okay, so now that it was her turn to visit the place, it did seem a tad foolish. Unlike Becky and Asia, she didn't need encouragement to date. Heck, her calendar stayed booked. She considered herself the quintessential party girl.

Her only problem was finding a man who could keep her interest, because so far no one had. Most were selfish and shallow and set in their ways— meaning they had no room to adjust to a woman who was also set in her own ways.

But she'd devised the plan, and it had worked brilliantly to bring Asia out of her self-imposed celibacy and to help Becky shed her unfounded insecurities.

So how dare Ian call her plan foolish?

She needed to bring Ian Conrad down a peg, and fast—before his dynamic manner started to turn her on. Sheesh, sometimes she was such a female, enjoying all that macho arrogance. "Did George, perchance, mention what kind of man I was looking for?"

Ian's eyes darkened a bit more, until they appeared more black than blue. He stared at her, his gaze so probing Erica felt pinned in place. She couldn't look away, and he wouldn't look away. "Yeah, something about sex slaves."

Despite herself, Erica's face heated. Becky was liable to be a widow even before she tied the damn knot, because Erica seriously considered killing George. She hid her turbulent thoughts from Ian, unwilling to let him know how the conversation disconcerted her.

Instead, she shook back her hair, propped her hands on her hips, and slowly smiled. "Should I presume you're here because you're willing to fill that role?"

"As a sex slave?" He grunted. "I'm here because I want you to stop dodging me."

"I don't." Her reply was fast and automatic. How dare he suggest such a thing? She didn't dodge anyone—not even big, buff men who were a little too tempting and a lot too overwhelming.

"Bull. You'll flirt and tease with every timid weak-kneed jerk in the factory, but you're always cautious with me, never quite letting loose."

"That's not true." She didn't let loose with anyone.

"And no matter how many times I manage to corner you long enough to have a conversation, you're still jumpy as hell."

"Ha!"

"You're jumpy right now, Erica." With one finger, he touched the racing pulse at her throat. His voice gentled. "I know I intimidate some people, but—"

He'd noticed her uneasiness? And here she thought she'd concealed that with plenty of sarcasm. Ian Conrad was just too damn astute for his own good.

Through her surprise, she managed a credible laugh. "You, intimidating? Be real, Ian. So, you're big? So what." So, Erica reminded herself, he was big and calmly autocratic in a way that would make any sane woman think twice about getting too close.

Unlike many of the men she'd dated from the factory, Ian wasn't in a managerial position. His work was physical—and suited his large, hard frame. Compared to the guys in suits, he looked deliciously rugged and capable in his work clothes. Very capable. Very manly. Maybe too manly.

Halfway through the day he'd be all hot and sweaty, his brown hair damp against his nape and forehead, his shirtsleeves rolled up to show off thick forearms. And his jeans were always well worn, snug on his tight butt and long muscular thighs and a heavy . . .

She nearly shuddered, just thinking about it, then covered that innate reaction by checking her nails and striving for a look of indifference. She did have to do that around him a lot, it seemed. But it wasn't her fault he exuded such raw, powerful appeal. "Ya know, Ian, it's hard for you to intimidate anyone when you're always quiet as a church mouse."

"Until I have something to say. And Erica, I have plenty to say to you."

That sounded like a warning, causing her heart to lurch and regaining her attention. He could be so damn intense, and yes, intimidating. She'd never admit it out loud, but it was a little thrilling. If she'd been truthful about her fantasy and what really turned her on, then . . . but no, she'd claimed to want a sex slave, and damn it, she'd stick with that story. "Yeah, all right, big boy. So speak up."

Trying her best to be casual, Erica propped her hip on the edge of her desk and crossed her legs. To her annoyance, though she had a lot of leg showing Ian never looked away from her face.

But oh so slowly, the corners of his mouth curled and wow, that gradual smile had a devastating effect on her equilibrium. It was wicked and sensual and suggestive, just hinting at what outrageous things he might do.

And then he did it, again with a distinct lack of haste that had Erica near to bursting with anticipation. By the time he stepped up, firmly clasped her knees in his big hands and drew her legs apart so he could stand between them, Erica was ready to swoon when she'd never considered herself a swooning type of woman.

Stunned by his daring, more than a little breathless, she stared up at him. He wedged himself closer—and in the process spread her legs more. She felt the rough denim of his jeans rubbing the tender insides of her thighs, felt the tensed steel of his muscles, his carefully restrained power.

"Listen up, Erica." He was again so close that if she leaned forward one measly inch she'd be kissing him. "I want you. I've wanted you since I first saw you months ago."

One breath, two . . . "That right?" Damn, her voice still sounded like a squeak.

"Mmm. You're bossy as hell, gutsy, a little too outspoken and risqué, but all in all, I like it."

Some of her sensual haze dissipated, replaced by annoyance. "What's with all the insults?"

"Just telling it like it is. You flirt too damn much, tease without regard to consequences, and avoid any man who might come close to matching you. But you won't avoid me. Not anymore." His midnight eyes glittered dangerously. "Isn't that right?"

Annoyed by her own desire to submit, Erica pushed away from him, only he didn't let go of her knees and he was such a solid hulk he sure as hell didn't budge. Instead, she almost fell flat on her desk, sending papers scattering to the floor. She caught herself on her elbows but it was still an ignominious position, and Ian in an aggressive mood wasn't a man to be taken lightly.

Straightening seemed a high priority but before she could manage it, he lowered himself over her. With the impact of an electric jolt, she felt his hard abdomen press against her soft belly, his groin nestle against hers. Oh, wow.

Her legs, literally hanging over the end of her desk, sprawled wide apart to accommodate his muscular hips. If anyone walked into her office right now, she'd have a lot of explaining to do—that is, if she could find any breath to speak, which was doubtful given how she panted.

When she realized just how quickly and easily he'd aroused her, she stiffened in alarm.

Ian snuggled closer and murmured, "Shhh, relax," and none of the flustered anxiety she suffered sounded in his tone. "Everyone's gone to a meeting. We're all alone."

And that was supposed to reassure her when all she could think about was wrapping her legs around his waist? So unlike her! So . . . submissive.

He cupped her face and smoothed her chin with his thumbs. His touch was sexual, but also tender, and Erica got flustered all over again. "Now tell me you'll forget this sex slave business and give me a chance to show you how good it'll be between us."

He oozed so much confidence, she couldn't help but believe him. And she wanted to agree, she really did. But old habits were hard to break, so she raised her chin, narrowed her eyes, and smiled her most taunting smile.

"You want a chance, Ian? Then meet me at Wild Honey after work, and plan on playing. Because I'm not about to back out of my deal with Asia and Becky and that means I need a sex slave. It can either be you—or it can be someone else. You decide."

A taut stillness settled over him, but his eyes remained bright, turbulent. "You're pushing me," he accused, still stroking her chin with an incredible gentleness in direct contrast to his tone. "I have to wonder if it's because you really expect me to back off, or because you're hoping I'll push back."

Erica gulped. "Just . . . just telling you the rules."

Damn it, she'd stammered, so she quickly tried to compensate. "You do know how to follow rules, don't you, Ian?"

She waited for him to lurch away. She waited for a dose of masculine anger, or at least annoyance. She waited for the typical male response.

What she got instead was a soft sigh and a butterfly kiss that came and went before she could even appreciate it. Resigned, he growled, "Have it your way, lady," and to Erica's astute ears it sounded like another warning, which had her heart beating double time.

In excitement and challenge.

She was still contemplating all the things he made her feel when he straightened, caught her elbows, and pulled her upright so fast her head swam.

"I'll be there," he said, and chucked her chin. "But just remember, turnabout is fair play."

Now *that* was a warning, no two ways about it.

He released her and Erica almost slid off the side of the desk into a molten puddle. He left much more quietly than he had entered.

Lord have mercy. What had she gotten herself into?

Ian smiled once his back was turned. Sexy, sultry Erica had looked so stunned, so confused, maybe even annoyed.

And definitely intrigued.

For months now he'd been studying her, getting closer to her, though she didn't seem to realize it and she sure as hell didn't cooperate. But finally, he knew just how to get her where he wanted her—which for starters was in his bed, under him, her body open and willing and hot.

He'd seen the subtle signs, the prickly temper, the contempt she veiled behind sharp teasing, and he knew Erica Lee was a woman in need of a good, long ride. Not some half-baked quickie, which seemed to be the speed most men preferred these days. He liked things longer, deeper, more intense. When he made love, he liked to take his time, to appreciate every nuance, to wallow in the sensations.

And so did Erica. He'd bet his eyeteeth on that.

From the very first glance she'd turned him on, and he spent a lot of time contemplating what a perfect match she'd be, in more ways than one. Sexually she'd be ideal. He thought of the different ways he'd take her, how he'd make her muscles burn, her skin sweat, her body melt. Once he got inside Erica, he wouldn't stop pleasuring her until she throbbed in satisfaction from her ears down to her dainty little toes. He'd leave her every nerve ending tingling and begging for more.

From him.

But Erica liked to play games and he'd never been a player. He did things his way and only his way. So he'd dredged up patience and watched for the right opportunity.

In the meantime, he'd gotten to know her better and he liked what he'd learned. He liked her. A lot.

She was a hard worker, always on time, rarely calling in sick. And she was loyal. No one could question her dedication to her friends. Ian knew she truly cared about Asia and Becky. They were a trio.

On top of those fine qualities, it had only taken him moments to recognize her intelligence, which gratified him since he had no tolerance for stupidity. Erica had a quick wit, a sharp sense of humor, and a massive chip on her shoulder that should have weighed down her slender body, but instead kept her backbone rigid and her shoulders stiff in cocky defiance.

Once he got her naked, though, he'd rid her of that rebellion. She'd bend to him—and enjoy doing it. He'd see to it.

"Hey, how'd it go?"

Ian stopped, startled to see George and Cameron standing just inside his basement office. Management rarely ventured into the gloomy bowels of the building, as they liked to call it. Ian preferred to call it quiet and private.

Whenever one of the suits wanted to see you, you were summoned upstairs.

Yet there they both stood, expectant, impatient. Hell, he hadn't even been aware of taking the elevator down, he'd been so engrossed in his plans for seduction.

Ian shouldered his way around George and dropped into the enormous leather chair behind his sturdy metal desk. "I hope you two don't expect a blow by blow report."

George scowled. "No, of course not. But we don't want her unhappy either."

Cameron leaned against the wall. "If you manage to piss Erica off, she'll tell Asia and Becky and—"

"And ruin your marital bliss, yeah I know." Ian leaned back and surveyed the two men who, due to short association, couldn't quite be called friends yet, but were certainly on their way there.

The fact that they actually cared about Erica helped a lot in gaining his respect. "Everything's fine. I'm not going to make her mad or unhappy. Just the opposite. But you know Erica. She's bound to do some blustering before she settles down."

"But it will be just bluster? You're sure of that?"

Ian shrugged. He wasn't about to tell them that Erica's grumbling would turn to soft moans soon enough. "I'm meeting her at the shop after work tonight. Just avoid her till then and you should be in the clear."

George turned to Cameron. "He's awfully damn confident, don't you think?"

"Yeah." And then, with a dose of suspicion to Ian, "Just how well do you know Erica?"

Ian almost laughed. They honestly expected her to chew him up and spit him out. Neither of them had understood Erica's subtle signals, but because the sexual chemistry Ian shared with her was enough to choke a horse, he'd recognized her silent pleas for satisfaction on a gut level.

She was a complex woman, more so than most. She intrigued him, amused him, and made him hot enough to burn. He looked forward to discovering all the facets to her personality. He looked forward to calling her his own.

He needed to reassure Cameron and George, and he tried to do that without telling them things that would be private between him and the woman under discussion. "I know what Erica hides, and what she wants exposed."

Judging by their expressions, they didn't believe him.

Cameron's brows rose and he almost laughed. "God, she's going to hang you by your balls."

Groaning, George said, "I should never have gotten involved in this. When you told me you wanted Erica, I really thought you'd use a little more finesse."

"She's not a cactus that has to be approached carefully," Ian said.

George gave him an incredulous look before turning away. "I should have called a halt the second you told me this harebrained plan." Hands deep in his pockets, he began to pace. "Becky is going to be so upset."

Ian could clue him in on a way to get around Becky's temper, but George didn't look open to coaching. And anyway, a man in love could be very prickly about hearing his woman's name mentioned—especially by another man.

Then George chuckled and said, "I guess I'll be doing some making up." He rubbed his hands together. "I do love how sweetly Becky forgives me."

Ian grinned. Maybe old George knew just what he was doing after all.

Cameron pushed away from the wall. "It's not that I don't find this fascinating, but I need to get back to work. So just tell me if things went according to plan."

"Perfectly. I told her George here had spilled the beans to two men—"

George whirled around. "Two?"

"—but that I didn't know who they were."

"Shit, shit, shit."

Ian barely hid his grin over George's distress. "She wouldn't admit it, but she's embarrassed."

"Erica?" Cameron asked with a fat dose of incredulity.

"We're talking about Erica Lee, right?" George seconded, just to make sure there was no confusion.

"One and the same." Ian frowned at both men. "She's first and foremost a woman, you know."

"Gotcha."

"Whatever you say."

If he hadn't needed their help, Ian never would have confided so much to them. What he did with Erica, the way their relationship evolved, was nobody's business. But she was skittish at the idea of giving herself to him, so after he'd heard the gossip of how the other two couples had met at the porn shop, he'd cornered George and Cameron before things could progress without him, and he'd insisted he be included—for Erica. "Being embarrassed makes her more likely to accept me before either of the two imaginary guys can make a move."

At least with George and Cameron, he knew they cared about Erica without being romantically involved with her. Not only were they both already in solid relationships, but they spoke about Erica with the fond exasperation they might have doled out to a pesky younger sister.

Cameron chuckled, but he could barely be heard over George's grumbling about ending up in the doghouse.

"Hey, I'm all for making the little witch squirm," Cameron said. "It's only fair."

She'd squirm all right, Ian thought, but not the way they meant.

"Amen," George added. "God knows she loves

to dish out the barbs, and I've got the holes in my hide to prove it. It'll do her good to get knocked off her high horse."

Ian had no intention of bringing Erica down, but he did expect to get all that energy and attitude normally used for sarcasm funneled into a new direction. When he thought of Erica concentrating fully on him, his muscles clenched in anticipation.

"Just don't hurt her," George tacked on. "I mean that. She rubs me the wrong way sometimes, but deep down I like her."

Ian eyed him. "Deep down, huh?"

"Same here," Cameron added. "Erica can be a little hard-edged, but she has a good heart."

"When I'm done," Ian promised with a smile, "she'll be thanking you both."

Neither of them appeared convinced, given the way they rolled their eyes and snickered. But they did finally leave his office, giving Ian the opportunity to plan. He tilted back in his chair and propped his booted feet on the desk. He was semi-hard and had been since first walking into Erica's office. She'd looked downright edible in her miniskirt, her glossy black hair loose, that taunting smile. And those slanted green eyes . . . His hands curled tight. Damn, he could just imagine how sexy she'd look in the middle of a screaming climax.

He closed his eyes and concentrated on breathing.

Afterward, he thought, once Erica was softened up and more relaxed with the release of sexual tension, they'd talk. Her guards would be down and she'd be open to him, emotionally vulnerable.

The image of Erica curled beside him, all womanly warm, was almost more satisfying than the idea of taking her sexually.

It was definitely as big a turn-on.

He'd never get rid of his boner thinking like that. To distract himself, Ian pulled out a pen and paper and started jotting down notes. He'd need to make a few purchases at Wild Honey and he wanted things that would give the most impact, items that would rock her feminist foundation.

He put body oil at the top of the list, and worked his way down from that—and all the while, he smiled in anticipation.

Chapter Two

Erica was in the lounge waiting when Becky and Asia finally strolled in. They took one look at her and balked. Becky even tried to turn around to sneak back out but Asia snagged her arm and dragged her to the table.

"My, my, my," Erica quipped. She hadn't been able to locate George, so Becky and Asia would become the recipients of her discontent. "Don't you two look apprehensive. Now why would that be, I wonder?"

Asia plopped down into her seat and even rolled her eyes. "Knock it off, Erica. You're terrorizing Becky with all that nasty sarcasm."

Wide-eyed Becky showed a lot more caution in seating herself. "Are you mad?"

Erica shot her a look. "Now Becky, why would I be mad? Just because your honey manipulated things a bit for me?"

Becky nodded, making her dark blond curls bounce. "George told me that he was trying to help you out by telling someone about the plan, but—"

"Do you know who he spoke to?" Though Erica asked the question casually, curiosity burned inside her. Who besides Becky, Asia, Cameron, and George knew about her risqué plans?

According to Ian, all of Cuther. Erica bit back a groan at that possibility.

"He didn't say," Becky ventured carefully. "And I didn't think to ask, not after he told me that Ian Conrad had overheard it all and that now you and Ian are . . . well . . ."

Suddenly Asia leaned forward. "George and Cameron said you're going to play sex slave with Ian."

There was a priceless look of scandalized trepidation on her friends' faces. Trying not to laugh, Erica said, "That's right," and she was proud of how cool she sounded—as if the idea didn't give her a little apprehension herself.

"But with Ian Conrad?"

Erica's reaction had been the same as Asia's, but she shrugged. "Yeah, so? What's wrong with Ian?"

With a worried look, Becky said, "Nothing's wrong with him, exactly."

Asia agreed. "Nope. Not a thing."

Fidgeting, glancing at Asia, Becky said, "Except that he's, well . . ."

"Enormous," Asia supplied.

Becky nodded. "Yes, enormous. Perfect description. And maybe . . ." She searched for the new word.

"Forceful."

"Exactly. Very forceful." Becky looked quite concerned by that fact.

Maintaining her lazy pose, Erica looked first at

Asia, then Becky. "He's so quiet, how do you know he's forceful?"

Asia pushed back her long brown hair and propped her chin on a fist. "Maybe it's because he's so quiet, and still everything gets done. He'll have some guys start working on wiring something and if they don't get it right, he doesn't say a word, he just has this . . . look."

"He does have a look," Becky said.

Asia shivered. "All the new guys stammer around him."

"So do the women," Becky confided. "I've heard them asking him out, coming on to him. And you know what he does?"

Despite herself, Erica was fascinated. "No, what does he do?"

"He gets this little smile and this real gentle look in his eyes and, oh, man, it's . . ."

"Devastating." Asia sighed.

"And then . . ." Becky bit her bottom lip, building the suspense.

"Then?" Erica prompted her.

"He says no."

"No?"

"That's right, no. He turns all the women down."

Erica snorted. Ian Conrad was not a monk, and he sure didn't strike her as the type who favored celibacy. The man oozed sexuality out of every pore. "Like I'm supposed to believe that?"

"It's true. Ask them. Yesterday in the ladies' room they were speculating about whether or not he's gay."

After a disgruntled huff, Asia rolled her eyes. "Wounded vanity. Just because a guy's selective . . ."

Erica started laughing. Sometimes her friends were downright nuts. "I had no idea you two had taken so much notice of him. And here you're both supposed to be happily involved women."

"We noticed you noticing," Becky explained, "so naturally we paid closer attention."

Erica studied her two best friends—her two *guilty* best friends. "And then you sicced Cameron and George on Ian to set me up because you thought I'd need help with that?"

Asia flattened back in her chair. "No way! We told you that was an accident. George was just talking about it—"

"About me."

"Yeah." Asia grinned. "But you give them both such a hard time, you know they're dying to see how this turns out for you."

"They're dying to see me get my comeuppance, you mean."

"Not true." Becky appeared affronted by such an idea. "George is actually a little worried about you."

"Worried? Why?"

Becky's voice dropped to a whisper. "Ian makes everyone nervous. He wouldn't have been my choice for you."

Damn, if they kept this up, *she* was going to get more nervous. And she was plenty anxious enough already without any added help.

Hoping to convince herself as well as her two friends, Erica boasted, "I can handle Ian, don't you worry about that. He might seem like the big, quiet, intimidating type, but he's still just a man, and like all men, he'll—"

Becky suddenly looked beyond her, and her

face blanched. She elbowed Asia, who followed Becky's gaze and then immediately slid lower into her seat. Her cheeks turned red.

No, Erica thought. *No, no, no . . .*

Warm breath touched the back of her ear, along with the hot scent of a big man who'd been hard at work. "Just a few more hours, Erica, and you can see just how well I handle."

Erica stared at Becky and Asia, willing either of them to lend a calming influence to help even out her tripping heartbeat. But they weren't looking at her. No, their panicked gazes were directed over her shoulder.

At Ian.

Now how in the hell had he gotten behind her?

Becky and Asia were horrified enough for all three of them, so Erica refused to join in. Instead she fashioned a snide smile, slowly twisted her head around to face him, and met his oh-so-close piercing blue eyes dead on. "Hey, Ian. Skulking around the break room, are you?"

"Repairing a busted circuit, actually." He surprised her by crouching down next to her seat, which put him slightly below her. In her experience, a man always chose a position of power, choosing to tower over a woman in an effort to intimidate her with his size. That Ian should lower himself beside her, giving her the advantage of looking down on him, was curiously touching.

But even with him practically kneeling, he was so big she still felt surrounded—by his strength, his scent, his blazing intent, which one and all could easily see given the way he devoured her with his eyes.

He braced one hand on the back of her chair so

that his hot wrist touched her nape, sending tingles down her spine. His biceps, already impressive enough, bulged even more. His other hand clasped the edge of her seat, causing his fingertips to brush up against her hip.

She started to lean back to escape some of that overwhelming masculinity. The smile that Becky and Asia had just warned her about suddenly tilted his sensual mouth. Erica halted, then forced herself to relax. Or at least, pretend to relax. With him practically in her lap, his face level with her breasts, she felt so wired she couldn't draw a breath.

He swiveled his head toward her friends, finally releasing Erica from that piercing gaze. Everything inside her went liquid with relief, even her backbone. She had a hell of a time staying upright in her seat.

"Ladies," he murmured by way of greeting.

And her friends, both mute ninnies, just gaped back at him.

His smile widened, looking more like a crooked grin. "Now don't be embarrassed," he chastised in a gravel-rough voice. "It's okay that you were talking about me. I'm sure you just wanted to reassure Erica, right?"

After a moment's hesitation, their heads bobbed comically.

"Yeah. That's what I thought." He pinned Erica in place again. "Not that you need reassurance, do you, Erica?"

Where had her voice gone? It took her a painful three seconds to find it, and that annoyed her enough that her natural self-confidence returned. "Of course not. As my personal slave, you'll do anything and everything I say. Isn't that right?"

Very gently, he asked, "Do you really think so?"

Her back stiffened, in alarm, in dread—maybe a little in relief. "Are you telling me you've changed your mind? Are you backing out now?"

He looked at her mouth . . . and looked some more. A little unsettled, Erica squirmed. They were all so quiet, she thought she could hear Becky and Asia breathing; she knew she could hear the erratic knocking of her heartbeat against her breastbone.

Finally, Ian broke the nerve-stretching tension. "Naturally not." He came to his feet with an amazing fluid grace considering his size. Then he touched her chin. "One warning, though. Be very careful what you instigate because you never know how it might turn against you."

Damn him! Insults and more threats. She would not put up with it.

Erica surged to her feet too—a ludicrous affectation since she only reached his shoulder. But she did poke him in the chest, and found out he was so hard she nearly broke her finger. Wincing, she said, "Quit trying to intimidate me, Ian Conrad, or I'm liable to just call the whole thing off."

He grinned, caught her finger, and cradled it to his chest in a manner that felt oddly protective. "But I don't intimidate you, isn't that right?"

Still staring at her slender hand caught up against that broad granite chest, she blinked. "What?"

He took a step closer to her, forcing her to tilt her head back to maintain eye contact. "I refuse to believe you'd back out on me now just because of a little uncertainty. After all, Asia and Becky went through with it and survived just fine."

After holding silent for the whole damn visit,

her friends started sputtering over having their sorry butts dragged into the conversation. Ian spared them an apologetic glance, saying, "Ladies, it's hardly a secret," then continued to Erica, "Trust me, you're woman enough, and you're definitely ballsy and brazen enough, to do what they've done. Isn't that right?"

He'd challenged her, the rat. Erica slanted her eyes and gifted him with her own small secret smile. "You betcha. I wouldn't miss this for the world."

He didn't seem the least put off by her inference. He even nodded in satisfaction. "Perfect." He glanced at the silver watch on his thick wrist. "Four more hours, then I'll see you at Wild Honey. We'll pick up a few things before we head to my place."

"Your place?" She raised a brow, a little amazed at his authoritative manner considering he'd agreed to be her slave. "Did I say I wanted to go to your place, Ian?"

"No, but you did specify that we'd meet right after work and since one thing after another has broken down today, I'm sweatier than usual. I'll have to shower."

"Maybe I'll let you shower at my place."

He smiled at her taunting way of saying maybe. "I'm not going to wallow in my own sweat all day, not even for you, so forget it. Besides, if we're at my place you can walk out whenever you decide you've . . . had enough."

Another challenge, as if she'd be the one to cry uncle. Her teeth clicked together even as she managed another not-so-sweet smile. "I can always just order you to leave."

That actually made him laugh and the sound of his humor was so unexpected, so deep and masculine, it gave her a small thrill. Her toes curled inside her shoes, but not by so much as a twitch did she give herself away.

When he saw her facade of disgruntlement, he laughed some more. Erica tapped her foot on the floor, waiting for him to get over his chuckles. Finally he wiped his eyes, but his grin remained as he said, "Order me to leave, huh?" and then, with a touch to the tip of her nose, "I suppose you can always try. In fact, I think I'd enjoy that."

And once again, he turned his back on her.

Erica stood there while he saluted Becky and Asia, who mumbled farewells, then she watched him leave the lounge. Every woman he passed visually noted his progress with sly, covetous intent. The men just got out of his way.

"Oh, my."

"Good Lord."

Erica didn't want to look at her friends because she knew what they were thinking, even before their muttered exclamations. She was thinking it, too. The difference was that her heart pounded and her body felt tight and hot, and it wasn't all because of apprehension. Ian's forceful nature scared her a little—and excited her a lot.

"Erica, sit down before you drop."

Becky added in a whisper, "She does look dazed, doesn't she?"

Erica shook herself. She had a reputation to maintain. "Dazed? Don't be silly. He's just a man." She sank into her seat and pretended her knees weren't shaking and her skin wasn't flushed.

"There's no *just* to it," Asia said. "Whatever he's got, he's got it in spades. I'd be very, very careful if I were you."

Becky mumbled, "If I were her, I'd hide."

Laughing, Erica propped her head on her hand and considered the situation. She'd be walking a fine line between maintaining control and enjoying him for the man he was and what he made her feel. Eventually, she'd let him drive her wild with his dictatorial ways. But first, she'd show him a thing or two about control, about women, and about Erica Lee.

For a man like Ian, being a slave could prove a formidable task. Already she imagined the things she'd tell him to do, things that would excite him—but keep him from satisfaction. It'd be frustrating for her too, but at least she'd prove her point.

Who she'd be proving it to, she wasn't sure yet.

Thanks to a last minute snafu with an ancient air-conditioning unit, Ian found himself behind schedule. Only five minutes late, but he'd been looking forward to this all day, and he just knew Erica would try to give him hell about it. Thinking of the way her eyes burned green fire whenever she got riled, he grinned.

A few seconds later he strode into Wild Honey. He maintained a steady pace, but he didn't allow himself to rush. Given half a chance, Erica would have him wrapped around her little finger and no way would he allow that. He barely glanced up as he passed the checkout counter and the tables of books and magazines.

Erica wouldn't be loitering in the front of the

store. No, the little witch would be in one of the fetish sections—and he knew exactly which one.

He found her standing in front of an aisle of domination wear, fingering a heavy leather dog collar with silver studs. Knowing her thoughts, he stepped up silently behind her and growled low, "Unless you want to end up wearing that thing, I'd suggest you put it back down."

She'd been so lost in thought her whole body jerked with his first words. "Damn it," she snapped even before whirling around to face him. The leather collar was gripped tight in her hand. "Can't you ever make a normal entrance?"

In contrast to her near shout, Ian's words were calm and quiet. "Into a porn shop? What would you consider normal?"

She scowled, then mumbled, "For such a big guy, you're awfully good at sneaking around."

"Next time I'll clear my throat." He deliberately made his tone patronizing enough that she couldn't possibly let it pass.

She didn't. Her brows drew down, her eyes glittered with annoyance, her mouth opened—and Ian leaned down and kissed her.

They were in the middle of a porn shop with a few customers milling around, but that didn't stop him. At the moment, a tornado couldn't have stopped him.

He'd thought about tasting her all day.

On the most basic level, her innate sexuality called out to him. Because he was a big man and could easily cause harm with his physical strength, he'd learned early on to control his reactions in all things. He kept an iron grip on his anger with men, and he tempered his sexual drive with women.

But with Erica, he had a feeling he could let loose in every way and she'd handle it—and him— just fine.

Focused on that fact, he curved his hands around her neck and used his thumbs to tip up her chin. Her eyes widened just before he took her mouth the way he'd wanted to take it since first meeting her.

A small, very feminine sound escaped her and a heartbeat later she went soft and warm. He watched her thick black lashes drift shut, felt her hands curve against his chest. The hard leather of the collar she still held dug into his left pectoral muscle.

Her lips were full and soft and opened more to allow the slide of his tongue. There was no gentle prelude, no tentative exploration. In so many ways, he'd been thinking of Erica as his since the moment he'd learned what she and her friends had planned. The reality of having her here now, soon to be his in fact as well as fantasy, was almost more than he could survive.

He kissed her deeply, loving the hot, damp taste of her mouth, the way she kissed him back, her expertise. The sound of their accelerated breathing echoed in his ears. Damn, he was a hair away from losing it.

He pulled back the tiniest bit, saw the excitement and reciprocal urgency on her face, and kissed her again.

The collar dropped to the floor.

Because they weren't alone and he didn't want her to suffer any regrets, he eased away, releasing her slowly, pressing small damp kisses to her chin, her cheek, her throat. "This way," he murmured, and carefully stepped her around the forgotten collar.

With a naturalness that normally came from long association, she nestled into his side. He kept his arm around her, his hand curving over her shoulder. In his opinion, she fit against him perfectly.

For the moment, she seemed docile enough.

A smile tugged at his mouth, but he resisted it. If he laughed now, Erica would not only go back for the collar, but probably a leash as well.

"What are we doing?" she asked when he stepped up to the back counter where an array of oils, exotic scents, and lotions were displayed.

"Making a few purchases."

"But I haven't decided what I want yet."

He knew what *he* wanted, so again, he smothered his satisfied grin. "It's your day, right?"

Wearing a suspicious frown, she nodded.

"So I figured I should pamper you."

One brow rose. "Pamper me how exactly?"

"How's dinner, a massage, and a long bubble bath sound?"

"Like heaven, but what's that got to do with sex?"

He almost said, *You're kidding, right?* but then he saw she was serious. Damn, but she must have been with a bunch of losers if she didn't understand the pleasure in setting the mood and indulging in extensive foreplay.

He gave her his own frown while carefully deciding how to word his answer. "Sex is best when both people are totally into it. I want you to be as comfortable and satisfied as possible. We're getting together during dinnertime, so I want to feed you. You've worked hard all day, so I want to relax you. Anything sexual you want, anywhere along the way, you just say so and believe me I'll be more than happy to oblige."

"You think so, do you?"

More bluster. He'd taken her by surprise, so naturally she got defensive. It was odd, but as often as not, Erica touched his heart as much as his libido.

He stroked his hands over her glossy black hair and lowered his voice more. "Erica, there isn't anything you can ask me to do to you or for you that I won't enjoy. I thought you already knew how much I want you."

The signs of arousal were easy to see on her face; the color in her cheeks, her expanded pupils, her parted lips. Still, the words from her mouth weren't encouraging.

"And if I want to watch you squirm? If I want to see how you deal with waiting?"

If he didn't know her so well, Ian might have been duped. But he did know her and the little darling wanted him, she just wanted to see how far she could push. Well, two could play that game— but only one would win, and he already knew when the night was over, Erica would be his.

He touched her mouth with his thumb. "I've been waiting months already. I can survive a few more days." Turning away, he picked up a small decorative bottle of massage oil. The label claimed properties that would leave your skin tingling and your nerve endings alive. Erica was such a sexy little thing, he doubted he'd need the oil, but maybe . . .

Erica snatched it out of his hand. "What do you mean you've been waiting months?"

Except for one quick, questioning glance, he

kept his back to her. "The day I first saw you, I wanted you. There hasn't been a minute since that I haven't wanted you." He fingered a massage mitt—some fuzzy contraption far too small for his hand—then moved on to the bubble bath. He could feel Erica standing just behind him, befuddled, annoyed, brimming with nervous uncertainty that she'd do her best to hide.

He gave her half a minute to mentally chew on what he'd said before facing her again. When he stared down at her, she met and held his gaze by sheer force of will. She had guts, his Erica, and he admired her more every moment he spent with her. "Sometimes I wonder if I'll ever stop."

She swallowed. "Stop?"

"Wanting you." Then he shrugged, dismissing the moment of heavy sexual tension and again turning back to the products. "But we'll work that out this weekend." He handed her the bubble bath.

She accepted it automatically. "Work what out?"

"How we really feel about each other."

"Bu-but that's absurd!"

"Stammering?" He draped his arm around her again and headed them both toward the checkout. "Not at all. I like you a lot, but it's hard to say how much when all I can usually think about is getting inside you."

She stumbled and would have fallen if he hadn't caught her.

"Wait a minute." Annoyed, she tried digging in her heels.

He kept walking, sweeping her along with him. "I have only so much patience, honey."

"But . . . what is this about a weekend? We're

getting together for one night and one night only."

He snorted, but otherwise kept his thoughts to himself. She sounded panicked enough without him telling her why he needed a whole weekend. One way or another, he'd convince her, once he got her alone.

"Damn it, Ian, I am not committing the whole weekend to you."

She could really dent his ego if he let her. Not that he would. He said only, "Why not? I figure it'll take me at least that long just to get used to seeing you in my place."

"Yeah?" Like a dog on a bone, she jumped on that. "Well if you don't want me there, then . . ."

"Oh, I want you there all right."

"Blast it, Ian." She jerked to a halt, forcing him to do the same.

"What's wrong now?"

In typical Erica fashion, she tossed her head, sending her silky mane of hair to fall behind her shoulders. "You keep throwing out these obscure comments in between insulting me and threatening me." Her nose lifted. "I don't know that I want to spend a whole weekend with you."

Ian took in the sight of her, from the determined tilt of her head to the bold fighter's stance. "Look at it this way," he whispered, "there's a whole lot of bossing around you can do in two and a half days. We both know you'll enjoy that."

"But you won't."

"Wanna bet?" He had her flustered, not that he minded. Gently, he relieved her of the oil and bubble bath. She stayed there in the center aisle while he paid for their purchases. With the bagged items in one hand, he again drew her close and led her out the door.

The late afternoon sunshine glinted off her hair, highlighting the blue-black depths. When he started to lead her to his car, she again balked. "I have my car with me."

"I thought we'd ride together."

"No way. You said it yourself—I should be able to leave when I want to."

She had him there. "All right. Would you like to follow me to my place, then?"

"Do you need to stop for groceries?"

Shaking his head, Ian said, "No. I have everything I need already at my apartment."

She looked skeptical, but didn't cavil. "All right. I am curious to try out these culinary skills of yours."

"I promise you won't be disappointed—in anything." Silently, they walked to her car across the scorching pavement. Ian waited while she unlocked the door and rolled down the window to let in fresh air, then he said, "Erica?"

She dug her keys out of her purse, pretending to ignore him, which was absurd considering every line of her body bespoke her awareness. "Hmmm?"

"You're going to enjoy yourself, you know."

He'd meant to reassure her, but apparently he hit a hot button. She slanted a narrow-eyed look at him over her shoulder, then slowly turned to him in full battle mode. Her voice was low and mean and sarcastic. "Oh, I'll enjoy myself all right. After all, I'll have you at my beck and call, tending to my every whim . . . right?"

He loved her like this, all prickly like a hedgehog, full of feminine challenge. Because he couldn't help himself, he smiled the tiniest bit. "Okay."

His easy agreement only annoyed her more. Her mouth flattened and her brow beetled. "If I stay the whole weekend—"

She was staying, all right. One way or another, he'd make sure she did.

"—then prepare yourself, because you'll be seeing the real me."

Curiosity rose in tandem with anticipation. "Meaning?"

"Meaning I don't always look like this." She indicated her face, hair, and chic clothing. "When I'm at home relaxing—my home or yours—I like to be comfortable. That means no makeup, no polite work manners. No frills."

No clothes, he silently added. *And even better than that, no inhibitions.*

Ian's smile widened though his voice remained infinitely gentle. "I have a very strong constitution, Erica. I think I can handle it."

She glared at him a moment more, then dropped into her car and slammed the door. Through the open window, she growled, "Maybe you can and maybe you can't. But make no mistake: you can not handle *me.*"

Chapter Three

He had a nice home. His apartment was on the third floor with an impressive balcony that looked out over a wooded back lot. A creek ran the length of the apartment complex, softly churning, housing a duck or two and surrounded by a multitude of flowers and birds and butterflies.

"That's my favorite part," he mentioned when she went straight across the living room, past the kitchen to look out the double glass doors on the far end of his dining nook. He detoured into the kitchen, opened a few cabinets, ran a little water, and seconds later Erica felt him come up close behind her. His breath touched her ear. "I always wanted to make love on the balcony, late at night so no one would see. You can hear the creek and see the stars."

Peeved at the idea of him sexually entwined with another woman, she said, "Yeah? So have you?"

"Nope."

"Why not?"

"I never had the right woman here before."

Erica's brain froze. *Right woman?* Surely, he wasn't

suggesting that *she* was the right woman? Never in her life had any man labeled her such.

But she had to admit, the idea of climbing atop that big muscular body with the fresh air surrounding them and the sounds of nature just beyond appealed to her too.

She shook herself. "Show me around your apartment."

"All right." His hand, like a burning brand, pressed at the small of her back. "Let's start in the kitchen."

Erica's eyes glazed over at the expanse of tall cabinets, the enormous refrigerator, and high-tech stove. She wasn't much of a cook herself, but she appreciated how functional a kitchen like his would be.

He'd set out two thick pork chops, a fat zucchini, and a plump ripe tomato. Her stomach rumbled; she might not enjoy cooking, but she definitely enjoyed eating, especially after a long day at work.

"It's a hobby," he explained. "Would you like something to drink?"

"Tea?" Erica found it somewhat amusing to watch a man as large as Ian move with such economic grace. He still wore his ragged jeans and sweaty work shirt, but he looked elegant in the kitchen, waiting on her.

He took a glass from the cabinet, filled it with ice from the automatic ice maker, and poured in a dark brewed tea. "Sugar or lemon?"

She shook her head and accepted the tea. He was full of surprises, she found. She couldn't help but comment on the neatness of his home. "You have a cleaning lady?"

"It's just me so I don't need one." He handed her a napkin and resumed the tour. "There's only the living room and the little dining room here."

Only didn't quite describe it. The room was large, with heavy masculine furniture and very little decoration other than a few framed prints on the wall and a scattering of family photos on a mantel over an electric fireplace. But still it looked very put together, and somehow homey and warm.

He flipped a switch and the fireplace lit up. "It doesn't give off heat," he explained, then continued down the hall. "My bathroom."

Erica peeked into the wholly masculine domain. Done all in cream with a glass tub enclosure rather than a curtain, it was spotless at best, near barren at worst. Other than a toothbrush in the holder and an electric razor plugged in, there were no personal items about.

It smelled of Ian, of his aftershave and soap, and his own unique, earthy scent. Her heart did a little flip as she breathed in and accepted the now familiar reaction in her body. She loved his smell, so masculine and raw and . . . Ian.

She was still a little goggled when he took her hand, otherwise she might have protested. Having her hand engulfed in his much larger one made her feel small and weak—and she hated that. She made a habit of not letting men feel superior in any way. But Ian tugged her only as far as the next door.

"My spare room. I use it as an office since it isn't really big enough for a bedroom."

"You work at home?"

"No, but I prefer to keep things organized and

this way they are. I grew up with my father spreading the bills across the dining room table." He shrugged. "I didn't like that."

Fascinated by this glimpse into Ian as a child, she turned to him. "I saw a bunch of pictures on your fireplace. Brothers and sisters?"

"Six. Three brothers, three sisters." His grin went crooked, a little self-deprecating. "It's not easy to make ends meet with that many mouths to feed, so my dad was forever fretting over the bills. It's not easy to find your own space either. My brothers are slobs despite the way my mother kept at them. And my sisters have always collected knickknacks, so—"

"So you now relish your own place, which you can keep as you like it." Erica hadn't expected such an outpouring of personal confidences. Most of the men she knew clammed up if you asked anything even remotely private.

Ian proved to be very different from any other man she knew.

"That's about it," he said, and moved her farther down the hall. "This is my bedroom." He pushed the door open and ushered her inside.

While Erica took in the king-size mattress, tall armoire, and long dresser, Ian crossed his arms and leaned against the door frame.

"What about you?"

She stepped farther into the room to explore. There was another set of glass doors that also opened onto the balcony. "What about me?"

"Any brothers and sisters?"

She halted in the process of smoothing her fingers across the plush, dark blue coverlet neatly spread over his bed. Ian's hot gaze could be felt on

her spine, in her heart. He was so intense sometimes that every fiber of her being was aware of his
attention.

Fashioning a cavalier smile, she turned. "Naw,
no siblings at all. Just me and my mother and
whichever man she was with at the time."

His brow rose. "Your mother's boyfriends lived
with you?"

Erica rolled her shoulder in a negligent shrug.
Damn it, she hadn't meant to say so much, but
now that she had, she found talking about it more
difficult than it should have been. "Mom often
trusted the wrong guy, that's all."

He hadn't moved. He still stood casually in the
doorway, thick arms folded, ankles crossed. But
suddenly he appeared more tense, more alert.
"Wrong in what way?"

Feeling like a coward and blaming Ian for it,
Erica strode to the glass doors. She tried to open
them but they were locked and her fingers fumbled without success.

Big hands settled on her shoulders and a soft
kiss touched her temple, setting her heart to a furious gallop.

They were in his bedroom, alone, and he'd just
kissed her . . .

Without a word, Ian reached past her and
opened the lock, then slid the door open. As soon
as that was done, he again settled at her back,
holding her loosely.

Erica didn't move. Part of her immobility was
caused by sheer enjoyment; she liked being this
close to Ian. Her body liked it too, warming and
softening in all the right places just because he
touched her, because his scent surrounded her.

But she held still too, because she felt foolish. So far, Ian had managed to drag every unwanted emotion from her with little effort. She wouldn't keep allowing that to happen. She *couldn't* allow that to happen.

She reclosed the door. "Wrong in that she thought each of them was the love of her life."

As if there'd been no awkward break in the conversation at all, Ian nodded. "Some people find that special person early in life, and others have to wait."

She forced herself to move away from him. Keeping her gait casual, she retraced her steps to the kitchen. Ian followed. "What about you? Ever found that special someone?"

"No. You?"

She laughed. "I'm not at all convinced special people exist, at least not in a one-on-one-forever kind of way."

"So cynical." He pulled out a stool for her. "What about Becky and Asia? They're your friends and I know they're happily involved. You expect them to crash and burn?"

Why did he push her? She flipped her hair back and shrugged. "I don't know. Their relationships are too new to tell."

"George and Cameron would be crushed."

She grinned. "No, they'd just give me hell and harass me and tell me to mind my own business."

"You like them?"

"Sure. They're good to Becky and Asia." She felt compelled to add, "So far."

Ian studied her a moment longer before shaking his head in an indulgent manner. "You want to keep me company while I cook?"

Erica had really expected him to jump her bones the minute they were alone in his apartment. She was mildly put out that he didn't, and yet fascinated with all he shared. Hoping he'd share even more, she opted to stay close rather than set the tone by leaving him alone.

"Sure." She started to seat herself, but was taken by surprise when he relieved her of her tea, set it on the counter, and then hefted her up to the bar stool.

Standing far too close, his hands still at her waist, he gave her a small grin and asked, "Comfy?"

His strength constantly amazed her—and turned her on. He'd lifted her as easily as he might have lifted a child. She cleared her throat. "Yeah."

He continued to look down at her, to hold her and smile. Then he leaned down for a kiss.

Erica knew she should tell him no, that she should deny him or at least reprimand him for not following the dictate of their agreement, which meant she was the boss and he was the slave. She should pull back right now. Or better yet, if she waited until he almost kissed her, then he'd really . . . Wow. He tasted so incredibly good.

Without conscious volition, her hands crept to his wide, hard shoulders. His cotton work shirt was soft, and she could feel the flex and play of muscle and bone beneath. Her fingers dug in with an effort to get him closer. She opened her mouth and felt the brief foray of his damp, velvet tongue, and . . .

"Damn." He straightened over her. "I forgot, I need to shower."

Erica blinked, trying to bring herself back around. She'd been so lost in that hot, devouring kiss. All she really wanted at the moment was more—of that kiss, of him, of how he made her feel, and his delicious, clean-sweat scent. She reached for him, but he shook his head.

"Sorry, honey. Shower first, then we can play all you want." He turned to the stove—turned his back on her—and set a pot full of water on to boil.

Erica went rigid.

"I'm going to go ahead and get the food started, then jump in the shower. I promise I won't be more than five minutes. That is"—he glanced over his shoulder and caught her fuming—"unless you want me to shave?"

Erica eyed the beard shadowing on his jaw, which made him look like a dark rogue. "No." Damn it, her voice sounded like a croak again. She cleared her throat and squared her shoulders. "You can shave later while I watch."

Both his brows lifted. "A voyeur, huh?" He sounded vastly amused by that. "I'm game."

"Of course you are," she said through her teeth, "because I'm the boss, so whatever I say is okay with you."

"Right."

Within seconds he had the thick chops sizzling on the range-top griddle, set on low, and he started out of the room with the admonition, "Be good—at least until I get back."

Annoyed more with herself than him, Erica snatched up her drink and went to the glass doors. At least this time she knew how to open them, so she sauntered outside, dropped into a padded chaise, and stretched out her legs.

The blazing sun had disappeared behind gray clouds without her realizing it, and the air smelled of an impending storm. She loved storms, found them sexy and energizing, and at the moment, they certainly matched her turbulent mood.

How could she teach Ian a lesson when all he had to do was look at her and she got tongue-tied?

The aroma of cooking pork drifted out to her, but she wasn't about to tend to dinner, too. That wasn't the deal, and she had to keep at least some part of the original bargain pure. She checked her wristwatch and saw it was six thirty-six. She'd give him the requisite five minutes he'd claimed, then she was leaving. And she'd have a legitimate excuse for walking out, too, given how he'd started things out.

A humid wind blew in, tangling her hair. Not that she cared. She turned her face up, closed her eyes, and tried to relax.

Not more than three minutes after that she heard Ian whistling in the kitchen. Ha. She wouldn't move. Let him come outside and find her. She waited, but all she got was the sounds of food being diced and dishes being rattled.

She stubbornly kept her eyes closed and maintained her feigned position of comfort. In truth, she felt as wired as a ticking bomb waiting to go off.

Then gentle fingers touched her head, smoothed her windblown hair behind her ears, and drifted down her neck. She was aware of Ian crouching beside her, fresh from his shower, big and powerful and imposing.

He leaned closer to her, brushing his mouth over her cheekbone, her ear, down her throat. "Tired?" he asked, in a voice low and rough and gentle.

Erica slanted her eyes open—and found herself

face-to-naked-chest with him. Stunned, she quickly straightened and looked at the rest of his body, but he had on jeans. Just jeans. Butter soft, well worn jeans that weren't properly buttoned, likely due to his haste in getting back to the food. His bare feet were big and lean.

God, she was lusting over his feet.

She looked back at his body, at that strong abdomen, the impressive, muscular chest lightly covered in dark hair, and she wasn't sure if she should be relieved or disappointed that he'd grabbed the damn jeans.

No words came. Ian shirtless was a sight to enjoy. He remained balanced on the balls of his feet, his arms draped loosely over his bent knees, his eyes direct, unflinching, watchful. His brown hair was damp, brushed straight back from his forehead, and he still had those sexy whiskers on his cheeks and chin. His eyes seemed bluer than ever, and as she absorbed his presence, he again came forward to kiss her.

She again let him.

It seemed she had no willpower around this one hunk of man. Somehow, she ended up lounged back with him caging her in, his mouth eating at hers, slow and deep and oh, so thorough. His whiskers rasped her delicate skin, but gently, as if he knew exactly what he was doing.

Tentatively, she touched his chest and felt his astounding heat, the heavy beat of his heart, the taut silk of his shoulders, the crisp hair over his chest. Her hands flattened on him, her fingers spreading wide. "Ian?"

He groaned as if in pain, then levered himself away. "Damn, you are a temptation."

He said it like an accusation, confounding her.

"My chops are burning." His crooked grin was back, more endearing—and frustrating—than ever. "Stay put, relax while I finish dinner, okay?" With that, he touched the end of her nose, straightened with a grimace that eased once he readjusted himself, and strolled into the kitchen, again whistling.

Erica flopped back in her seat, utterly speechless. She was losing and she knew it. And even worse, he knew it. Using almost no effort at all, he had her panting after him and she couldn't let that continue. Somehow, some way, she had to get control so that he was the one panting.

She had to turn the tables on him.

Ian tried but failed to ignore his straining boner as he diced tomatoes, sliced zucchini, and seasoned the light sauce for the linguine. Having Erica alone in his apartment was enough to tempt a saint, and God knew he wasn't a candidate for sainthood. She'd surprised and aroused him with her quick capitulation each and every time he touched her. Of course, he'd known they'd be great together, a fact that had driven him nuts for the past few months. But now that he had her where he wanted her, he'd expected to have to work for it.

Apparently, Erica had expected the same. Grinning, Ian peeked out the glass doors at her, saw her frown and mulish expression.

She was conniving something, he could feel it.

And his anticipation grew.

Seconds later she strode in, all saucy and in control once more. She perched on the stool while sizing him up. Or admiring him. With Erica, it was hard to tell.

He glanced at her over his shoulder. "You should get more comfortable." Pretending to be struck by his own words, he shook his head. "No, I said that wrong, didn't I? I'm your slave for the weekend, so I should get you more comfortable."

As he spoke, he wiped his hands off on a dishcloth.

Erica's smile was slow and wicked, just the way he liked it. "All right. What do you suggest?"

"When you get home from work, what's the first thing you do?"

"Kick off my shoes."

"We'll start there, then." Without hesitation, Ian went to one knee in front of her and lifted one slim leg. Her shoes were leather wedges that tied around her ankles. Very sexy. He propped her foot on his thigh and loosened the lace, then slipped the shoe off.

She wore stockings, and for a moment, he enjoyed the silky feel of them against his palms.

He was involved in imagining her legs around his waist when she offered him the other foot.

Ian took his time removing this shoe, while noticing that his lowered position and the way her leg bent gave him a peek at her iridescent peach panties. She knew it too, the little witch.

"It's warm today," he murmured, most thoroughly distracted. "Why don't we take these stockings off too?"

Erica stood, again placed her foot on his thigh, and said, "All right. They're thigh-highs, not panty hose."

"I noticed."

"Do it slow."

Ian's heartbeat quickened. She was in full boss mode now, and damn, it was exciting. Without looking away from her, he took quick note of the food, using his nose to determine how much more time he had.

The scents of sautéed veggies joined the other aromas in the room. The chops were almost done, and the pasta wouldn't last more than another minute without being overcooked.

He leaned in to reach beneath her skirt, putting his face even with her belly. Eventually he'd have her in this exact same position again—but she'd be naked.

As if she'd heard his thoughts, she inhaled. Moving as slowly as he could manage given the trembling in his hands and the thundering of his heart, Ian trailed his fingers up her right leg until he encountered the warm, firm flesh of her bare thigh. He'd love to feel that flesh on his jaw while he tasted her. He'd hold her naked bottom in his hands and control her while she bucked and cried out a climax . . .

"Ian?" Her shaky voice drew him back.

"Just making it slow—the way you said." He allowed his fingertips to graze the crotch of her panties—and his heart almost stopped when he realized they were damp.

His control snapped and his muscles went slack. He leaned into her, his jaw against her pelvis while he inhaled the spicy scent of her sex.

"Ian?"

She sounded as breathless as he felt. Disregarding her orders, he quickly rolled the stocking down her leg and removed it, tucking it into her shoe.

Bracing her hands on his shoulders, she offered her left leg and he went through the routine again. But he only touched her thigh this time, not wanting things to progress so fast that he ruined his plans. When the second stocking joined the first, he didn't stand. Instead, he looked up at her, met her heavy, darkened eyes, and wrapped his arms around her hips.

Keeping his eyes locked on hers, he leaned forward until he could kiss her belly through her soft cotton shirt above the waistband of her skirt. Her lips parted on an indrawn breath. Nostrils flaring, he opened his mouth and gently bit. She was soft, just as a woman should be. Very edible. He'd enjoy nibbling on her everywhere once he got her complete acceptance of him as her man.

The kitchen filled with the sounds of their accelerated breathing. Suggestively, easing her into his command, Ian nibbled his way lower.

Her eyes closed and her hands on his shoulders clamped tight, stinging in force.

The leather skirt felt slick and impenetrable, drawing him to a halt. "You know what I think?" he rasped while noting the way her breasts rose and fell and her legs were braced apart. "I think you should be dessert."

Her eyes snapped open. For one long moment, she looked disoriented, and then she shoved away from him with a flushed face and a noticeable dose of annoyance.

Giving her room to collect herself, Ian went to the stove. He removed the browned chops, arranging them on two plates on a tray. He lifted the pot of linguine from the burner and emptied it into a strainer. While steam rose in his face, adding to his inner heat, Erica approached. Without her shoes, her petite stature was more obvious than ever. At least, she was petite next to him. He supposed she stood around five-feet-six, an average height for most women.

Her fingertips skated along his naked spine, making his stomach clench. "Speaking of dessert, I'm wondering if you shouldn't be naked while you do all this."

He almost snorted. Once again, she'd taken him by surprise. While water ran over the pasta, rinsing it, he faced her with a smile and his hands on his fly. "Want me to shuck the jeans? Just say the word."

Her eyes widened, but quickly narrowed. "Not just yet. I'm afraid you'll be a distraction and I am hungry."

"For food?"

"That too."

Giving her her due, he saluted. "You're the boss."

Under her breath, but not quite under enough, he heard her mutter, "Now if we could both only remember that."

"You want to eat on the balcony?" He seasoned the pasta, mixing in the sauce and zucchini and topping it off with diced tomatoes and freshly grated Parmesan cheese. "It's cooling off a little, so it won't be too uncomfortable."

"I think it might rain."

He looked her in the eyes and said, "You won't mind getting a little wet, will you?"

Her nose lifted into the air. "I'll wait outside. You can serve me." And off she went, her hips swaying, leaving Ian to grin behind her.

Twenty minutes later, when she was halfway

through her meal and he was almost done, she gave him a genuine compliment. "This is absolutely delicious." Up until then, she'd been quietly eating, and he'd been quietly watching her.

Because he'd just taken his last bite of pork, he merely nodded in acknowledgment of her praise.

During the meal, the sky had darkened considerably but Ian hadn't bothered with the outside light. He'd considered getting a candle, but the breeze had picked up so there didn't seem to be much point. Besides, the dim evening suited Erica and her exotic looks. In the deepening shadows, her eyes were more luminescent, her skin softer. And the charged, humid air repeatedly stirred her scent, keeping him on the keen edge of awareness.

A heavier gust of wind brought the promise of an energetic storm. Erica held her hair away from her face and studied him. "I had no idea you were such a good cook."

"I'm good at a lot of things."

She swirled linguine around her fork and asked, "Such as?"

Ian leaned back, getting comfortable while she finished. Just watching her mouth as she chewed, her throat when she swallowed, turned him on, proving he was in dire straits. He liked the way her lips closed around her fork, how he got the occasional peek of her tongue . . . "I'm the best electrician around."

She waggled her fork at him. "And modest, too."

He shrugged. "Modesty is overrated. Did you know I've considered setting up my own shop a time or two?"

"So why haven't you?"

Because I like working with you. He shook his head. "The timing isn't right yet. Maybe soon."

She looked a little downcast by the idea that he might leave the factory, which encouraged him. "What else are you good at?"

"Building things. Someday I want to build my own house."

"All by yourself?"

"With subcontractors, but using my designs and direction. I'd like a place isolated away from neighbors. In the woods maybe, with a pond or a creek nearby."

"Wow. That sounds wonderful." At that moment, Erica looked softer than he'd ever seen her. She wasn't bristling, wasn't erecting barriers to keep him away. She looked almost . . . dreamy. "I like my privacy too."

He sent her a look. "Really?"

The dreamy expression faded, replaced by teasing. "Hey, even us party girls like our downtime."

"So you wouldn't be averse to living quietly?" He hadn't expected that. In fact, he'd thought the living arrangements might be his biggest obstacle.

"Someday. So when do you plan to build this dream home?"

Ian pushed his plate away and crossed his arms over the table. He saw Erica's gaze skirt to his chest and then, with marked determination, come back to his face. Since her body fascinated him, he was glad for some reciprocal interest. "When I marry and settle down."

She, too, pushed her plate away. "Got a woman in mind for that?"

Before he could think it through, he said, "Oh, yeah." *A beautiful, intelligent, stubborn woman*—who suddenly looked ready to strangle him.

Well, hell. He'd certainly set himself up now.

Chapter Four

Erica drew up straight, making Ian regret his hasty admission. In a flash, she was on her feet, pacing to the railing behind him, her every step filled with barely restrained anger. "Strange." She looked out over the back lot. "I can't imagine a woman fitting into your life."

Ian twisted to see the rigid line of her back. She looked cute standing there in her short skirt, her legs bare, her hair dancing in the wind. "No? Why not?"

She huffed. "Just look at how you live. All neat and orderly with things just so. Men your age are very set in their ways."

"A truism? Is this from experience or supposition?" Or from watching her mother? A string of boyfriends, she'd said, all of them wrong . . .

"Men don't like to change just for a woman."

She hadn't bothered to look at him when she made that ludicrous accusation. "Maybe a woman would be the one changing."

Whipping around, she glared at him. "Typical

male attitude," she all but spat. "The woman is always the one who needs to adjust."

Ian stood. With every minute he spent near her, he better understood her. "I just said maybe, Erica. No reason to bite my face off." He moved closer to her until she braced her hands behind her on the railing, but couldn't lean any farther away. His eyes on hers, his hips nestled close to her pelvis, he said, "Seems to me if two people are in love and ready to build a life together, they both ought to do some adjusting."

"Ha! What adjusting are you willing to do?"

She flung the words at him, as if she expected him to be totally inflexible. How could he be inflexible when she already had him wrapped around her little finger?

She didn't know that though, and part of his plan was not to tell her. She needed a man to match her, and love her, otherwise she'd grind him under.

He stroked her cheek, bent till his mouth touched hers. "For the right woman, I'd do whatever I need to." His words were an explanation she couldn't yet understand, only because she didn't know she was the right woman. But before the weekend was over, she'd figure it out and she'd know he had done whatever he needed to—including duping her, with George and Cameron's help.

Erica flattened her hands on his chest to keep him from kissing her. He allowed her to put a small space between them.

"Who's the woman?"

"What?" He'd been so close to taking her mouth, so lost in the best part of his duping, mainly getting her in bed, that his thoughts were scattered.

"This paragon you hope to marry and settle into

the woods with. Who is she? Someone we work with?"

A slow smile took him by surprise. Why, she sounded jealous. "It doesn't matter. She doesn't want me that way. Yet."

"So I'm here to fill the time?"

Damn it, how had he gotten into this exchange? Ian locked his jaw, measured his words in his mind, then mentally shrugged. He'd give her some truths and see what she did with them. "You're here because we're sexually attracted to each other."

He half expected her to deny it, but she only pursed her mouth. "You want me enough to risk alienating this other woman? What if she finds out about this weekend?"

"She'll know because I don't keep secrets." He lowered his voice to a growled whisper. "And yeah, I want you more than enough."

"For a weekend."

He couldn't very well tell her he wanted her for a week, a month, a hundred years. "So what about you? Are you always honest?"

"Brutally."

That made him laugh.

"It's not funny, Ian. A lot of guys expect women to sugarcoat things, to always cater to their macho egos. But honesty is important to me."

"Yeah?" Damn. What would she think when she found out he'd finagled their weekend from the start?

"If I don't like something I'm going to say so, and if a guy can't take it, tough."

"I'm not exactly fragile, Erica."

"Not your body, no. But male egos are far more delicate than—"

On behalf of males everywhere, he felt he had to interrupt. "You can be as honest with me as you want. Feel free to tell me exactly what pleases you, what you like and don't like." She looked skeptical, so he added, "I want to hear it."

She gave a sharp nod. "Fine. I don't want anyone to try to change me. And I definitely don't want anyone to try to control me."

Ian sighed. If he took her words to heart, all of his plans would be wasted. But he didn't want to change her. He just wanted her to stop trying to be so tough, to accept him and how he made her feel. As to controlling her, well, only in a few sexual situations where he knew she'd enjoy herself.

He cupped his hand over her shoulder and trailed it down her arm until he could lace his fingers in hers. "Speaking of control . . . I promised you some service, remember?"

Just that easily, she went breathless. "Of course I remember. It's . . . it's our deal."

"So you want to soak in the tub while I put away the dishes? When I'm finished I could help you with your bath."

A little more color bloomed in her cheeks. Embarrassment, or excitement?

"Help me how?"

"However you want. It's your show." He started backing up into the apartment, tugging her along with him. The idea of having his hands on her naked, wet body damn near took his knees out from under him. If there was any justice in the world, he'd have her tonight because waiting any longer than that would be torture. "I'll wash your back, your feet, your hair."

"I just washed my hair."

Such an inane comment for Erica. He loved it. He loved her. "Then we'll skip that part. You're in charge, so what you say goes."

They reached his bedroom and Ian opened the closet. "Help yourself to a robe or a shirt or whatever you'll feel most comfortable in. I'll get the bath water ready."

She stood in the middle of his floor and bit her lip.

Ian wanted to hold her, to coddle her, to lay her atop the mattress and make slow, heated love to her. But more than that he wanted her trust. "I'll be right back."

He wasn't gone for more than a minute. Once the temperature of the water was adjusted and the tub began to fill with bubbles, he went back to her. She'd pulled out his old terry cloth robe and had it clutched in her hands.

"Erica?"

"Hmmm?"

"You're not shy about getting naked are you?" He approached her slowly, more because he had to hold himself back than because he was afraid of rushing her. "Remember, no matter how damned tempting you are—and believe me, you're plenty tempting—I won't do anything that you don't want me to do."

She nodded. "Right." And then with a frown, she said, "I want to ask you something first."

"Shoot." They stood five feet apart and not touching seemed almost impossible.

Slowly her head lifted until their gazes connected. "Why me?"

His brain went blank. What could he tell her that wouldn't blow his whole plan? That lust at first sight had morphed into love rather quickly? That wasn't the way to handle Erica. "What do you mean?" he asked, stalling for time.

"I know you keep talking about sexual chemistry and all that. But there's more to it. Why focus all this energy on me? You know, Becky tells me that a lot of the women at work try to get your attention."

"Yeah?"

Nodding, she said, "They think you're gay because you ignore them."

He grinned at that.

"You think that's amusing?" She looked more confused than ever.

"Am I supposed to be insulted over someone else's assumptions? Let them think what they want."

"But . . . why aren't you interested in any of them?"

He drew a long, deep breath. Time for a few more truths. "You want me to bare my soul? All right." He held out his arms. "I'm a big man."

Her gaze dropped to his lap, making him laugh. "I didn't mean that, although everything about me is . . . proportionate."

Judging by the way her eyes widened, she understood his meaning. He was a big man, from his feet to his intelligence and everywhere in between. "I meant that my size intimidates people, especially women."

"The women at work?"

He waved a hand. "They're silly, hiding in the bathroom and gossiping. So, yeah, they'd probably be the type to jump over a look. Ever since I've been a teenager, I've had to hold back. My temper, my attention. And my sexual drive."

"But you figure I'm different?" She sounded a little awed by that.

"From the moment I saw you flirting and taunting and driving all the guys nuts, I knew I could let loose with you and you wouldn't turn tail and run."

Touching her became a necessity so he took one long stride and closed the space between them. He caught her shoulders and brought her to her tiptoes, close to his chest. "I know if I grumbled, you wouldn't get afraid. You'd just grumble back."

"Damn right, so don't try it."

"Yes ma'am." He kissed the end of her nose. "But I am just a man, so if I forget or lose my temper, you won't quail, will you?"

She snorted, but asked with a scowl, "Just how violent do you get when you lose your temper?"

"I get loud, not violent. And that's enough to send most women running."

The very idea set her off. "I don't run from anyone!"

"And I don't hurt women. Ever. I'd sooner break my own arm. I swear it."

She nodded. "I believe you. But don't think you can get away with yelling at me either."

The things she said made his heart full to bursting. Gently, he said, "If I did, I wouldn't mean anything by it. Besides, you'd just yell louder."

"And longer."

He laughed. "When I have you under me, small and vulnerable, you'll love it. You'll take what I give you and want more and you won't ever feel overpowered."

Her lips quivered and a pulse raced in her

throat, but she thrust up her chin. "I'll demand my turn on top."

"Yeah." His voice went low and hoarse. "That's what I figured." She started to lean up to kiss him, and Ian said, "The bath is probably ready to overflow."

He hustled her out of the room and down the hall. The tub was full, but he caught it in time. Kneeling, he shut off the water, set a thick towel on the ceramic floor just outside the tub, and turned— in time to see Erica unbuttoning her shirt.

Apparently, their exchange had emboldened her. Ian dropped back onto his ass with a thump and watched, spellbound. She smiled as she slipped each button free, knowing she drove him crazy and enjoying it.

"I told you that I take my shoes off when I get home, but know what else I like to take off?"

"Your clothes?" Damn, he sounded hopeful.

"Sometimes. But my shoes and my bra are always the first to go. Both are so constrictive. You won't mind if I spend the weekend barefoot and braless, will you?"

He shook his head, rendered mute by the sight of pale flesh visible through the gaping shirt. Any second now he'd see her breasts. Be strong, he told himself. Do not start groveling. Or drooling. Drooling would be bad, too.

And here he'd thought this would be the easy part.

She shrugged the shirt off her shoulders and tossed it at his face. "Fold that for me."

"Right." He dropped it to his lap, unwilling to look away for even a second.

She reached behind herself and dragged down the zipper on her skirt. "Ian?"

"Mmm?"

"I need you to help me. Tug this down my hips, okay, so I can step out of it."

Oh, good Lord. He moved forward on his knees and reached for the skirt. But that close to her, his hands automatically went to bare flesh. He shaped her waist, loving the fine texture of her skin in contrast to his rough palms. Her belly was gently rounded, smooth and pale, and her navel made only the slightest indent. He had to kiss it.

"Ian? The skirt."

He cleared his throat and gathered what meager control he had left. He just hadn't counted on the effect of her nudity. He felt like a ravening beast, hungry, in heat, ready to conquer. He wanted her under him—now.

The skirt was tight and had to be worked down. Her panties almost came with it, tripping his heart and freezing his breath in his lungs, but at the last second she caught the waistband and kept them on her hips.

Her bra matched her panties, and the shiny peach shade did interesting things to her rich black hair and ivory skin. It also did interesting things to his dick, making him swell to a full, demanding erection.

Through the thin material of her underclothes, he could see the darker circles of her nipples and a neat triangle of pubic hair between her legs. Still on his knees—a position now somewhat familiar with Erica—he reached up for the front clasp of her bra, then waited.

"Go ahead," she whispered.

Ian had been in his teens when he'd mastered getting a female's clothes off her. He sure as hell didn't fumble now. The bra clasp opened and he drew the material apart. She lowered her arms and the straps slid down, then off so that the bra landed on the floor.

Her nipples, not pink but a deep mauve, were tightly puckered, making him groan. She didn't have large breasts but they were soft and round and this was Erica. He'd wanted her for so long, he almost couldn't remember ever not wanting her.

Erica curved her hand around his neck. "I want you to kiss me."

His gaze snapped to hers but he didn't need more encouragement than that. Oh, he knew what she intended: to make him hot, then make him stop.

She wanted some payback.

But hell, he was already hot, and stopping wouldn't be easy for her, either. Eventually she wouldn't want to stop. He knew he was right about that.

He lifted himself a little higher until his face was level with her torso. Wrapping his arms around her he tugged her close, tilted his head, and drew her left nipple deep into the wet warmth of his mouth. He sucked, not hard, but he wasn't the least bit timid about it either. His nose pressed into her plump breast and she smelled so good he was already breathing hard.

Her body arched and her hands knotted in his hair. Ian tugged, using his tongue to tease, to flick and lick. Then he sucked some more until they were both shaking.

"That's enough," she whispered, but without much insistence.

"Not yet." He moved to the other breast. "Gotta be fair."

"To you?" she asked on a sigh.

"To these." And he kissed her right breast with the same enthusiasm. Within moments, Erica moved against him, her belly nudging his chest, her legs shifting with the need to get nearer. He stroked her shoulders, down to the small of her back, and finally over her firm cheeks, kneading and plying the resilient flesh, helping to grind her against his body.

When she was all but lost, he hooked his thumbs in her panties and pulled them down her legs. Leaning back, he looked at her. Her green eyes were smoky with desire, her nipples wet from his mouth, her whole body quivering. With one finger, he stroked the silky black curls on her mound, up, down, pressing in just the tiniest bit until he felt her small, taut clitoris. She groaned.

Jesus, she was the most appealing woman he'd ever seen.

And she was his.

He stood and scooped her into his arms; at the same time, Erica hugged him, pressing her face into his throat. "Where are we going?" Her voice was deep, affected by sexual need.

Regret stung him, but he didn't head for the bedroom. Not yet, he told himself, not just yet. "You're going into the tub and I'm heading to the kitchen." His voice was unusually gruff.

She jerked her head back. "What?"

Lowering her into the now tepid water, he said, "Relax. Soak. When I'm done with the dishes I'll help you wash then dry you off and give you a massage."

The water level was high, all but covering her except for her breasts and rosy nipples. He turned away, ignoring her slack-jawed surprise while struggling to contain himself. He would have liked to whistle, but his mouth wasn't working right at the moment and no way could he pucker.

Just as he reached the hall, he heard a furious splash, followed by a soft moan of dismay. He had her right where he wanted her.

Unfortunately, she had him in the same position.

Only she didn't know it, and he did.

Erica scrubbed herself with a vengeance. Let him help? Ha. She'd let him rot, that's what she'd do. He'd had his chance and he'd walked away. She'd been willing, damn it. Willing and needing and . . .

The problem, at least to her mind, was that when he got near, she couldn't seem to remember that she was the boss. She just went all soft and female. She hated going soft and female.

It made a woman weak and left her open to misuse.

She didn't have enough fingers and toes to count the men who had used and discarded her mother. Her mother would give a man everything—her heart, her home, often even her paycheck. And eventually he'd leave her, devastated and financially broke. They'd had to struggle so many times because of the scoundrels that her mother had grown fond of.

Erica prided herself on being different. Unable to accept her mother's lifestyle, she'd gained her independence early on and she protected that above all else. She said and did exactly as she pleased and never would she let a man dictate to her.

Yet Ian had only to touch her and she lost herself.

She needed to rethink this whole thing. Really, what was it she wanted? She lifted one finger: Ian naked. That would be very sweet on the eyes, not to mention how much her hands—and her mouth—would love it.

She lifted another finger: Ian making love to her. Yes, that would be heavenly.

A third finger went up: Ian at her mercy.

As if a lightbulb went on, Erica suddenly realized she could have all that with only one simple ground rule. Before he touched her again, she'd spell it out to him, then it'd be on him to maintain control, rather than on her.

Now why hadn't she thought of that sooner?

She sat up in the tub and sluiced off the clinging bubbles. She wasn't going to get any cleaner and no way could she relax. She'd just stepped out of the tub when Ian came back in.

He stopped in the doorway, his blue eyes nearly incandescent as they tracked every inch of her body. Subtly, the muscles in his chest and shoulders grew tight until the strength in his upper body was clearly defined. His hands curled into fists.

"Damn, you look good."

The bottom dropped out of her stomach at the way he said that and how he looked at her. She lifted a hand. "Don't come any closer."

His back straightened. "What?"

"I mean it, Ian. We have to talk first."

He looked troubled, and aroused. "Let me help you dry off, then we'll talk."

"No! I'm the boss, right? Well I say we talk first." Gaining a little momentum on her attitude, Erica crossed her arms beneath her breasts and waited.

Slumping back against the door frame, Ian cupped one big hand over his crotch and winced. "I'll wait, but I don't know if John Henry will. Jesus, Erica, I'm about to explode here."

Caught between a laugh of triumph and overwhelming excitement, Erica looked at the straining erection beneath his jeans. Yep, he was plenty in proportion. She gulped. "You walked away from me."

"No easy feat, I don't mind telling you. But you're the one who set up the rules—that I'd wait on you. I'm trying to do that."

She wouldn't let him fool her again. "I want you to make love to me."

He jerked straight. "Yes."

"What do you mean, yes?"

"I mean, yes. Hell, yes. I'm more than willing."

This time she did laugh. "But I have some stipulations."

His biceps bulged. "Name them."

Oh, Erica could easily see why women got nervous around Ian Conrad. In his hunger, he looked savage and hard and ready to conquer. Only he'd never conquer her. "It has to be just sex."

His eyes narrowed, intense and bright. "Come again?"

Well, damn, now he was starting to make her nervous. "I don't want you muddying the waters with too much talk, unless it's sex talk. And no more playing games."

"Games?"

She sighed. Well, she could admit a little, and then he'd have to do the same. "We've both been doing it and you know it. This business of one-up-manship has to stop. We'll both be naked, and if you have any skill at all, we'll both enjoy ourselves. Period."

For three seconds he looked ready to erupt. His jaw was locked tight, his body tensed as if for attack, and anger practically vibrated off him. Then he let loose with a string of stinging curses that made Erica's heart leap in shock. "Ian!"

He turned away, paced two steps and came back. "No."

That drew her up. "What do you mean, no?"

"I mean no." He stared at her hard. "I want more than just sex."

Her jaw worked several times before she could get the word out. "More?"

He advanced and she—damn it—backed up. Her naked fanny smacked into the ceramic tile wall and in the next heartbeat Ian pressed into her front. "I want everything from you, Erica Lee. Everything you have to give."

Because she didn't understand him, she went on the defensive. "You want to control me."

"I want your trust." He pressed a finger to her mouth, halting her denial. "Before you say it, they are not the same thing. I know you keep men at a distance for a reason. I suppose some of what you told me about your mother is to blame for that."

She tried to speak, but he leaned down and briefly kissed her, silencing her with the warm press of his mouth, the gentle sweep of his tongue. "I want your body, your humor, your cocky sarcasm. I want you, Erica. Right now, but tomorrow too."

Her mouth touching his, she asked, "And the day after that?"

"Always."

She jerked back so fast her head cracked on the wall, making her wince. "Damn it."

With a huff of annoyance, Ian's hand opened over the back of her head and rubbed. "Don't be nervous with me."

"You do not make me nervous."

"Not physically, no. You want me too, I can tell that much." He settled his hips into the notch of her legs. "But you're nervous because you're not sure if I'm for real. You're afraid you'll start to like me, to trust me, and I'll walk away."

"Your ego is massive."

"Erica." He pressed his forehead to hers. "Can't you let go just a little?"

She wanted to so badly that it scared her. Then a thought occurred to her and she glared. "What about this woman at work who you want to marry and carry off to the woods?"

By small degrees, he gathered her tightly to him. Erica couldn't draw a breath without feeling some part of Ian, without inhaling his scent. She couldn't move a millimeter without her lips touching his, her body rubbing into him. Once he had her locked close, he whispered, "That's you."

"Me?" She barely squeaked the word out.

He nodded, bumping his nose into hers.

"But I thought . . ."

"Shhh. Drop your defenses just until tomorrow

morning, and then we'll talk about it again. I promise. I'll explain everything."

"And until then?"

"I'm going to make love to you." He kissed her softly. "And I'm going to fuck you." The kiss turned raw and demanding, almost frightening in intensity.

He wrapped one arm beneath her bottom, one across her back, and lifted her. "I'm going to drive you wild, sweetheart, which is what you deserve considering how wild you've made me."

It all sounded wonderful to her, savage and gentle, raunchy and sweet. Everything she'd ever wanted, and too much to resist. She laced her fingers in his hair and managed a smile. "Okay."

Relief darkened his face, wrought a groan from deep inside him. "I'll prove to you that you can be yourself with me and I'll love it."

She almost believed him.

Without thinking about it, Erica wrapped her legs around his waist and returned his kiss. He started walking them to his bedroom and the friction of his rough denim between her open legs inflamed her. He kept kissing her, deep and long, and then she felt her feet touch the floor.

Within seconds, Ian had the coverlet stripped off the bed. He opened a night table drawer and removed a whole box of condoms.

How considerate, Erica thought, wondering how many of them they'd use, but glad they wouldn't have to worry about running out.

"Ian?"

He lifted her onto the bed, stretching her out crosswise, then stepped back to strip off his jeans. Erica rose to one elbow to watch, her breath suspended, her fingers curled into the sheet. He pushed the denim down his long legs and stepped free, then stood there a moment to let her look.

His pelvis was a shade lighter than the rest of his body. His legs were long and muscled, and his big, narrow feet were braced apart. Her gaze slowly rose again until she stared at his erection. He was long and thick and she swallowed hard. "My, my."

Naked, macho, and to her mind, perfect, Ian climbed onto the bed beside her. Erica wanted to spend at least five minutes just looking at him, absorbing the sight of him, but he didn't give her the chance. He tangled his hand in her hair, took her mouth in a ravaging kiss, then didn't stop kissing her. Not that she wanted him to stop.

If she were honest with herself, she'd admit that she loved his caveman approach, loved the feel of his big hands now roaming her body, gripping her behind, kneading her breasts. She even enjoyed the rasp of his whiskers. From the first, his bold, assertive manner had drawn her. She didn't like wimpy men, but she did like Ian. A lot.

Maybe too much.

She'd wanted him for a long time, she just hadn't wanted to acknowledge it. Now that she had, she felt free—free to indulge her secrets, her desires.

Maybe on Monday she'd thank Cameron and George for speaking out of turn. If they hadn't, who knew what type of guy she might have ended up with? But because of them, she had Ian. And with Ian kissing his way down her throat to her breasts, she knew she was lucky indeed.

Chapter Five

Ian knew he should slow down a little, but he couldn't. He cupped one soft breast, thumbed her nipple, then drew her into his mouth for a soft suckle.

Erica squirmed, trying to get closer to him. Putting one leg over hers and pinning her hands above her head, he held her still. When he expected to hear her complaints over the restraint, he got a surprisingly hot moan instead.

Ian lifted his head to look at her.

Why, the little sneak. She liked being controlled sexually. And he liked taking his turn at control, at least in bed. Out of bed, well, Erica's independent nature was part of what he loved.

After transferring both her hands into one of his, he used the other hand to stroke down her body to her belly. "Can I reverse the order?"

She gave him a blank, anxious look.

"Seeing you like this . . . I want to fuck you first, and make love to you after."

"Yes."

He was so hard it hurt. "Let's see if you're wet

enough yet." Holding her gaze, he pressed his fingers lower, through her dark curls and over slick flesh. Her body arched.

"Open up for me, Erica."

Her throat worked as she swallowed, then slowly her legs parted.

He looked down to where his large hand completely covered her. "Bend your knees. I want to see you."

Without hesitation, she did, opening herself fully to him. He took in the sight of her pale thighs laid open, her damp curls, and her glistening vulva. He pressed his middle finger deep. She groaned hard, her hips lifting, her eyes squeezing shut.

"Nice and wet," he murmured, pleased with how her muscles squeezed his finger. "God, the things I want to do to you . . ."

He pushed another finger in, testing her, filling her. She was aroused enough, wet enough, that there would be no discomfort for her. He pulled out and found her clitoris again, at the same time bending to catch a nipple in his teeth. Her moans turned raw, her body moving with his hand, and suddenly it was too much. He'd waited for this moment, for this woman, too long to hold himself back.

Ian sat up, startling a groan of protest from Erica though he didn't take time to explain. He caught her knees in his hands, spread her legs wider until he could see every glistening pink inch of her sex. He heard her gasp even as he bent, tasting her with his tongue, licking and finally sucking. Erica became frenzied.

He hooked her legs over his shoulders and

caught her hips in his hands to keep her still. She tasted hot, sweet, like a woman should. Her fingers locked in his hair, holding him closer to her as she cried out and twisted, as the sensations built and expanded.

"Ian."

With utmost care, he held her swollen clitoris in his teeth for the concentrated rasp of his rough tongue.

Erica came. She cried out in a nearly soundless scream, her legs stiff, her heels digging into his shoulder blades. Before her last shuddering breath had subsided, he was reaching for a condom.

Erica lay there, limp, a little sweaty. Smiling.

Damn, he loved her. In record time he had the condom on and had settled between her thighs. "You'll take me deep, won't you sweetheart?"

Her smile of contentment faded as he again hooked her legs and held them high. He outweighed her by a hundred pounds easy, was big and hard where she was slim and delicate, and still he settled against her.

"Tell me, Erica." His cock nudged against her sensitive lips, swollen from her climax. In this position, she was completely vulnerable—and they both knew it. "Tell me you want all of me."

She lifted her hands to his chest, a futile effort to hold him back. Her nails bit into his pectoral muscles as he began pressing inward.

"Tell me."

She panted. "Yes."

Her compliance, combined with the wet velvet grasp of her body on the head of his dick nearly forced him into an early release. He gritted his teeth. "Then relax for me."

She gave a choked laugh. "Can't."

He pushed in another inch and heard her inhalation of discomfort. Biting off a groan, he said, "You're gonna have to, babe." He felt himself sweating, felt his every muscle quivering with the effort it took to hold back. "You're clenching. Relax and let me in."

She took three shallow breaths, then one long, deep one. She closed her eyes, loosened her grasp on his chest, and nodded.

Through his intense concentration, Ian summoned a smile for her. "I love you, Erica."

Her eyes popped open again, huge and stunned, and he thrust in hard, filling her up and obliterating his last trace of control. He was so deep, a part of her—his woman—that holding back became impossible.

Alive with acute, burning pleasure, he stroked in and out and just when he felt his stomach coil, felt his balls tighten and knew he was about to lose it, Erica began countering his thrusts. He heard her raspy breathing, saw the heated rise of pleasure on her face, and he came, aware of Erica joining him, of her body milking his. Aware of the perfection of the moment.

He slumped on top of her, replete, boneless. His weight wrought a moan from her, reminding him of her position. "Sorry," he murmured, then carefully lowered her legs. Turning his face inward so he could taste the salty warmth of her neck, he rumbled, "You okay?"

She grunted, making him smile again. Damn, from the day he'd met her she'd amused him even while setting him on fire. They were both damp, sticking together, and he never wanted to move.

"Give me a second," he said, "and I'll make love to you."

This time she choked, but the sound turned into a low laugh. Her limp arms came around his neck and she contrived a halfhearted hug. "You're something else, Ian Conrad."

That perked him up. "Something better than what you've known," he agreed. "Someone you can trust."

"Maybe."

He lifted his head to growl at her. "Your second's up."

"What?"

"It's time to make love to you." She started to protest, to laugh some more, and Ian kissed her quiet—then went on kissing her for a long, long time. When she tried to wiggle out from under him, he flipped her onto her stomach and kissed her spine, the small of her back, her dimpled bottom.

By the time he finished with that, Erica was again squirming with need. He turned her over, cradled her gently, and this time he took her slow, cherishing her body and showing her that she not only made him crazed with lust, she overwhelmed him with love and tenderness too.

After nearly two days of uninhibited debauchery, Erica was badly rumpled, lazy, and still so sexy Ian wasn't sure he'd ever stop wanting her. It was nearing ten o'clock on Sunday morning, and he still couldn't glance at her without feeling a rise of sexual awareness. He couldn't hear her breathe without wanting her. And her laughs, her taunts, drove him to the very edge of lust.

Every single thing they'd done had felt like foreplay. He'd showered with her, wanting only to let
the hot water ease her sore muscles. Instead, he'd
taken her against the wet tile wall with the enthusiasm of a schoolboy on prom night.

He'd pulled out the massage oil, intent on fulfilling his end of the bargain. But Erica lying on
her stomach with her beautiful back and shapely
ass showing proved more than he could take. The
oil got set aside while he kissed her all over, occasionally shocking her, definitely thrilling her. He'd
drawn her to her knees to take her from the back,
holding her breasts in his hands with his thrusts so
deep he hadn't lasted more than five minutes—
which was fine since Erica had started coming in
half that time.

In the midst of steamy sensuality, there'd been
very little personal grooming. Ian let her use his
toothbrush and he remembered brushing her
long silky hair once, only to muss it again when he
carried her out to the balcony to fondle her under
the moonlight. He liked having her outside.

Late Friday night, the storm had rolled in,
spraying rain on them, leaving them both damp
and windblown. Erica had tasted especially fine
with her skin dewy.

Thinking of it made him want to taste her again.
Down boy, he told his overenthusiastic cock. *Enough
already. Let her rest.*

Saturday morning everything had been fresh
from the rain, sparkling clean, and they'd lingered
in bed beneath a ray of sunshine slanting in through
the open window. Seeing Erica lit by the sun made
him more determined than ever to get her to that

house in the country, where privacy would allow them to make love outdoors as often as they liked.

Ian was amazed at his stamina. He'd always had a strong sexual appetite, but he'd never been so insatiable that he couldn't seem to stop. Of course, he'd never been with Erica. And he'd never been in love.

She hadn't bothered with makeup at all, but her slanted green eyes looked sexier than ever, especially when they were soft from a recent climax, as they were now. He knew he should get up and cook her breakfast. They hadn't had a full meal since Friday night; Saturday they'd only snacked so neither of them had to leave the bed for long. She had to be getting hungry. He was starved.

But then Erica tucked her head into his shoulder and hugged him, and Ian knew he wasn't ready to move yet.

"I am so exhausted," she teased.

Touched by a modicum of guilt because he'd awakened her from a sound slumber a few hours earlier by sliding into her from behind, Ian asked, "Are you glad now that you stayed?"

"Yes." She tilted her face up to see him. "You are imposing, intimidating, insatiable, and very sweet."

Most of that he couldn't deny, but . . . "Sweet, huh?"

"Surprisingly so."

Perhaps now would be a good time to come clean, while she was still calling him *sweet*. He knew she'd want to go home tonight since they both had to work in the morning. But damned if he was ready to let her go. "There are still a few things we need to talk about."

She yawned and nestled back into his side. "What kind of things?"

He didn't want to start a fight, not when she seemed so peaceful and trusting. But he wanted to start their new relationship with a clean slate. Feeling possessive, he cupped her breast and said, "About why you keep men at arm's length."

She laughed. "I dunno about that. You're pretty close." She reached down and encircled his penis, which was thankfully at ease for the moment.

"Physically." He bit the bullet and added, "But you know I want more."

She again looked up at him. "Really?" At his nod, she looked very satisfied—and a little shy. "You think there's something about that porn shop that brings people together? I mean, look at Asia and Cameron, and then Becky and George."

"And me and you?"

"I do like you, Ian. Everything about you. Most especially your honesty."

His stomach twisted with dread. "My honesty?"

"That's right. You told me up front what you wanted and why. If it wasn't for you being so honest about the whole thing, I think I would have bailed out on you."

He couldn't bear the thought that he might have missed this special time with her. "Erica, honey . . ."

"I suppose I should be honest too, huh?"

His admission died in his throat. "I'd love for you to trust me enough to tell me about yourself."

She nodded, causing the silky weight of her hair to glide against his ribs. "You were right about why I don't open up to men. I've never told this to anyone before. Not even Becky or Asia. But my mom . . . well, she was confused. And weak. She always thought she needed a man around and there was always one willing to hang on her. They used her. For sex, for money. She took care of them, playing house and pampering them—until they walked away."

Ian rubbed her scalp, kissed her forehead. "I'm sorry. But you have to know I'm not like that."

"I do know it." Again, she twisted to look up at him. "I kind of think you're the type who would resent relying on a woman for anything."

"Not true. I'm relying on you to keep me happy." He caught her chin on his fist and lifted her face more. "You're fast becoming a requirement in my life."

She grinned, but didn't look like she believed him. "I grew up with men hanging around the house. I hated it. When they were there, my mother thought she had to be perfect. She'd get up early to put on her makeup and fix her hair because otherwise she'd get complaints and insults. It made me so damn mad, but the more I tried to convince her that we didn't need them, the more distant we got with each other. She never relaxed, never let herself just kick back and enjoy life." Erica shook her head. "She tried to get me to do the same, but I fought her every inch of the way."

"You're your own person, Erica, not a replica of your mother." He kissed her temple, hoping to reassure her. "She made her choices and you make yours. That's how it should be."

Erica lowered her face and hugged Ian. "There was another reason why I refused to primp for them." She took a deep breath. "When I was about sixteen, the men started looking at me differently."

Ian stiffened with a mix of disgust and rage. "They didn't—"

"No." She gave him a teasing pinch, deliberately lightening the mood. "I wouldn't have allowed that and you know it."

Ian squeezed her so tight she gasped. Erica just didn't realize how susceptible she was as a woman. She considered herself tough, but from her toes to her eyebrows, she was feminine and soft and certainly weaker than the majority of men.

She'd spent more of her life building bravado than any female should ever have to. "You're sure no one ever . . ."

"I'm sure. When I was seventeen I moved out."

Startled, Ian tipped her chin up. "Seventeen?" She'd been so damn young.

Erica shrugged as if it was no big deal. "I spent a year working, staying with friends, moving around a lot. I eventually landed here, and after working my way through a two-year technical college, I started at the factory as an office assistant."

Ian gave a mental salute to the divine hand of fate for delivering her into his path. He'd always be thankful for that. "How are things with your mom now?"

She was silent for a long moment. Her fingers teased at his chest hair, and Ian felt her press a soft kiss to his side. "She died when I was twenty-two. Ovarian cancer. I hadn't seen her for a long time, and I didn't know she was sick until it was too late."

"Jesus, Erica, I'm so damn sorry."

She crawled on top of him, kissed his chin, the bridge of his nose, then his mouth. "You have nothing to be sorry for. But thanks."

"Do you ever see your dad?"

"Never met him. Mom told me he didn't know she was pregnant, and by the time she was showing, he was long gone. Soon after I was born, she'd moved on to a new man."

"And so you've always been fiercely independent."

"It's not just that, you know." She propped her pointy elbows on his chest and put her head in her hands. "Guys in general are pigs."

"Is that so?"

"Yep. They work hard at pretending they care just so they can get you into bed, but then spend the mere two minutes they need there to get off."

"Not always true."

She grinned. "So I'm learning."

He hated to think about it, but he said, "You've picked some losers, haven't you?"

Instead of getting angry at that observation, she nodded. "Yeah, and I was beginning to think I was like my mom, that all I could pick were losers."

"Wanna hear my theory?"

"I don't know. Do I?"

He swatted her delectable behind. "Yeah, you do." Both hands now holding her bottom, he said, "Because of your mother's choices, you've always thought you had to control everything to prove you were different, independent and able to do your own thing. That naturally meant you chose guys who'd let you have control."

Her eyes narrowed. "I still have control."

"Over yourself." He squeezed her butt. "That's all anyone should want to control. I don't want to control you, and you don't need to control me."

"Because you're not going to use me?"

He nodded. "And because I love you, I don't ever want to see you hurt."

She went still. "That's the second time you've said it."

"Keeping count?"

"Maybe."

"Want me to say it about a dozen more times?" With Erica lying naked atop him, it was getting difficult to carry the conversation. He could feel her pubic hair on his belly, the soft cushion of her breasts on his abdomen. "It's true, you know. And I think you care about me too."

She didn't admit it, which bugged Ian, but he knew she needed time. "You're a strong, intelligent woman, Erica. You need a strong man, not a weak-kneed ass."

Her shoulders started shaking, and seconds later she burst out laughing. Ian rolled her beneath him, spread her legs, and settled against her. Her laughter died.

"You know I'm right."

Breathless, she said, "I'm willing to admit it's possible."

"Because you care about me too?" Damn it, he was pushing her after all.

"Because you drive me wild." She grabbed his ears and took his mouth. Her kiss was meant to get him off track, and it damn near did. But he was used to her tactics and he wanted to clear the air once and for all.

"Shh. Erica, wait." He stroked his fingers through her hair, spreading it out over his pillow. "Let's finish talking first, okay?"

"Talk?" She sent him a mock look of surprise. "Did I finally wear you out?"

He couldn't resist kissing her. "Never. I could make love to you for a lifetime and not be done. But this is the first time we've really talked about personal stuff, and there are things I want to tell you."

She sighed theatrically. "All right. Spill your guts and I'll try to be attentive."

"You're such a generous woman."

She laughed. "Quit stalling."

He was stalling, but Erica's reactions were unpredictable. She was as likely to walk out on him as she was to understand. But damn it, he did love her. That had to count for something. And he knew she cared for him too, even if she hadn't admitted it.

Somehow, he'd get her to tell him. She could get mad, but before she left his apartment, they'd have an understanding.

Ian drew a deep breath, and said, "I set the whole thing up."

She didn't explode, but only because she didn't yet understand. "Set what up?"

"Our meeting at the porn shop."

"I know. You overheard George and Cameron and . . ."

"No, sweetheart." He rubbed her arms, trying to prepare her. "Like I told you, almost everyone at the factory knows about the deal you three ladies had. I knew you'd be next and there was no way in hell I could stand the thought of you playing sex games with some other man. I wanted it to be my turn."

She stiffened beneath him. "Your turn?"

"You kept shying away from me," he growled. "I wanted a chance to prove to you how good we'd be together."

"What did you do?"

The time for truth. "I approached George and Cameron and they agreed to help me." She didn't comment on that, so he continued. "I knew just showing up at the right time wouldn't work with you, Erica, not the way it had with Becky and Asia. You wouldn't have a single qualm about ignoring me or telling me to get lost so that you could choose some spineless jerk to play with instead. So I challenged you."

Erica didn't speak, but like a volcano ready to erupt, he felt the tension building in her.

Damn, her silence hurt almost as much as the lethal look in her eyes. He held her shoulders and gave her one firm shake. "I lied about overhearing George and Cameron. I confronted them, convinced them to go along with my plan, and they . . . well, they did."

"I see."

Ian didn't trust her soft tone. "Don't be mad at them, Erica. They made me swear I wouldn't hurt you. Hell, they dogged my heels like two mother hens, worrying about you."

"What a lovely image."

"Your sarcasm is misplaced. I told you I love you—"

"And you told me you lied, and that my friends all know it. One big joke on Erica. I bet they thought you'd teach me a lesson, huh? That you'd turn the tables on me—and you did. Did they laugh about it?"

"No." He hadn't expected her to be hurt, but judging by her tone and the dampness of her eyes, she was exactly that. It made him feel sick and helpless.

"Have you been giving them blow-by-blow reports on your progress?"

Ian's own temper started. "You know better."

Her eyes were solemn, her gaze direct. "Right before you confessed, I was thinking how little I knew. About men, about myself. Now I'm doubly sure that I'm an idiot."

"The hell you are! You're an intelligent woman, damn it."

"Would you mind getting off me?"

Ian drew a breath and reached for control. "Yes, I would mind. I want you to understand. I want you to tell me that you care about me."

Erica opened her mouth, but a furious pounding on the front door interrupted what she might have said. Ian twisted to stare out toward the hall, cursed, and refused to budge.

"Aren't you going to answer that?"

"No."

"Then I will." She tried to slide out from under him.

"No." If he let her get away now, she'd go back to avoiding him. He just knew it. "Erica—"

The pounding on the door increased. It sounded like there were a dozen fists hitting it. "God damn it!" Ian exploded, and then to Erica, "I don't suppose you'd stay put while I go see who's trying to break down my door?"

"Yeah, right."

Sounding very put upon, he muttered, "That's what I thought." He pushed himself away and watched as Erica scrambled to her feet. In a show of temper, she snatched up the sheet and wrapped it around herself.

Ian sighed, opened a drawer to pull out boxers, and stepped into them.

Erica hustled up beside him when he started out of the bedroom. "You're going to answer the door in your underwear?"

They went through the hall and into the living room. "No, I'm going to tell whoever it is to get lost in my underwear."

And then he heard George call out, "Better open up, Ian, before the female battalion knocks it down."

Ian and Erica looked at each other in surprise.

"Erica! It's me, Asia. Becky's with me. Let us in."

Erica slugged Ian in the stomach, making him grunt. "You told them all we'd be here?"

He scowled right back at her. "Of course I didn't. They probably figured if you weren't at home, you must be here. We did have a detailed discussion in the break room, if you'll recall."

Looking sheepish, she said, "Oh, yeah."

Ian jerked the door open. "Did someone plan a party and not tell me?"

Asia gawked at him, her gaze moving over his naked chest and down his body until Cameron cleared his throat. Becky started to look too, but George quickly covered her eyes. He glared at Ian. "Good God, man, put some clothes on."

"Why? You're not staying."

Somewhat flustered, Asia shoved her way past him. "Erica, we had nothing to do with this. George and Cameron didn't tell us. I can't believe Ian had them lying to us."

Ian rolled his eyes while Cameron barked, "I did not lie to you, damn it. I just didn't tell you about it."

"A lie of omission!"

Ian gestured to George, who still had Becky's eyes covered. "Looks like you might as well come in too. I'd like to shut the door to spare my neighbors all this drama."

George, still blinding Becky, hustled her in and kicked the door shut.

"George?" Becky asked.

"Yeah, sweetheart?"

"What am I missing?"

He kissed her temple. "Just Ian in his underwear."

She tried to pull his hand from her eyes.

Erica had gone back into the bedroom, Ian assumed to get dressed. Instead, she returned with a pair of his jeans and a T-shirt. "Try for a little decency, okay?" She tossed them to him.

"You wouldn't like me decent." She scowled, but when he winked at her, she actually flushed. Maybe, just maybe this would prove a timely interruption. God knew he'd been floundering on his own.

Ian stepped into his jeans just as Becky got George to turn her loose. "Well, heck. I miss everything."

"I'll get naked for you just as soon as we finish this misguided mission."

Becky turned to George, smiled, and said, "Promise?"

Asia cleared her throat. "Can we all remember why we're here?"

"I know why I'm here," Erica said, keeping the

sheet tight around herself. "But no one told me we were planning an orgy."

"Damn," Cameron said to George, "I don't think we're dressed for an orgy."

Asia elbowed him. "Becky and I were worried all along about you getting tangled up with *him*." She glared toward Ian. "And it looks like we were right."

"You were?"

Asia leaned closer, and in a stage whisper said, "Erica, he set the whole thing up."

"Yeah, I know." Erica crossed her arms over her chest and nodded. "He told me."

Asia drew back. "He did?"

Ian threw up his hands. "What do you have against me?"

Very matter-of-factly, Becky said, "You're big."

George choked, making Becky blush and swat at him. "George! I didn't mean *that*."

Rubbing his eyes, Ian asked, "God knows I probably shouldn't ask, but what's wrong with being big?"

"You're dictatorial too," Asia claimed.

They were worried about him being heavy-handed with Erica? He shook his head. "Yeah, so is Erica and you like her."

Cameron nodded. "He's got ya there, honey."

"People are nervous around you," she insisted.

"Not Erica." Ian turned to her. "Are you, sweetheart?"

"Certainly not." Erica sat down on the edge of the sofa, making certain the sheet covered what it should. "I don't see why you and Becky are all up in arms. It's not like this is anything new. Cameron lied to hook up with you, pretending he hadn't overheard your fantasy about spanking."

Ian's head jerked around so fast, he almost knocked himself over. Spanking? Asia and Cameron?

He stared, fascinated. The newlyweds both flushed, and said almost in unison, "That was a misunderstanding."

"And Asia, you hand-picked George when you found out Becky was into bondage."

Bondage! Ian eyed Becky with new insight. And here he'd always thought her to be shy and innocent. Maybe he needed to reevaluate.

"Erica," George growled while shoving a giggling Becky behind his back. "One of these days . . ."

"Oh, give up, George. Becky's not fine china. You're perfect for her, just as Cameron is perfect for Asia."

Ian stood right in front of Erica. "And I'm perfect for you."

She peered up at him. "You lied to me."

Frowning, Asia sat down beside her. She no longer looked so certain in her mission. "But as you said, Cameron lied to me, and I still love him."

"Yeah. I'm working that part of it out in my head."

Becky sat on her other side. "George lied to me too, but only for a little while. He admitted to me that it was a setup. And you know what? I remember he said he would help set you up with the perfect guy too. I just didn't know he'd think Ian was perfect."

George stepped forward. "I didn't, but Ian did. And why not? He's crazy about her. How much more perfect can it get?"

Cameron added, "We are talking about Erica here, remember. She scares most guys to death."

Erica tossed a throw pillow at him. "I never scared you."

"That's because I knew Asia would protect me." George nodded.

"It's heartwarming that you're all so concerned about her. Really." Ian looked at Erica. "But I think we can work things out on our own."

Cameron cleared his throat. "Well, I don't know about that. I feel rather protective."

Asia nodded. "Me, too."

Becky smiled at George. "We all do."

Laughing, Erica said, "Now why would you all feel protective of me?"

Ian knelt down in front of her. "Because they love you as much as I do. And if you're still keeping count, that's three."

Erica looked small and very uncertain sandwiched between her friends with their men crowding close to their sides.

"Three what?" Becky asked.

Erica's eyes went soft and dark. "Three times now that he's told me he loves me."

Asia and Becky were mute. Cameron said, "I believe him. God knows he's worked hard enough to get you here."

"Damn right," George agreed. "And I think Erica loves him too."

Ian raised a brow. "You do?"

"Sure. She's been defending you since we got here. Damned if I've ever heard Erica defend a man before. Usually she's ripping them to shreds."

Slowly, Ian's grin spread until he thought he might burst with satisfaction. Erica had been taking his part, defending him to her best friends. The look she gave him now was part wary, part annoyed. She was such a prickly woman sometimes. "Tell me you love me, Erica."

Cameron and George quickly seated themselves on the arms of the sofa next to their respective women. "I don't want to miss a word," Cameron said, despite the way Asia tried to hush him.

George said, "I wish I had my video camera," and Becky elbowed him hard.

With everyone looking at her, Erica naturally went cocky. "Yeah, sure, I love him."

Four mouths fell open. Ian just continued to smile.

"I mean, what's not to love? On top of being gorgeous, the man's a great cook, a talented electrician, and he plans to build a house off in the woods." She looked at Asia. "I always wanted to live in the woods."

"You did?"

Erica nodded. And then to Becky, "And I've always had a thing for the big macho guys."

"You have?"

"Oh, yeah." She slid off the couch to land in Ian's lap. He toppled onto his rump, but kept her locked in his arms, near to his heart. "I just didn't realize it until Ian came along."

"Does this mean you're getting married?" George wanted to know.

Erica laughed. "That better be what it means."

"Great. Then we're out of here." He pulled Becky to her feet. "Trust me, love. They want privacy."

Asia and Cameron stood too. "We'll go," Asia

told her, "but I expect to hear from you soon with all the juicy details."

Erica gave a sly grin. "I'm not sure you're old enough to hear these details, Asia. They're juicier than most."

Cameron laughed. "A challenge!" And to George, "You think he's trying to outdo us?"

"Sounds like. I don't know about you, but I'm heading home to add to my repertoire on sexual deviations. The way these three gossip, you can't protect your manhood closely enough."

Becky snickered.

Asia took Cameron's hand. "A good idea. Cameron and I will do the same."

"Such a grand exodus," Ian noted once the door had closed behind them all. "Should we put out the same effort, you think?"

"I believe you already have." She toyed with his chest hair and asked, "All that stuff you did . . . it really was wonderful. You're wonderful."

"I told you that for the right woman, I'd do whatever I needed to." He gave her a lecherous smile.

"So it was just to wear me down?"

"No, it was to get you ready." He kissed the end of her nose. "They call it foreplay."

"Well, it worked."

Maintaining his hold on Erica, Ian came to his feet and headed for the bedroom. "Shall we see if it'll work again?"

"Am I still in charge?"

"For a little while longer. Then it's my turn." He entered the bedroom and placed her on the bed. Leaning over, being as serious in his declarations as he could be, he said, "That's what marriage is all about, you know. I love you, so I want you to be happy. You love me, so you want me to be happy." Then he asked, "Right?"

A teasing, very sexy grin eased into place. "Yes."

"Yes?"

She laughed. "Yes. I love you."

Ian snatched her up for a strangling hug. Laughing, Erica forced him back a bit, then said, "You know, as long as I'm still in charge, where's the massage oil?"

His expression warmed and his eyes grew dark. "You're ready for more pleasure, are you?"

"Absolutely." Erica shoved him to his back, then straddled his hips. "And I figure getting to rub your big gorgeous body all over is probably as much pleasure as any woman deserves."

"You want to use the oil on me?"

"That's right. And any man as controlling as you, ought to be able to control himself while I do this. So lie quietly . . . and let me love you."

Ian smiled. "Well, when you put it like that . . ."

Please read on for an excerpt from Jude's Law *by Lori Foster, available now!*

When it comes to love, he plays to win

There's only so much frustration a guy can handle before he gets a little nutty. For Jude Jamison, his frustration has a name—May Price. She's everything the former Hollywood bad boy actor came to Stillbrook, Ohio, hoping to find: open, honest, lovable, and full of those luscious curves you don't find on stick-figure starlets— curves May doesn't seem to appreciate in herself. Every time Jude tries to get close to the skittish businesswoman, to take her in his arms, she thinks he's joking. Joking? Joking does not involve lots of cold-shower therapy.

Time for new tactics. If May can't respond to his compliments and sexy innuendos, he'll just have to spell it out for her. Jude Jamison is going to lay down the law for May Price. And after that, she'll have no delusions about just how much he wants her . . .

He blamed May Price for his new affinity toward lush curves. Before meeting her damn near a year ago, he'd been more than satisfied with willowy models and leggy starlets.

Now, Jude Jamison couldn't get the voluptuous Miss Price, or her very sexy body, off his mind. He wanted her. He *would* have her.

But so far, she hadn't made it easy for him. Hard? Yeah, he stayed plenty hard. When it came to May, nothing went as he intended. Thanks to his fame and acquired fortune, he usually only needed to make himself visible and women were interested.

He liked it that way—or so he'd thought before May challenged him with her resistance. She didn't care about money or fame. No, May liked his interest in art. Specifically, she liked his interest in the art she sold in her gallery.

Trying to make headway with May brought back memories of his youth, when getting laid made the top of his "to do" list and occupied most of his energy. He'd worked hard on sex back then, and he'd had the time of his life.

He still enjoyed sex, but without the chase, it didn't seem as exciting. Hell, it had almost become mundane.

May made it exciting again.

In fact, she made everything exciting. Talking with her left him energized; laughing with her made him feel good; just looking at her gave him pleasure—and often had him fantasizing about the moment when she'd give in, maybe loosen up a little, say yes instead of shrugging off his interest as mere flirtation.

He'd turned thoughts of that day into a favorite fantasy—May out of her restricting clothes and her concealing glasses, with her hair loose and her expressive eyes anxious, seeing only him.

He adored her dark brown eyes with the thick fringe of lashes, the way she looked at him, the way she seemed to really see him, not just his image.

But before he could make moves toward getting her in his bed, he needed to go the route of casual dating. She was different from the other women he'd known. More old fashioned. In no way cavalier about intimacy. And she had a big heart.

He appreciated those differences a lot, but thinking of his failed come-ons left him chagrined.

She took his best lines as a joke. Added sincerity left her unconvinced. And at times, she didn't even notice his attempts at seduction. Yet subtlety wasn't his strong suit. She left him confounded, and very determined.

May wasn't an insecure woman. She wasn't shy or withdrawn. Open, honest, and straightforward—that described May. But no matter what Jude tried, she found a way to discount his interest.

He decided the local yahoos in Stillbrook, Ohio,

were either blind, overly preoccupied, or just plain stupid when it came to women. For May to be so oblivious to her own appeal, they sure as hell hadn't given her the attention she deserved, the attention *he'd* give her—in bed.

It had to happen soon. With his financial status and number of investments, not to mention the propositions from two other factions, a slew of daily business details demanded his attention. But until he had May, he couldn't concentrate worth a damn.

Hands in his pockets, shoulder resting on the ornate door frame of May's small art gallery, Jude watched her with the piercing intensity of a predator.

Time for new tactics. She hadn't reacted to compliments and innuendos, so he'd spell things out for her instead. After tonight, May would have no delusions about what he wanted with her.

As she bustled across the floor, bouncing in all the right places, he visually tracked her, soaking in every jaunty step, each carefree movement. She hadn't yet noticed him, but she would. Soon.

Anticipation curved his mouth.

No matter the location, no matter the occasion, May always became aware of him within seconds of his entrance. She could deny it all she wanted, but the awareness went both ways.

Fighting it would do her no good.

Jude played to win, always had. If May knew anything at all about his history, she knew that much. And for right now, he intended to win her.

It didn't matter that her denial made sense. It didn't matter that, despite the attraction, she probably feared him—with good reason. He wouldn't let it matter.

Hell, he wouldn't even think about it.

Ignoring the curious gawking of everyone else in the main room of the art gallery, Jude wove his way toward May. She had her profile to him and, as usual, her suit jacket showed wrinkles from an uncomplimentary fit, likely caused by her impressive rack. The seat of her knee-length skirt hugged her generous ass. And somehow she'd snagged the back left leg of her nylons.

Like the finest fetish garb, her rumpled wardrobe made her that much more enticing.

He couldn't help but think about the voluptuous body she tried so hard to hide. Because most women flaunted their assets, her modesty amused him. Well used to bold seductions, her attempts to be demure dared him. Everything about her made his imagination go wild.

What type of panties did she wear under that asexual clothing? Cotton, or something slinky and slippery and barely there?

Soon enough he'd discover the answers for himself.

He was still studying her ass when she finally sensed his approach. Her animated conversation fell flat, and she whirled around to face him, almost dislodging her wire-framed glasses. He liked the front view as much as the back. Slowly, he brought his attention away from the notch at the top of her thighs, to her belly, her breasts, and up to her flushed face.

Their gazes locked, and Jude smiled.

Regardless of the crowd around her, he didn't bother to hide his intent. He wanted her, and she could damn well deal with it.

Connect with Us

Visit us online at
KensingtonBooks.com
to read more from your favorite authors, see books
by series, view reading group guides, and more.

Join us on social media

for sneak peeks, chances to win books and prize packs,
and to share your thoughts with other readers.

facebook.com/kensingtonpublishing
twitter.com/kensingtonbooks

Tell us what you think!

To share your thoughts, submit a review,
or sign up for our eNewsletters, please visit:
KensingtonBooks.com/TellUs.

More by Bestselling Author

Lori Foster